SEXY
STRANGERS

SEXY STRANGERS

EROTIC STORIES

EDITED BY
RACHEL KRAMER BUSSEL

CLEiS
PRESS

Published in the United States by Cleis Press, an imprint of Start Midnight, LLC, 221 River Street, Ninth Floor, Hoboken, New Jersey 07030.

Printed in the United States
Cover design: Jennifer Do
Cover image: Shutterstock
Text design: Frank Wiedemann

First Edition.
10 9 8 7 6 5 4 3 2 1

Trade paper ISBN: 978-1-62778-329-3
E-book ISBN: 978-1-62778-542-6

Contents

vii   *Introduction: Hot Strangers, Hot Times*

1   *Skate Date* • ANNITA TERCIO
12   *A Body in Motion* • SULEIKHA SNYDER
25   *Waxing Gibbous* • D.J. HODGE
35   *Away Game* • SPROCKET J. RYDYR
49   *Take Tuesday* • LIN DEVON
61   *Hot Neighbor Guy* • KATE SLOAN
74   *Second Season* • ASH DYLAN
88   *Ken's of Kensington* • FRIEDRICH KREUZ
100   *Our Reflection in the Mirror, Mirror* •
      JESSICA LEIGH ROODE
106   *Private Beach* • A.J. HARRIS
116   *Charlotte the Pirate Queen* • DR. J.
130   *Untamed: A Modern Primal Love Story* •
      NIKKI RAE
142   *Life's Too Short* • SIENNA MERIT
154   *Parc-aux-Cerfs* • JORDAN MONROE
166   *Half Angel* • KIKI DELOVELY
175   *In the Zine Library* • EM FARRIS
187   *The Boy Toy* • LYNX CANON
197   *Hunger* • LYDIA LOOMIS
209   *The Doctor* • BARTHOLOMEW MAXWELL
219   *Ember and Ash* • OLEANDER PLUME

227   *About the Authors*
232   *About the Editor*

Contents

INTRODUCTION:
HOT STRANGERS,
HOT TIMES

There's nothing like the thrill of encountering a stranger and feeling that initial spark, that intuition that even though you don't know this person, they could be someone you want to get naked with. That's the premise of *Sexy Strangers,* where encounters between neighbors, dates, rivals, and others who appear in the lives of the protagonists turn thrillingly sensual.

In these stories, lovers meet in all sorts of ways, from roller skating to beaches to sex clubs to libraries. Wherever they find each other, there's a moment when they know: This is someone I want to get naked with. There's a lot more to these sexy stories than casual sex, though. Whether or not these encounters extend beyond their initial sizzling start or are whole in and of themselves, these passionate stories bring all the heat of that initial discovery.

The lovers you'll read about get to know each other in the most intimate of ways, fueled by various desires—for hot sex, for someone to offer them lust and longing and attention that they aren't getting elsewhere. In many of these stories, a stranger helps unlock an aspect of a character's sexuality which has been hidden away, or which they haven't been able to fully access on their own. These strangers exchange kisses and touches and orgasms as well as deeper gifts, in many cases, as they encourage their new lovers to try something new, whether it's exhibitionism, voyeurism, sex toys, BDSM, role-playing, or particular locations, positions, or sensations.

Every character you'll read about in *Sexy Strangers* is changed in a powerful way by what happens when they strip naked before a new lover, when they communicate in a very particular way about who they are and what they want. They offer the permission these sexual seekers have been looking for to embrace their most uninhibited selves and have the kind of sex they've either dreamed about or couldn't have imagined themselves actually doing.

In "Life's Too Short" by Sienna Merit, the protagonist succumbs to the sexual charms of the bartender she's had her eye on, making the most of the title saying. "She was a hungry, merciless wildfire when she got going. I was breathless looking at her." That same energy is present throughout these stories, a rush to say yes, to explore, to go to those places, literal and figurative, that are a little (or a lot) edgy, daring, and often combine a mix of nerves and arousal. That balancing act of trusting someone new to learn how to read their body's roadmaps, of going with the unexpected without knowing what will happen beyond the immediate moment, that drives the erotic tension in these stories. I hope they whisk you away with their sexual frenzy and leave you breathless as well.

Rachel Kramer Bussel
Atlantic City

SKATE DATE

Annita Tercio

*P**lease, please, please let no one else be here,*** Darby thought to herself as she parked her car.

She checked her phone: 7:30 a.m. She glanced at her stuffed tote bag on the passenger seat. She reviewed her mental checklist one more time. Water: check. Elbow, wrist, and knee pads: check, check, check. Cute stripy socks: snug around her calves. Stretchy retro shorts that skirted the edge of being cheeky: settled into the crease of her thighs. Brand new roller skates: teasing her from the top of the bag. Daring her not to fall on her ass.

"Am I really going to do this?" she said aloud to herself. She peered out the car window at the smooth concrete surface of the reservoir. Morning sun filtered through the tall trees and birdsong emanated from the branches. Otherwise, the street was quiet. She studied the slice of pavement visible from the gate. No one glided past. Later in the day it would be hopping, with everyone from parents chasing toddlers on tricycles to the local derby team practicing drills. The reservoir was the place to go if you wanted to be on wheels. Smooth, flat, big, completely fenced in, and free.

Which is why Darby was there. Just hopefully early enough to spare herself the embarrassment of others witnessing a six-foot-tall, forty-seven-year-old woman attempting to roller skate again after last attaching eight wheels to her feet decades ago.

"This is ridiculous," she said aloud. She looked at the skates. Bright green suede. Sparkly laces. Matching suede toe caps. She'd really gone for it. She'd been wanting to try skating again for over two years, ever since she'd walked past a man sitting on the floor of his garage, clearly mid clean-out, strapping on a pair of skates he'd just unearthed from some dusty box in a corner. He looked giddy. Something about the look on his face, of rediscovering something that must have once given him pleasure, had struck her. She hadn't felt joy for quite some time, and now, in her post-divorce-fuck-it-I'm-going-to-reclaim-myself-and-have-some-goddamn-fun phase of life, she'd decided to stop withholding from herself. Seek freedom. Seek joy. Play.

So when her chosen skates came back in stock she hit "complete purchase" before she could even talk herself out of it. Three days later, they were at her doorstep.

She touched the silky suede of the skates. Damn they were pretty. And expensive. Darby exhaled, grabbed the tote, and got out of the car.

Nerves tingled in her fingers as she laced the skates tightly around her ankles. Once on, she looked down at her long thighs, a little more muscled of late due to her newfound love of squats. She adjusted her pink-striped tube socks as the metallic threads of her laces caught the sunlight. Unconsciously, she grinned. Double checking the Velcro of her pads, Darby flipped herself over onto her knees and stood up, lunging on one leg, then the other. She wobbled a moment but then remembered all the tutorials she'd watched online. Keep your knees bent. Core tight. Shoulders straight. Look ahead. Breathe. Relax.

She flashed to herself as a kid. She used to skate up and down the driveway, on the back patio, weaving and turning for hours. The only reason she'd stopped was because she'd hit a growth spurt in her early teens and her brother's friend, staring up at her from his sneakers, had looked at her yellow overalls and immediately nicknamed her Big Bird.

A breeze rustled across her neck and bare arms. The sun washed over the bare pavement, empty except for her.

"Fuck it," she said and pushed off.

Just like that, Darby was skating. At first her strides were tentative. Then she adjusted her balance from her heels to the balls of her feet, the skates' leather snug against her shins. The wheels rolling over the pavement thrummed under her feet and with each passing minute, her movements grew more fluid.

She picked up more speed and leaned into a turn, relishing the momentum pushing her into a gentle arc.

She giggled aloud. "I'm doing it!" she said to herself. She rolled back to the spot where she'd dropped her bag. She found her earbuds, popped them in, cued up her favorite 90s playlist, tucked her phone into the top of her sports bra, and before she even had a chance to think, turned around on one foot and propelled herself forward with her toe stop. She giggled once more. *Fuck age, fuck self-doubt,* she thought.

Gliding across the smooth concrete, music thumping in her ears, sun kissing the tops of her shoulders, Darby skated. Back and forth. Round and round. With each revolution across the expanse of the reservoir, the muscle memory returned. She swung her hips from side to side, her feet swiveling in response. She pushed with her left foot, then drew a C with her right, zooming into a quick turn and stop. "What?!" she shouted, laughing out loud. Yes! This is why she wanted to do this again.

Remind herself that life was more than work, paying a mortgage, wasting time on dating sites with men who told her they thought she seemed great but they preferred—in the words of one man a whopping one inch shorter—to be the taller one "because it just felt more natural." All her life she'd never understood how on one hand, long legs were desirable, but then, when she showed up sporting her thirty-three-inch inseam, or even worse, wearing heels, men balked, afraid that somehow her natural genetics threatened their masculinity.

When she'd first tried on her skates, daring only to stand on her bedroom carpet in front of her full-length mirror, she couldn't help but think: *I look like a giraffe.* Standing that close, she couldn't even see the top of her head in the reflection. But now, skating, gliding, turning, bouncing to the music, she didn't feel like a giraffe. She felt graceful. She felt strong. She felt . . . hot.

Pushing harder, she lifted her arms above her head. She snapped her fingers in tune to the music. Janet Jackson's "That's the Way Love Goes" came on and something about the slow beat, the clench of her ass and thigh muscles, the growing summer heat, all of it, made her rake her hands down the front of her body like she was in a music video. Her nipples puckered at the feel of her fingertips. The tip of her clit pulsed.

She giggled. Darby was literally and figuratively feeling herself.

Why had she waited so long to get back on skates? She turned again and—

Shit.

Someone else was there.

In a shady corner a man was sitting on a cheap fold-up camping chair. He was bent over, furiously lacing inlines to his feet.

How long had he been there? Had he seen her?

He sat up and looked straight at Darby before she could look away. If she hadn't panicked, she could've kept skating with her hands away from her fun zones while looking right past him in an attempt to signal she had no idea he was there. Then she could nonchalantly skate back to her bag, plop down as if she hadn't just gotten there ten minutes before, take off her skates, and go home for a vibrator session and a second cup of tea.

He lifted a hand and waved. A gesture to say, *Hey. Since it's just us here it would be weird if we didn't acknowledge each other.* Darby waved back weakly as the man slowly stood up.

Well, fine. She wasn't alone anymore. He probably didn't see her shaking her ass and pinching her own nipples, right? He'd probably just arrived. Next time she'd get here even earlier, maybe before—

"*MERDE!*"

Somehow, in the two seconds since they'd exchanged waves, the man had managed to fall. Had he even . . . skated? Darby wondered. But there he was, legs waving in the air and the camping chair resting on his back.

Instinctively she skated toward him, taking her earbuds out. "Are you okay?" she called out.

As she neared, he pushed the chair off himself, yelling out, "*Merde!*" once more but less forcefully. He pushed his legs out in front of him as he struggled to set the chair upright.

"Are you—" she started to ask again but cut herself off. She was going way too fast. She jammed a toe stop down but it bounced and skidded behind her. She grabbed the fence to break her momentum, wheels clattering and sliding from underneath her. "EEEEEE!" she squealed as she somehow managed to get her feet back under her.

"I'm okay. You?" the man said with an accent.

Darby looked down at him. What were the chances? He was adorable. Dark salt-and-pepper hair curled out from under a hat. Even under the brim she could see that his eyes leaned toward green. He was dressed simply, in gray shorts and a light T-shirt that somehow showed a trim body without actually being tight. His tan calves curved gracefully into new black inlines.

Darby wanted to climb right up and over the fence and disappear.

She also wanted to climb right on top of him.

"I'm still standing," she said, pushing the thought away and attempting to smile. She realized she was clinging to the fence. Finger by finger she let go, trying to look casual. "Looks like you took a nasty fall."

He nodded, smiling at her. He made no attempt to get up. "Yes," he said. It sounded like "Yusss." He looked both friendly and confused. In a handsome way.

"Well," Darby said. Wow. His smile was . . . something. "Good luck!" she called out as she carefully turned, suddenly stricken that she was on roller skates. In tube socks. Wearing tiny 70s retro-style shorts she'd bought for $17 off Amazon. And that she was eight hundred feet tall looming over a charmingly sexy man sitting on the ground. Who, she noticed, was trying not to look at her legs.

She smiled again as she pushed off, fumbling as she attempted to put her earbuds back in.

"AHHH!" she heard from behind her. "*Merde, merde, merde!*"

Without thinking, she whipped around. Her speed spun her into a three-sixty and her arms flew up as she rocked back, but just as quickly she bent her knees and flung her arms forward, reestablishing her balance. The man, on the other hand, was on all fours, trying desperately to catch purchase with his skates but instead his feet rolled helplessly behind him. He managed to grab hold of the fence with one hand and through force of will and a comically wide stance, got up in a crouch. He glanced at Darby and, laughing, gave her a meek thumbs up.

She couldn't help herself. Darby skated back, going slower this time and managing to drag her toe stop without it stuttering over the pavement.

"Grab the fence with your other hand," she said. "Step your feet closer. Then you can pull yourself up."

He glanced at her again. His cheeks were red. Fuck he was cute. "Sorry," he said. It sounded like, "sa-REE?" Darby put it all together. Not only was this man completely inept on skates, he was French and barely spoke English. And then, in a nanosecond, right back on his ass.

What the hell was happening this morning?

Darby laughed. She'd been worried that she looked like a giraffe and yet this man might actually be one, albeit reincarnated in a taut French man's body.

Holding up his index finger, he reached into his pocket and pulled out his phone. With a few taps he spoke into the microphone and then held it out to her. She leaned down and saw that he had translated himself. "I'm sorry, my English is bad and so is my skating. I'm here visiting family."

He took the phone back, tapped again, then held it for her, waiting for her to speak.

"My skating is not so good either," she said after a pause, defaulting to self-effacement.   He read her words and then looked at her in shock. He muttered some words into the phone. Darby couldn't understand a single one of them, but the way his words slid around in the back of his throat made her want to bend down and watch his tongue.

He held the phone out. "You are joking. Your skating is

beautiful! You are a graceful gazelle." Just as she took her eyes off the screen, she noticed his eyes traveling up her legs. He quickly averted his gaze. Darby watched his face flush deeper.

He mumbled into the phone. "Apologies, I am just embarrassed to be trying this around such a beautiful woman." Normally she'd roll her eyes at a line like that, but then he covered his face with his hands, letting out a soft laugh that ended in a sigh. His hands were gorgeous. Thick veins carved into the backs of them, indicating an easy strength. He spoke again into the phone. "It is impossible to stand in these things!"

She laughed. Hm. *Maybe you don't need to stand,* she thought.

He dictated into the phone once more, his voice lower this time: "You looked like you were having a nice time by yourself before I interrupted."

She stared at him. This time, he didn't glance away as he gazed up at her. A soft grin pulled at his mouth. So he *had* seen her feeling herself. Figuratively and literally.

Grabbing the fence for stability, she motioned for the phone.

"Did you have a nice time watching?" she asked. Heat flooded her cheeks, but she didn't break her stare.

His eyes flickered wide for a moment as he read her translated words.

"*Oui,*" he said. He put the phone down.

She pushed on her toe stop, inching closer. Her shadow covered his face. He licked his lips. On her skates she towered above him. Her hand sweat as she clung to the fence. *Darby! What are you doing?*

He reached a hand toward her. Before he touched her, he caught her eyes, waiting. "Please," she whispered, nodding.

He traced a finger across the top of her sock. His touch was warm and his fingers firm. His hand curved around her calf before he slid his hand up, middle finger pressing up the back of her knee. Instantly chills traveled up her hamstring, her ass, her spine. Her skin puckered and she watched his mouth edge open.

She dug her right toe stop into the pavement and swung her left leg to the other side, balancing atop her other toe stop and grasping the fence with both hands. Her legs formed a triangle over his head. She looked down at his face. He looked incredulous, like he couldn't believe what was happening.

Neither could she. But that didn't stop her. She came here for fun, right? She bit her bottom lip as she let go with one hand, shifting the soft terry cloth of the shorts over to expose her pussy.

"Do you want—" she started to ask.

"*Oui*," he sighed. She bent her knees, lowering down, jamming her skates into the fence to hold herself. She started to think of how awkward she must look, femurs jutting out to each side, but then her thoughts stopped as she felt his hands slowly, reverently, travel up and down the backs of her legs and then his mouth as he gently kissed the insides of both her thighs, his green eyes looking up at her the whole time. He took over pulling the fabric away to display her folds, and she held the fence with both hands and spread her legs even more as his mouth moved over her clit.

At the moment he first tasted her, they both groaned. He used just the tip of his tongue and the edges of his lips, barely circling her, alternating licks with soft kisses. She started to pump into his mouth, meeting every restrained lick. Darby did not know this man but she knew he was teasing her, so she teased back, feeding him her pussy and then pulling away. The warm pressure of his tongue against her clit felt so good, and he ran his other hand under the back of her shorts, cupping her ass and pulling her closer. She pushed into his mouth even more, wanting to feel his entire tongue flat against her clit and lips. His tongue pressed and circled and then dipped lower between her slit.

She started to buck against his mouth, grinding her clit against him as he lapped at her. He was moaning just as much as she was, and she watched as his mouth dove deep inside her thick, wet lips. She ground against him, simultaneously wanting his tongue deep inside her walls and yet pressing around her clit. Her head fell back as she spread for him even more. The hand on her ass slid forward and she felt him press a finger at the edge of her opening. "Oh, fuck, yes," she moaned, and slowly he slid it inside her.

As he filled her with one finger, then two, all she wanted to do was fuck this man's mouth and hands. As his fingers curled deep within her and his tongue and lips licked and pressed and sucked all over her hard, pulsing clit, that's exactly what she did. She circled her pussy all over his mouth, the pressure building inside her into a pulsing heat. Clutching the fence with one hand, she let go with the other to grab the back of his head as she bucked into him until her thighs shook and the waves of her orgasm overtook her. She rocked her pussy against his face, coming and coming against his tongue until finally the waves subsided.

"Oh, my God," she whispered. His hands squeezed both her asscheeks, pulling her down. She edged her hands down the fence and somehow maneuvered her legs and skates under her so she was sitting next to him, her legs stretched out, muscles quivering.

She picked up his phone. He tapped on it a few times and held it to her. "I thought by getting here early I'd have this place to myself," she teased.

As soon as he read her words he smiled. His mouth was wet

with her. He dictated back. "I wanted to learn how to skate before a birthday party later today. I didn't plan on making a fool of myself before a stunning woman skating on the most gorgeously long legs I've ever seen."

Reading that, she actually blushed. *Darby! You just came on this stranger's mouth!* "I'm sorry you didn't learn how to skate," she replied.

He looked straight at her as he dictated. She didn't need to see the phone to know what he said: "I am definitely not sorry."

Thinking about her knee pads, she was about to offer something more to him when the reservoir gate clanged. They both looked and saw a young woman cautiously step forward, skates slung over her shoulder, scanning the perimeter and then, when she saw them, try not to look disappointed when she realized she wasn't alone.

"Tomorrow?" she said into his phone.

He nodded enthusiastically.

"Good," she said, not so nonchalantly standing up. "It's a date." She laughed. "A skate date."

A BODY
IN MOTION

Suleikha Snyder

The woman who'd just paid a premium for twenty minutes of his time looked like a teacher at a private school. Or a movie librarian. The stereotype of a prim and bookish girl with her glasses and her button-down blouse and what were probably orthopedic shoes. They were black and thick-heeled and looked really comfortable—which was something Luke really appreciated, given how much time he spent on his feet on any given day. She'd introduced herself as Meena, and he had no doubt it was her actual name. She didn't seem to be afraid of being seen here. No, her fear was something else. Her hands were knotted together on her pressed-together knees . . . but only for as long as it took her to realize that. She swiftly placed her palms flat on the seat on either side of her. The knees, encased in faded brown corduroys that were almost trendy, stayed closed. Just as the drink on the table to her left stayed untouched.

It was the second of her two-drink minimum, according to

Tracy, who'd served her out on the floor. Meena had done what was required but knew her limits. A fact she didn't hesitate to make clear. "I don't want a lap dance," she said in a quiet but clear voice. "Can you just be sexy?"

He fought back the laugh the earnest question brought out of him and toed off his shoes by the door. The last thing he wanted to do was embarrass her. That wasn't the job. That wasn't what she'd paid for. That wasn't what she deserved. "Yeah," he said softly. "I think I can be sexy for you." What's more, he *wanted* to.

He'd worked the private room dozens of times. Danced for plenty of customers. Sometimes, he just let the music guide his motions, his body literally a well-oiled machine. They were usually too lubricated themselves—on too many cocktails—to notice. But this time, as the familiar strains of Usher's "U Got It Bad" came over the speakers, he took his cues from *her.*

Meena tilted her chin up as he began to roll his hips, her knuckles white as she clutched the edges of the leather banquette. So brave. Like she was readying for a fight and not a dance. She had something to prove by being here, whether it was to herself or someone else, he couldn't guess.

Luke made no move toward her. He stayed where he was, just toying with the buttons of his shirt. Most of his one-on-one sessions started the same way. With one question. "What turns you on?" he murmured. "What's going to make you feel good?"

"I have no idea anymore," she blurted out, with the same huff of surprised amusement he'd held back. "Not being here. Being at home. Watching you on TV instead."

She preferred distance. Her sex objects removed and untouchable. Safe. He got that. Sometimes, after all of the groping and grabbing he endured in this club, he'd go home not wanting to be touched at all. Even an accidental brush from people on the train felt like sensory overload. Or, worse, a violation. And the last thing he needed was for her to feel that way.

"Pretend I'm on TV then," he suggested with a smile. A genuine one. "Just a really good flat-screen."

She laughed again, loosening her death grip on the seat. *That's my girl.* "Please. The only thing flat about you is your abs," she said with the moxie that probably got her in the door of Cloud9 in the first place.

He looked down at the abs in question, still covered by his white shirt. "Are you sure about that? Maybe we should find out. You know, for science."

Her battle-ready posture curled as she smothered a giggle against her palm. And the apprehension in her eyes turned into a sparkle. Humor got her going. It engaged her brain. Revved her engine. Good. He could happily work with that.

"Alexa, play 'Pony' by Ginuwine," he said, glancing up at one of the ceiling speakers for effect.

Meena's brown eyes widened behind her glasses. "You do *not* have an Alexa in here." Her voice rose in disbelief.

"No, we do not," he confirmed with a grin as he went to the tablet on the wall and manually skipped through the private room's playlist. Most women were happy with the basic *Magic Mike* experience—though they'd long since retired the Ginuwine song because all the dancers were sick of it. The routine was to woo them and whisper to them and make them a part of the performance. Make them feel like a partner and a sex object at the same time. Touch and tease and tantalize. That wouldn't work for this prim and private person.

No. Not so prim. She wasn't as fragile and fearful as he'd assumed. "Beatles or Stones?" he asked over his shoulder.

Her volume went up another notch. "You cannot *possibly*

strip to The Beatles," she declared, so confident in her claim that she forgot to be anxious.

"Watch me," he challenged as the first notes of "Oh! Darling" filled the circular lounge.

And she did. Meena followed his hips and his shoulders *as* he came back to center and started to dance. Those intense eyes taking everything in. *It's a dare,* he thought as her lips parted and her cheeks flushed. She lost a bet. And she wasn't the kind of woman who reneged on a deal. Not with those buttons marching in a uniform line to her high collar. Her hands were fisted again. But not from nerves this time. *No.* As Luke pulled his white oxford from the waistband of his jeans and slowly went for his own buttons, he wondered if she might just be tempted to do it for him. Maybe she was itching to run her palms down his chest as he swiveled his hips to the perfect burlesque beat. If not now, then *soon.*

That's right, he urged her silently as he tossed the shirt onto the banquette next to her. *Be here with me.* Because if Meena wasn't there, wasn't *present,* then she was wasting her money and her time. That was one of the first things he'd learned when he started dancing at clubs like this to help pay his way through college. To connect. And the connection here was growing stronger by the second.

He held her gaze even as it roamed across his body. She was fascinated by his arms. And his shoulders. Both emphasized by his tight and sleeveless white T-shirt. His feet were bare, because it was easier to dance that way, and he felt her eyes there, too. Taking everything in. If she'd been laughing at the music pick initially, it was all gone now. Her pulse was probably beating wildly, because she loosened that stifling shirt collar, exposing the delicate brown skin of her throat. That smooth silk might be the only part of her he ever saw. And there was something magical about that. Something intimate in a way that wasn't about fucking her.

This was a trade, what he did in the private rooms. He stripped off almost everything, just so people could share a secret part of themselves. Their wants, their needs, sometimes their hopes and their sorrows. Even their anxieties and their doubts. "Can I come closer?" he asked quietly.

She just nodded, as if speaking might release the word "no." And that would defeat the purpose of her being here, wouldn't it? Whatever had made her walk in . . . now, it was making her stay. And so was he.

Luke reached behind his neck and grabbed his T-shirt, pulling it up and over his head. Always a crowd-pleaser. Not the only thing he was good at doing one-handed. And then he was just in front of her knees. They'd fallen open, but he knew better than to nudge between them. That was too much. Beyond the limits she'd established earlier.

Maybe it was research. Like she was a writer or a social scientist or a reporter. A private detective working for a suspicious husband. Luke had nothing to worry about on that score. He'd never taken liberties with a customer. Some of the other guys? Sure. They kissed and touched and made women come. They accepted phone numbers and offers of well-compensated dates. He didn't judge and he didn't tattle to management. It was their prerogative. But it'd never really been his.

Not even when someone was focusing on him the way Meena was now . . . or so he was telling himself. *Don't ruin it. Don't break. Don't cross the line.* The temptation to ask questions, to learn more, was strong, but he could resist it. He had to keep his mind on the work. No matter how curious he was about what had brought her here. Or how she looked as her walls came down.

She'd been pretty before, if a little too serious and severe and ready to jump out of her skin. But now, canting forward, close enough to reach for him, dark hair escaping her bun, she was bordering on fucking incandescent. The tension had drained out of her. Whatever hesitation she'd had, it didn't matter now.

He mouthed the song lyrics as he took off his belt and worked open his fly. And when his zipper came down, as far as they were both concerned, she *was* his darling. That was the job. *Don't forget that.* That was what she'd paid for. *And nothing else.* That was what she deserved. *More than this.* And this was why he worked at Cloud9 three nights a week and did two shows with the rest of the guys on Saturdays. *Right?*

Because everybody was a little bit beautiful during a dance.

She knew what the dancer saw when he looked at her. What she showed the world. Someone uptight and buttoned down. The bouncer at the door had almost refused to let her in. Same for the house manager and the pretty cocktail waitress who eventually told her how to book a private experience. For years, she'd been told where she didn't belong. Not at school amidst all those white faces. Not at college, in her STEM classes. Not in the research lab. Not in her marriage. She was so tired of it. Of being the odd one out, the nerdy one, the quiet one, the one who wasn't exciting enough.

It was time to remember who she was *inside*. The person with passion and ambition and the sheer will to accomplish anything she put her mind to. So here Meena was, at an all-male revue, thanks to a Groupon and alimony payments. Inches from a nearly naked man who was slated to lead a burlesque show at ten. *Luke,* her waitress had said, and he'd repeated it as he joined Meena in what they called "The Starlight Lounge." Now Luke was lowering his zipper as The Beatles trailed off into the opening strains of something by Otis Redding. He liked the classics, this guy. Or maybe he thought *she* liked the classics, which wasn't entirely wrong. But she found herself wryly asking, "Is the median age of your clients sixty-five?" before she could censor herself.

"*You're* still here, aren't you?" He didn't miss a beat as he peeled down his jeans . . . a move that shouldn't have been sexy, but somehow he made it so. He was handsome in that way that models were. Dirty blond hair and a shadow of pale stubble hugging his jaw. Suntanned and sleek with an eight-pack—confirmed for science. And if they weren't supposed to talk during one of these dances, he wasn't saying so. He seemed to be watching her as closely as she'd paid to watch him. His dark blue eyes, flecked with a gold that matched his five o'clock shadow, had barely broken contact.

Was that the gimmick here? At these *Magic Mike*-inspired clubs that had popped up all over the country in the last decade? To make people feel like they were someone's sole focus? It was effective. Too effective. Sometime in the last few minutes, she'd started to feel less uncomfortable and more at ease. And then she'd started to feel hot and sweaty. Her throat was tight. Undoing her collar hadn't helped. She'd worn her work clothes on purpose. Like that might be some sort of shield. A barrier between her and all the things she wasn't supposed to want . . . and the things she was afraid to reclaim.

She'd failed to account for one thing. For someone who'd only ever felt invisible, there was nothing headier than being seen. And nothing hotter than being heard. Luke had respected her request for no lap dance . . . and the one to *just be sexy*. What could be sexier than a man with rhythm and a sense of humor who actually listened to her? She knew now. A man with all of that who was almost brushing up against her bent legs.

"Can I come closer?" He'd asked so kindly, so politely, before taking off his T-shirt. When was the last time someone had asked before invading her space? She couldn't remember. But this beautiful man, this sexy stranger kicking off his jeans and standing before her in nothing but clingy black boxer-briefs, had shown her that respect. It left her breathless. Was that how starved she was for basic courtesy? Was that why she was leaning forward, near enough to reach out and run her fingertips along the grooves of his hip cuts?

Meena tried to keep her focus above his neck. She really did. But Luke's eyes were too insightful and his body was too tempting. So, when he sank to his knees and did some sort of sinuous arch, her gaze instinctively followed the curve down his shoulders and the taut stretch of his back. The globes of his butt in those snug shorts. She'd asked him not to dance up on her. She hadn't said anything about not fucking the floor.

Some sort of noise escaped her throat. A strangled squeak. He looked up at her, a smile pulling at his lips and a pleased glint in his eyes. As if they weren't blue and sparkling enough already. "You doing okay, darlin'?" The drawl of the last word was as strange on his un-Southern tongue as it was coming from a guy from Liverpool.

He was teasing her. And she was enjoying it. She was enjoying all of this. She couldn't have imagined that ten minutes ago. Or even before she'd made it through the front door. Dr. Meena Reddy—Dr. EverReddy or Dr. NeverReddy, depending on how the postdocs were feeling about her that week—was actually in a strip club by herself and having a good time. "I'm doing great," she said, still surprised that she meant it. She'd picked the most antithetical to her reputation excursion . . . but this was the most like herself she'd felt in a very long time.

"Good," murmured Luke as he stayed kneeling before her

and rocked back on his bare heels. "What you need from me now?"

She had him for ten more minutes. It wasn't nearly enough time to encompass what she needed. From him or from anyone else. So all she said was, "Come closer." *Come closer, I want more.*

He thought about it sometimes. That session with Meena.

"Come closer," she'd said. And Luke listened. Like he always did. Bending over her. Stroking her cheek with his fingertips as he continued to dance. Letting her explore as much of him as she was comfortable with. He'd pulled away from her semi-hard, both of them pretending not to notice. It wasn't unusual in this gig—dicks had a mind of their own, especially when you were miming sex acts—but Luke couldn't blame hip swivels and sexy oldies music. Not that time. Not with that woman.

Something about her *got* to him. Her bravado in coming to the club. Her determination to stay. And how she'd opened up in that room, laughing and wanting and asking and taking. She hadn't been back in since, and he had to tuck his disappointment away, like putting on a cock sock before stage shows. She hadn't left her number, or asked for outside contact. No propositions, nothing. Just "thank you" as she drained her second drink and walked out of the private room with her shoulders back and her head held high. He'd stood there, barefoot, clutching three twenty-dollar bills, remembering how it felt to have her hand on his chest and her knees bracketing his hips. And he'd wanted more.

Two weeks later, she was still on his mind. And there, in that room, as he danced for other people. He remembered her hair escaping her bun, those silky tendrils of black hair that had curled around his fingers when they were just inches apart. He thought about how she'd undone those top few buttons of her blouse. That little flash of exposed skin haunted him like she was the one who'd been nearly naked, not him.

Was her research concluded? Her dare completed and bet won? Luke was beginning to feel like a man obsessed. He did his shows at Cloud9, pulled shifts at the restaurant he'd worked at in undergrad, and tried to be present during his last kinesiology class of the term. But Meena was there with him at each and every place, in each and every moment. A lunch patron at Easton's played "These Arms of Mine" on the digital jukebox and Luke was glad for the bar in front of him, hiding his damn-near instant erection. The Beatles? Forget about it. It was like he had a Yellow Submarine in his pants. And the three twenties in his wallet Meena had left him as a tip . . . ? They stayed unspent. Like that somehow meant what had happened between them wasn't a transaction.

With a degree to finish and two jobs to juggle, Luke tried to reconstruct his life into something like normal. He had to move on. No more intriguing customers on the brain. So, of course, that was when she walked into it again. An hour into a dead Wednesday shift at the restaurant. Meena made straight for the bar in brisk strides. Near to the door as it was, they saw each other almost immediately. He tried not to drop the pint glass he'd been drying before he came around to her side with a "Hey."

"Hi." She gave him a nod, purse clutched tightly to her side in her go-to white-knuckled grip. "I went by Cloud9 last night, but you weren't working," she said, the explanation coming in a rush as she got flustered and focused anywhere and everywhere but his face. "They said I could find you here a few days a week."

It took Luke a few seconds to process that. Her, Meena the

mystery woman, actually seeking him out. And it wasn't just
in his slightly fevered imagination. *She's really here. She felt it,
too.* But he couldn't, wouldn't, assume. "You came looking for
me? Why?"

"I . . . don't know," she confessed with a laugh, gaze sheepish
behind the shield of her glasses. "But I can't stop thinking about
that night. Or you."

Something clenched low in his belly, hopeful and hungry.
But this was no conversation to have in the middle of Easton's,
where anyone could overhear or interrupt. "C'mon. Come with
me." He drew Meena into the storage room, which half the staff
used to hook up and smoke up. It locked and had a small window, hence the appeal. It served as an office and a break room,
too, sometimes. But right now, it was a private room, a cham-
pagne room, a VIP lounge. Where he and this utterly captivat-
ing woman could strip themselves bare. Metaphorically, if not
literally.

"I haven't forgotten either." It was an easy admission. As
easy as locking the door behind them. "That night was something special for me, too."

"It was the first time in a long time that I felt seen," Meena
said, as she unbuckled her coat with unsteady hands.

He gently knocked them aside and finished undoing the
three belts that held the leather jacket closed. "It was the first
time in a long time that I felt *anything*." Luke wasn't even kidding. If he'd opened her up, she'd blown him wide. "I wanted
it to last all night." With more buttons coming undone. More
layers revealed. More questions answered about what made her
tick. Then *and* now. "I want to *know* you."

Meena didn't resist when he pushed her coat down her shoulders and helped her take it off. She just looked up at him with
those brown eyes, worrying her bottom lip with her teeth for

a moment. But when she spoke, there was no hesitation in her voice. No passivity either. "I want to be known. I want to feel alive like that again."

Alive. Yes. That was what it was. This electric feeling coursing through his veins as he brought her close. She wore another conservative shirt—pale pink, with three buttons undone. He could see her pulse beating at her throat and the sharp slant of her collarbone. And when he tipped his gaze downward, there was the shadowy cleft of her breasts. Bra-less. *Fuck.* This was who she really was. This was why she'd gone to the club that night. No scores to settle. Just trying to remember, or awaken, the woman who would come to him with her nipples hard.

Luke leaned his forehead against hers, breathing in, breathing *her* in. Now he was the one coiled with tension. The one not sure how any of this was supposed to go. "Meena," he whispered, not even bothering to mask the awe in his voice. Because he was awake now, too. "Meena, you came back."

"I did." She didn't say "in more ways than one," but it was there nonetheless. In how she pulled back just long enough to slip off her glasses and tuck them away. In how she returned to center and right into his arms. Her hair was loose and wavy. Her lips were glossy and he caught the faint scent of cherries. And if her blouse was deceptively sedate, the black miniskirt and strappy shoes beneath were anything but. She moved against him like a pro dancer and a lover, hips swaying toward his, hands sliding down his back and gripping his ass.

It didn't need choreography. Undoing her blouse as she explored beneath his T-shirt. Tasting that tempting hollow at the base of her throat. Hiking her skirt up and locking her legs around him as they stumbled against the door. They didn't need music for this. They were making it. As he reached between them and rubbed her through the damp silk of her panties.

While she keened for more and he pushed the silk aside and put his fingers inside her. His heart was pounding in his ears. His dick throbbing in his jeans.

"What's going to make *you* feel good, Luke?" she gasped as she came apart riding his palm, too fast and ready for more.

"Just be sexy for me," he murmured, as he lowered his mouth to hers.

WAXING GIBBOUS

D.J. Hodge

A massive black bus pulls up to the campus entrance. Single file, we pile in. In front of me stands a pair of identical brunettes. It's safe to assume I won't be sitting with either of them. I'm without a security blanket. My friends aren't into the art scene, so I'm taking this trip solo. It's a big deal for me, branching out like this. I thought I'd feel more excited, but it's awkward. The closer I get to the bus, the more I regret my decision to come at all.

Without being obvious, I take a peek behind me. There's another friend cluster. Sighing deeply, I climb up the steep steps. I choose a seat toward the back. The seats are tall and plush, creating a false sense of privacy. Settling close to the window, I pull my phone from my bag and check my reflection. Brown skin, tired brown eyes, and a haphazard curly topknot stare back. Maybe I should have put more effort into my look today. Maybe I would feel better.

It's an interesting experience, being one of the few Black

students on campus. I'm both hyper-visible and invisible. Some days, I can get through the day without speaking to a single soul, and I love it. Other days, it's lonely and draining. Sitting by myself in the enormous double seats, today is the latter.

Leaning against the headrest, I glance out at the quad. We're in the infancy of winter. The transition from comfortably cool to bitingly cold has been slow and drawn out. Tugging at my long socks, I try my best to cover more of my thighs. I don't know why I thought a miniskirt without tights was a good idea in October.

"Before we pull off, I want to remind you of all the rules. You're all adults, so they shouldn't be too hard to follow," Professor Rhodes shouts from the head of the bus. Sitting up, I peek at him over the seats. The yellow overhead lights give his already ruddy complexion an unfortunate hue. Straightening his shoulders, he clears his throat. That combo usually means he's gearing up for a rant. I roll my eyes.

Before he can continue, there's a knock on the bus doors. Annoyed, Rhodes instructs the driver to open them. Then with his arms crossed, he waits for the offending party to climb the steps.

"Mr. James. Nice of you to join us. Did you miss the departure time when you received your invite?"

"Nope." The voice is deep and smooth. "Slept through my alarm."

I push my body up even more so that I can get a better look. I'm not disappointed. I've never seen him before. If I had, I'd absolutely remember. The man is handsome, ridiculously so—with skin the color of cherry wood stain. He reminds me of Black actors in the nineties, specifically Morris Chestnut in *The Best Man*. Grinning at an unamused Rhodes, his bright, white teeth shine under the lights. On his head sits a backward MHU cap, his short, tight curls peeking over the closure band.

"Take a seat, Mr. James. I'd appreciate it if you tried your very best not to disrupt us further."

"Sure thing." He winks, making his way toward the back.

"You can sit here!" someone yells from behind me.

"Or here!" another calls out, followed by a stream of giggles.

Whispers fill the bus, but none of it's clear enough to decipher. I'm positive he's the focus of all the chatter. Instead of walking past me like I expect, he stops abruptly.

"Mind if I sit here?" he asks, looking down at me. I've never seen anything like them, eyes the color of cinnamon, warm, rich brown with tiny green flecks. My brain momentarily slips out the side of my head.

"Uh n-no," I stutter like an idiot.

"No, it's not taken, or no, I can't sit here?" He raises a brow.

"I'm sorry, I didn't—"

"I know. I'm kidding." He chuckles, sliding beside me.

I attempt to make myself smaller, afraid I'll accidentally touch him. Embarrassed and a little uncomfortable, I focus on Rhodes as he rambles on about the rules. Somewhere between not leaving the museum premises and where the designated meeting spot is located, I feel my new seatmate staring at me. He does it blatantly, starting at my exposed thighs and slowly working his way up to my face.

"I'm Keith." He offers me his hand. I look down and find it almost completely covered in tattoos. A cluster of snakes, intertwined, sit snug between his fingers, traveling up toward his wrists. Stacks of rings sit on his thumb, ring, and middle fingers in various shades of gold, no silver. His nails are painted. The manicure is short and neat. The color, a dark navy. So dark it looks black. Keith turns his hand, and the color shifts slightly, appearing more purple. It's lovely against his deep skin.

"Joy." I shake his hand. It's warm and heavy. "Nice polish."

Keith smiles at me. It's even more glorious up close. Before I can release his hand, he flips mine over. Clutching my wrist, he looks at my nails—a stiletto set, extra long and extra sharp in matte black. He applies pressure to the center of my palm with his thumb in small circular movements. Reflexively, I press the very tips of my nails into his skin, just enough to pinch.

He smirks. "That wasn't very nice."

"Who said I was nice?" I take my hand back. Biting his full bottom lip, he shakes his head. Then he looks away, effectively tossing a cold bucket of water on the moment.

As the bus pulls off, I study Keith's profile. His whole body must be covered in tattoos. They spiral up his neck and behind his ear. Rose gold gauges, the circumference of my pinky, sit comfortably in each lobe. Girls walk up and down the aisle, deliberately ignoring Rhodes's "rules." They aren't subtle about their interest, as they find reasons to linger around him. Keith ignores us all, quietly pulling a tattered book from his backpack.

The cover is missing, and the spine is completely broken. Threads poke out from the center, dog-eared pages double the thickness. It's literally hanging on by its threads. I watch in disbelief as he folds it backward, bringing it closer to his face so that he can see.

"Problem, Joy?"

"What did you do to that book?"

"I read it," he says without looking up. "That's what you do with books. You read them."

"You can read a book without it looking like that by the end, I'm sure."

"Not if you love it enough."

Shifting my body, I watch him flip a torn page. "If you love it, wouldn't you make an effort to take better care of it?"

"Who says I haven't taken care of it? I touch it every day, carry it with me everywhere, and enjoy it thoroughly," Keith says, his voice low. He makes it sound almost sensual as his fingers slide across the page. "I think that qualifies as love and effort, don't you?"

"If you say so."

I catch a few words on the page. Nothing stokes my curiosity enough to eye hustle. So, I straighten up in my seat and settle in for a quick nap.

We pull up to the museum sooner than I would have liked. Swinging my arms over my head, I stretch my limbs. Keith glances at the hem of my skirt as it slides up my thighs.

"What's the name?" I ask as we step off of the bus.

"The name of what?" He looks down at me. Pins and buttons cover his long denim jacket. The most interesting of the bunch is a Bugs Bunny on a stool with a bare-assed Lola Bunny thrown over his lap, gloved hand in the air. Keith notices me noticing the pin and winks.

"The name of the book," I say pointedly.

"*Wide Awake.*"

"*Wide Awake?*"

"Yep."

"What's it about?"

Keith and I walk at the back of the class, taking in the grounds. I love fall. The lush trees bristle under the breeze. I adjust my socks, pulling them slightly higher on my thighs.

"It's about a vampire."

I raise my brow, and he shakes his head. "It's not what you think. Or maybe it is. At its core, it's a love story. A Black vampire finds himself trapped in the Deep South. He meets a free woman who plans to escape to the North and falls for her. She becomes the only human he's ever turned. In the field where he turns her, they spend the evening having the most depraved sex you could imagine."

"You read vampire smut?" I ask, taking a seat in front of a massive marble installation. "Interesting. Is it detailed, or do you have to use your imagination?"

"No imagination needed." Keith sits next to me. There's a mischievous glint in his eyes. "They play in each other's blood, amongst other things, and when the moon hits exactly three quarters, they die the little death."

"They come underneath the moon? That's nice if you can get past the blood play, I guess."

"They come *because* of the moon." He grins. "When it's over, they fall asleep in a barn, and in the morning, she's gone. So he spends the rest of the book trying to find her, recreating the moment whenever the moon enters waxing gibbous with whoever he can find."

"Do they reunite? Does he find her?"

He doesn't answer, standing instead. "Let's check out the Egyptian installation. I hear they stole some pretty dope shit for the display."

"All right." I sigh, popping up to follow him.

Keith is unlike anyone I've ever met. Everything he says is intentional, purposeful. If the thought doesn't add to our conversation, he avoids sharing it. We walk through the long halls, getting lost amongst the crowds. Keith knows something about nearly every piece. Things you wouldn't find on the information cards. He's tells me he's an artist and charcoal is his medium of choice. I tell him about my love affair with watercolor and how obsessed I am with my current piece.

I find myself engulfed in his energy. It's contagious and exhilarating. Before I know it, it's almost four. At the meeting point, Rhodes tells us we're free to explore but, we have forty-five minutes to board the bus.

"Wanna see the stars?" Keith whispers in my ear.

"The stars?" I look up at him.

"*When I consider thy heavens, the work of thy fingers, the moon and the stars, which thou hast ordained.*" He smiles.

"Psalms 8:3. You don't strike me as religious." I tilt my head.

"I'm not. Not anymore, anyway. Come on." Resting his hand at the small of my back, he leads me toward the back of the building. With the museum closing in an hour, the crowds have thinned out considerably.

"Wouldn't stars be something we'd see at the planetarium?"

"Yes. But they're hosting a mini-exhibition here. Cross promotion or something. It's to get people over to the Museum of Science for the real thing."

"That makes sense." I nod, following his lead.

The room is considerably large for a temporary exhibit. Keith and I are the only people there. I move to take a seat, but Keith pulls me to the side, and we sit on the carpet instead.

"It's better from down here. Trust me," he says.

We remove our jackets and lay them out before sitting on top of them. The lights go down, and I move closer to Keith, feeling a little afraid. I'm not the biggest fan of the dark. As if he senses it, he runs his hand across my shoulders and over my arm. My skin tingles from his touch, and I feel myself relax as we gaze at the starry projection. Keith lies flat on his back, comfortable in the space. The music starts, and a soft voice explains the universe's beginning. I feel his hand make its way up the back of my sweater. The warmth of his fingers and the texture from the rings create delicious sensations against my skin. Arching my back, I stretch my legs out in front of me.

"Join me," he whispers, his large hands circling my waist. When he pulls me down so that I'm basically on top of him, I go willingly.

His scent is overwhelming, woodsy, and rich. Keith's hands travel up the backs of my thighs, under my skirt, and across my ass. I moan into his neck as he squeezes my warm skin.

"You like that? Let's see what else you like." He chuckles, pulling my panties to the side. I don't stop him. Nothing about this day feels real. It's felt exciting and intense but never real. I don't want to think about what it is or isn't. I just want to feel. And at this moment, I want to feel Keith.

His rings against my clit make me dizzy. He strums at me until I feel like I'm going to break in two.

Just when I feel myself start to tip over, he pulls back. I whimper, and he kisses me. There's nothing soft or gentle about it. Keith is ravenous, palming my ass and rolling his hips against mine. Softly, I bite his bottom lip. He groans, flipping me onto my back.

"Ever get fucked in a museum, Joy?" he asks, dragging his teeth across my neck.

"Does this count?" I ask, shoving my hands down his pants.

"Oh, Imma make it count. Don't even trip." Leaning on top of me, he grabs his backpack. He's hard and thick in my hand. I drag my nails up his length, and he shivers. I don't think I've ever seen a man get a condom on so fast. I giggle as he licks my neck, running his hands up my thighs. When he slides into me, I hold my breath. There's a slight tug, but my body quickly adjusts. Keith lifts my sweater over my breasts, sucking and biting my nipples through my thin bra. The wetness between my legs intensifies.

"It's so fucking good. You know that?" He stares down at me.

I nod, pulling his shirt up so I can feel his skin. Then, pinning my leg back, he leans forward so his face is right above mine. I close my eyes.

"Don't do that. Look at me," he says, his forehead against mine.

"More," I whisper.

Everything feels tight. It's like he's cranked a lever to the limit and I'm straining for release. I grab his face, sliding my tongue across his jaw. His grip on my thigh tightens as I move my hips to meet his thrusts. It feels fucking incredible. My body tenses as he whispers a series of filthy things to me.

"Feels crazy, doesn't it?" he says, his lips against my throat.

"Harder," I plead, clinging to his neck.

Keith rubs my clit with his free hand, sending me swerving toward the finish line. Biting his shoulder, I dig my nails into him, and he hisses.

Then he pulls back. Working his hand up my neck, he pushes his wet fingers into my mouth. I suck them, lost to the pressure building in the deepest parts of me. The feeling spreads out, all-consuming, before engulfing me. I come, spiraling through the orgasm. Keith follows close behind, burying his face into my neck. We lie there, breathing heavily, waiting for our heads to catch up with our bodies. Finally, I shift, and he rolls off of me. We stare at the massive moon above us. I smile, and when I look over, I find him smiling too.

We make it back to the bus on time. Barely. I slide into a seat, and Keith follows. My body hums as I settle against the warm leather, sated. Keith rests his hands on his knees, breathing deeply.

"You never answered my question," I say, running my fingers over his knuckles.

"What question?"

"Does he find her? The vampire, does he ever find the woman he turned?"

Keith slides his hand up my thigh, settling it just under the hem of my skirt.

"Yeah." He grins. "He finds her."

AWAY GAME

Sprocket J. Rydyr

Going to a bar the night before her first ever away game as a pro soccer player is, Lindsay Lees knows, a terrible idea. She should be getting a good night's rest, especially since she hadn't been able to sleep a wink on the plane. She'll be a zombie on the field tomorrow afternoon.

But, well, her hotel bed is lumpy, her roommate snores like a damn freight train, and she can hear strangers having sex through the paper-thin walls. Who could blame her for sneaking out?

Her coach, probably, but she's determined not to think about that.

It's not like she's going to get wasted. She's not even going to drink. She'll be good and have some water, maybe get a head start on carbo loading with some bar pretzels, and just . . . lose herself in the crowd for a bit. Maybe do a little dancing, not enough to tire herself out, but enough to get her out of her own head. Soak up some local color, enjoy the atmosphere of a new and unfamiliar place.

And if it happens to be a dyke bar? If there just happens to be a neon labrys above the door that catches her eye from across the street and tells her "This is the one?" Then that's nobody's business but her own.

Lindsay indulges herself in a Shirley Temple—sugar is basically just deconstructed carbs, anyway—and a plate of nachos as she sits at the bar and people-watches. *This isn't a terrible idea,* she tells herself reassuringly. *This is a fantastic idea. I'll take a nap while Sheila is chowing down at the continental breakfast instead of rattling the windows with her snoring. It'll be great.*

Her eyes widen and a chip droops half forgotten from her fingertips as she catches sight of the handsomest butch she's ever seen in her life. *As a matter of fact, this is possibly the best idea I've ever had.*

The butch is standing at the opposite end of the bar, drinking some delicious-looking concoction decked out with a tiny cocktail sword pierced through a neat row of chopped fruit. She's got short-cropped, dark hair: mere bristles on the back and sides and shining waves swept back on top. One perfect wave falls over her forehead, brushing thick, dark eyebrows. *Like Superman,* Lindsay's idiot brain supplies helpfully. Neon lights paint medium brown skin with washes of pink and blue. Thick-rimmed glasses perch atop a ruggedly crooked nose. Dark eyes catch Lindsay's. Plush lips part in a sly grin, pearly teeth clenched lightly around a cocktail sword as they slide the last cube of pineapple from it.

Lindsay realizes that she's staring. And *sweating.* She takes a deep swig of her own drink to try to cool herself down. When she looks up again, the butch is gone. Disappointment sinks into her gut.

"This seat taken?"

Lindsay jolts nearly out of her skin.

A chuckle rich as fine chocolate warms Lindsay's ears. "Sorry, I didn't mean to startle you."

"N-no, it's fine!" Lindsay squeaks. *Squeaks!* Like the mousy, shy teenager with no idea how to talk to pretty girls she hasn't been in years. "And no, this seat isn't taken."

"Great." The stranger's smile is even more dazzling without a cocktail sword between her teeth. She slides onto the stool next to Lindsay's and, oh, Lord, she's *tall*. Lindsay has to crane her neck up to look at her even when she's sitting. "Stan," she says, holding out a hand.

It takes Lindsay a moment to process that this is an introduction. "Oh! Lindsay," she answers, shaking the stranger's hand. It's warm and firm, pleasantly strong. "Oh, shit, wait, should I use he/him pronouns for you?"

Stan smiles politely and gives a small head shake. "No, thanks. She/her is fine, they/them is better."

"They/them it is, then. She/her is good for me," Lindsay informs them.

"Duly noted. May I get you another?" Stan asks, nodding at Lindsay's drink.

I'm dreaming, right? There's no way someone this sexy is offering to buy me a drink. I hope I didn't hit my head or something. "Um, yeah! That'd be amazing. It's a Shirley Temple."

They smile and nod in approval before catching the bartender's attention and ordering another round of drinks for them both.

Wait, a virgin piña colada? Huh. Maybe they don't want me to feel weird about not drinking? That's sweet. Unnecessary but sweet. "Would you like some nachos?" Lindsay offers.

"I thought you'd never ask." Stan gives a sheepish little smile and it's so unfairly cute that Lindsay has to take a big sip of her drink to cool her blush. "I actually came here tonight because I had a craving for them. And then I see this gorgeous woman sitting here eating a massive plateful, and I just think . . . *kismet.*"

"You know, I don't really believe in fate, but if that's how I ended up sitting with the most attractive person I've ever met then I'm good with calling it that." *Oh, fuck, did I actually say that out loud? This drink is definitely nonalcoholic, right??*

Stan laughs, loudly and beautifully. "You're not so bad yourself," they tease.

"Yeah, right." Lindsay's joy sours a little in her stomach as the words tumble from her lips. She pushes the plate of nachos closer to Stan without even thinking about it, her mind suddenly filled with critical voices. Former coaches, high school teammates, team dieticians, her mother. *"Should you really be eating that?" "If you don't lose weight, you won't be able to keep up with your teammates." "Do you have any idea how many calories are in all that cheese?"*

She's proud of her strength and her speed, and certainly of her skill, but she's been the chubbiest player on every team she's played with since junior high. The muscles are there, and they're strong as hell—*thank you very much*—but they're padded with a layer of fat. The upside is that opposing players tend to underestimate her abilities, thinking she'll be slow or a bad jumper. The downside is, well, looking "out of shape" compared to her teammates despite being at the same fitness level. And never being allowed to forget it.

Concern flickers across Stan's face. "Did I say something wrong?"

"No, not at all," Lindsay replies, and it feels like a lie even though it's the truth. Stan didn't say anything wrong. The problem is with Lindsay.

Stan pops another chip into their mouth and chews it

thoughtfully. They finish off their drink with a loud slurp that makes Lindsay giggle. "How about a dance, then?"

"I probably shouldn't," Lindsay says grudgingly. "I've got a big day tomorrow."

Stan's lips twitch into a private smile, like they're holding onto a joke. "Mm. Me, too." Stan gives Lindsay an evaluating look, dark brown eyes tracing from face to feet and back up again, slow and sizzling. Lindsay shivers under its intensity. "You're in good shape," Stan remarks, which almost makes Lindsay scoff in disbelief. "I bet you could handle a dance or two without it negatively impacting your performance on the pitch tomorrow."

Lindsay blinks rapidly as the penny drops. "My . . ."

Stan grins, every inch the cat that caught the canary. "Lees, right? You're the new girl everyone's been clamoring about." They lean in close and lower their voice to a conspiratorial whisper. "I've been told to keep an eye on you." They wink.

Lindsay's stomach does a flip. "You . . ."

Stan's eyebrows lift in surprise and their grin fades. "Oh, hell, I thought you were just playing coy. You really don't recognize me?" They pull off their glasses when Lindsay shakes her head. "Contacts when I'm on the field. And, of course . . ." They roll up their sleeves to reveal extensive amounts of ink stretching up their forearms. Extremely distinctive and immediately recognizable ink. They smile when Lindsay's eyes widen with recognition.

"Holy shit," Lindsay blurts. "You're Constance Novar!"

"In the flesh," they admit. "But I'm just Stan to my friends. I hope we're still friends?" At Lindsay's numb nod, they continue, "I've got to say, my respect for your coach just went down. I would think she'd be having you use a photo of me for target practice."

"I'm really just a sub," Lindsay mumbles, embarrassed.

Stan smirks. "Well, lucky me."

Lindsay blushes. "Not, like, in a sex way . . . I mean . . ." She sighs when Stan laughs.

"Oh, come on; you walked right into it. You're being a bit *defensive*," Stan teases.

Lindsay purses her lips. "Maybe you're just being too *forward*," she snarks back.

Stan—Constance *fucking* Novar—gives her a smile of absolute delight. "Oh, good; I'm so pleased to meet a woman who doesn't run for the hills as soon as the puns start coming out."

"I guess they find them *offensive*," Lindsay replies, unable to keep the smile off her face. *This is so not how I thought Constance Novar would be if I ever met her. Them. Oh, my god, Stan is seriously Constance Novar! And they're a total nerd!*

"Maybe so." Stan chuckles. "So, Lindsay, how about that dance? Or are you scared to fraternize with the enemy now that you know who I am?"

"Shouldn't you be the one who's scared?" Lindsay counters. "I'm a terrible dancer; what if I stepped on your foot? You're a key part of your team's offense. I'll be lucky to get subbed in for the last five minutes."

"Hmmmm, you make an excellent point." Stan leans in close, dangerously close, guiding Lindsay's face with the touch of a fingertip to her chin until their lips are nearly touching. "Well, perhaps we should skip the dancing, then. Cut right to the chase?"

Lindsay swallows hard. "And wh-what would that be?" *Please, please, please be suggesting what I think you're suggesting.*

Stan traces that teasing fingertip along Lindsay's jaw, down the sensitive skin of her throat, and along her collarbone until it brushes the fabric of her shirt and comes to a stop. "Back to my place?"

Holy shit, score! Except, dammit . . . "My coach would be furious . . ."

"I won't tell if you don't. If she somehow finds out you can tell her it was reconnaissance. Checking out the enemy's moves." Stan leans back, breaking contact and giving Lindsay room to breathe and think clearly. "Up to you, though. We can hang out here and eat nachos all night if you'd prefer."

I should say no. Shouldn't I? Definitely. I should definitely say no. "My roommate's snoring is awful," Lindsay finds herself saying instead. At Stan's amused raise of an eyebrow, she adds, "I'd probably sleep better if I found another place to stay the night."

Stan's responding smile is radiant as a sunrise. "That could be arranged. I have a private room, as it happens. With a very comfortable bed."

"That does sound intriguing . . ."

"And I don't snore."

"*Sold.*"

Not only does Stan have a private room, they also have their own private entrance with its own set of stairs leading up to it. Lindsay doesn't even have to sneak in past their sponsor family. It feels illicit anyway.

Lindsay's teammates are sleeping soundly in their hotel rooms, and Lindsay is here: following a rival player up to their room, stopping every few seconds to kiss them again and again, both of them tripping over the stairs in their eagerness. She should probably be ashamed.

She isn't. She's nearly delirious with desire.

When Stan closes the door behind them and unbuttons their long-sleeved shirt, Lindsay's jaw drops. She'd known to expect a good amount of muscle—Novar has been a pro for years, even done a stint on the Mexican national team—but *damn*. She wasn't expecting this exquisite level of definition: perfectly sculpted deltoids, triceps shaped by the gods themselves, abs you could plane wood with. Lindsay is immediately overcome with the urge to taste every inch. She holds herself in check, seizing her lower lip between her teeth and feasting only with her eyes . . . until she sees the invitation in Stan's expression and realizes she doesn't *have* to restrain herself.

She dives in and worships. Stan struggles to pull their shirt the rest of the way off as Lindsay puts her mouth on every bit of skin she can reach. Together they stumble backward toward the bed, bouncing when they hit the mattress. It's just as comfortable as Stan had promised. It might as well be a bed of nails for all Lindsay notices. She tongues the chiseled grooves of Stan's abdominals. Nips the wings of their clavicles. Trails hot, open-mouthed kisses across firm pectorals and soft breasts; first over the fabric of Stan's sports bra, then over hastily exposed bare skin.

Stan hisses ecstatic profanity as they help Lindsay work their pants down their legs, revealing thick, strong thighs, boxer briefs sporting a damp patch in the center, rock-hard calves, shins marked with the scrapes and bruises that come standard with a soccer career under a layer of dark leg hair. *Holy hell. I might be the luckiest woman in the world tonight.* "Protection?" Lindsay asks, tracing a fingertip along the waistband of Stan's boxer briefs, causing their abs to twitch.

"Nightstand," Stan pants, tugging off their underwear and flinging it across the room. "Top drawer. *Fuck*."

Lindsay is only too happy to oblige them, fucking them hard and fast with gloved fingers as she sucks dark hickeys into their skin. Stan moans and grunts out what sounds like at least three different languages' worth of swear words as they ride Lindsay's fingers and curl their own into her hair, short nails scratching bluntly at her scalp. Sweat has never tasted better than it does trickling down Stan's washboard abs, pooling in their navel, mingling with the heady scent of their arousal.

Stan comes with a yelp and a spasm, shuddering hot and wet around Lindsay's pumping fingers. They come again two minutes later with a scream muffled against their own forearm, muscles tensing and releasing, twitching as they collapse against sweat-soaked sheets. *"Dios mío,"* they pant before huffing out a pleased laugh.

Lindsay peels off her glove and tosses it into the wastepaper basket next to the bed before stretching out next to them. She's uncomfortably hot under all of her clothes. *Should I undress? Will Stan think it's weird if I don't? But god, they're so sexy and I'm so . . . not.* She runs a fingertip slowly down Stan's stomach. Their skin is glistening with sweat, radiant and beautifully bruised from Lindsay's teeth. She kind of wants to ravish them all over again. "Holy shit, you're perfect," she murmurs.

"You're pretty damn perfect yourself," Stan replies, running strong fingers through Lindsay's short hair.

"Uh-huh . . ."

"Seriously, you're fucking gorgeous."

Lindsay pulls back so that she can properly side-eye them. "Yeah, right."

Stan props themself up on their elbows and locks eyes with her. "Hey, listen to me. You're stunning. You know that, don't you?"

"You don't have to flatter me. You've already got me in your bed."

Stan frowns, their forehead creasing. "It isn't flattery; it's the truth. Why would I have brought you home if I didn't find you attractive?"

Lindsay draws protective arms over her chest. "Wouldn't be the first time I've been somebody's pity fuck."

Stan's expression softens from indignation to sorrow. "Well, hell." They sit up and rub the fine bristles at the back of their head thoughtfully.

Here it comes. Some pretty lies to smooth over the fat girl's hurt feelings and get her all pathetically grateful for your attention. Or maybe some good old-fashioned flat-out rejection. Damn it, I'd really hoped that Stan wouldn't be like everybody else. Stupid, really.

"I'm sorry someone made you feel like that's all you're worth." Stan sounds unnervingly sincere. They hesitate, then reach out a hand, palm up. Lindsay doesn't take their hand, but she does resist the impulse to withdraw further. "For what it's worth, I promise you you're not here because I pity you. You're here because I walked into that bar tonight feeling lonely, and then I saw . . ."—they brush reverent fingers over Lindsay's cheekbone, drawing blush—". . . the most incredible beauty."

"Yeah fucking right," Lindsay scoffs.

They shake their head sadly. "I mean it. My jaw practically hit the floor when I saw you standing there." They cup Lindsay's jaw tenderly. "You're a knockout. Truly. Cheekbones for days. Beautiful eyes. Soft, full lips. Not to mention the sexiest curves . . . and the strength they hold." They lower their hand to Lindsay's upper arm, giving it a firm squeeze. Lindsay flexes instinctively and Stan grins. "Make no mistake, Lindsay. *I'm* the lucky one. You agreed to come home with me." They run their hand down to Lindsay's, lacing their fingers together. "Believe me, you're not the first rival player I've found in that bar. But you are the first I decided to take the risk for."

Lindsay blinks in surprise. "Wait, really? I figured me being your opponent tomorrow was what appealed to you."

Stan shakes their head, smiling softly. "There's a certain illicit thrill, I'll admit. But it's one I've never indulged in before. It never seemed worth risking my performance on the pitch." They shrug. "Until tonight."

Lindsay doesn't speak for a long moment, letting Stan's words settle over her. "I've never played an away game before," Lindsay says finally. "Professionally, I mean; I did in school, of course. But this is my first professional away game. It's . . . kind of a huge deal for me." She huffs out an incredulous little laugh. "I did *not* expect to jeopardize my performance with an affair with a member of the opposition." She looks up and meets Stan's eyes. They're beautiful: patient and understanding and simmering with heat all at the same time. "But . . . yeah. Like you said. I saw the most incredible beauty, and I just couldn't resist."

"Though you didn't recognize me as an opponent," Stan reminds her. "Perhaps that would have made a difference. Or maybe not. I knew exactly who you were when I caught sight of you. Didn't stop me." Stan gently withdraws their hand. "Do you want to call this off? Maybe it's too late for you not to 'sleep with the enemy,' but I'll understand if you'd rather go back to your hotel and your teammates. Especially if you still don't believe that you're here because I want you."

"I want to be here," Lindsay says decisively. Looking into Stan's eyes and seeing the unmasked desire there, she believes it. She believes everything.

"I want you to be here," Stan reaffirms, face brightening. "As long as you want to be here. You can sleep on the floor if you're not feeling, ah, amorous anymore. Or in the bed, and I'll take the floor. Or we can both take the bed and just spoon or whatever." Stan cocks their head and offers a suggestive smile. "But if you still want me as much as I want you . . ."

"I really fucking want you."

Stan's pupils dilate. They lick their lips and Lindsay follows the movement of their tongue, entranced. "Then let me show you how stunning you are." They raise an eyebrow in question. Lindsay answers them with a kiss.

If Lindsay had any lingering doubts about the honesty of Stan's professed attraction to her, they are swiftly dispelled.

This is no quick, hasty fumble in the dark. Stan turns on the light to see her better. They take their time undressing her, checking in with sincere brown eyes as they remove each item of clothing, waiting for Lindsay's nod of consent before moving to the next. Stan devours her first with their eyes, then their hands, then their mouth. Their touch is reverent in a way that Lindsay's never experienced before, slow but eager and devout. Stan makes hungry eye contact as they explore her body, present and engaged and clearly ecstatic to be right where they are: kissing Lindsay's ample thighs reverently before they dive between them.

Under Stan's touch, she feels beautiful. She feels strong. She feels desirable. She feels *hot*.

She shakes apart and comes back together once, twice, more. Stan would probably keep going forever if Lindsay didn't tap out. They dispose of the used dental dam and gloves before flopping down onto the mattress next to Lindsay, curling up beside her and playing with her hair. "How do you feel?"

"Exhausted," Lindsay admits with a satisfied smile.

"Exhausted and beautiful?"

Lindsay's smile deepens. "Exhausted and beautiful," she agrees.

"Mmmmm, then my work here is done," Stan purrs. They yawn. "Just in time. I'm ready to conk out."

Oh, shit, should I offer to leave? My legs are pretty much jelly right now, but I don't want to overstay my welcome . . .

"I'm gonna brush my teeth," Stan announces, kissing Lindsay on the forehead before bouncing back up from the bed. "There should be some fresh toothbrushes in the cabinet if you want to go next. I mean, you can leave if you want," they say hurriedly at Lindsay's surprised expression. "But it's cool with me if you want to stay. I promise I don't snore. We can set an early alarm if you want to try to sneak back into the hotel without being caught."

Lindsay's heart warms. "Sounds good to me."

The alarm goes off around four in the morning. Lindsay is slow to stir. She's so comfortable in this soft bed, in these firm arms. "Time to go?" Stan asks, voice husky with sleep, when Lindsay finally drags herself from the surprising comfort of their embrace.

"Yeah. You don't have to see me out; keep sleeping."

"M'kay," Stan mumbles agreeably into their pillow. They stay in that position until Lindsay unlocks the door. "See you later, gorgeous," they say then, waggling their fingers at Lindsay as she turns the knob.

Lindsay shakes her head and rolls her eyes, but her stomach doesn't twist in disbelief. She knows that the compliment is genuine. Stan thinks she's gorgeous even if she doesn't. It's a good feeling.

When Lindsay is subbed on in the eighty-fifth minute, she barely has time to make eye contact with Stan from across the width of the field. Stan looks, somehow, less sweaty and exhausted after nearly ninety minutes of intensely competitive soccer than they did after sex with Lindsay, and it's ridiculously gratifying. Stan gives Lindsay a smile that has her feeling alarmingly weak in the knees and follows it with a wink in the moments before the whistle blows.

Lindsay can't help but grin even as she takes a stray elbow to the solar plexus from one of Stan's teammates mere seconds after play resumes. Her legs burn more than they would have if she'd spent the night sleeping, and going up for headers is more of a challenge than usual. If she were a starter, she might actually be in trouble. *Although Stan certainly doesn't look like they're struggling.*

In fact, the closest Stan ever seems to come to struggling is as they're setting up for a free kick, when Lindsay gives them a subtle wave and Stan nearly trips over the ball. Lindsay can't hold back a giggle, drawing curious looks from the rest of the wall.

Okay, yeah. Definitely the best idea I've ever had.

TAKE TUESDAY

Lin Devon

"We've met," he'd said, and she'd known.

Two words sent two years of dating right down the drain. Well, two words and a great deal of eye fucking between her then-boyfriend Mick and the woman he was supposed to be meeting for the first time, Cassandra. It was one of those corporate after-hours functions where everyone gets to schmooze in fancy getups on the terrace of their newest development. Cassandra had headed the merger, and Mick, as head of accounting, had apparently been working closely with her for months. That he'd never bothered to tell Elisa, his girlfriend, that all those late nights had been spent alone in the company of the leggy blonde shark, was apparently no big deal. So there she'd been, introducing the two like an idiot after having met the woman at the bar, and it had all come clear. It still made Elisa's teeth grind three weeks and a relocation later. As she sat at her favorite lunchtime cafe sipping tea she recalled the way Mick had first denied it, then tried to gaslight her, then admitted the whole thing with an air of callous nonchalance peppered with maddening accusations of her prudery.

"You know what? It's natural." He'd shrugged. "It's what we're built for. It doesn't mean anything, just physical. And open relationships help everyone feel free, because at the end of the day we still choose each other. The physical stuff is just bodies doing body things. I know you're not like that, but it's you I choose to spend my life with. That's what's important."

She'd thrown a ceramic frame at his head. It missed, but shattered satisfyingly. She'd meant what she'd said then, right before slamming the door on him for good. "Both people still have to agree to it or it's just plain old cheating, Mick. I don't date cheaters, and I don't choose you."

She smiled into the fragrant steam. The shark could have him, chew him up, and spit him out if she wanted to. Elisa was relieved to be free of him. Her new apartment was the haven she'd been trying to create with Mick but was never able to. Her coworkers had rallied their support around her and ended up giving her the best few weeks she'd had at the ad firm. She was grateful beyond measure for them showing her what real affection looked like.

Now she sat at her go-to lunch spot nibbling a cucumber sandwich on the sunny sidewalk, thinking it didn't take much to set her on her feet again. That's when her feet got knocked right out from under her. Again.

He walked toward her from up the street like hot caramel poured into tailored slacks and a button-up shirt, a cap of waving dark hair over hazel eyes behind glasses. She could set her watch by him. Every Tuesday at 1:15 he strolled up the sidewalk, gave her a smile like tossing a small piano on her head, and went inside the cafe, her cafe, for coffee. Every Tuesday.

She was not obsessed. She was not rebounding. In fact this little ritual had been going on for five or six months now. He strolled up the walk, smiled, and went in. This, though perhaps enough to obsess lesser women, was not the reason she considered this their ritual.

When he came out of the cafe, he took the table on the other side of the door, sat on the opposite side from her, and sipped his coffee while reading a book. It was always the same. If she wasn't looking at him, she could feel those hazel eyes traveling to her over the top of his book. She'd look up just to catch him looking away. But slowly. He did not care if he was caught. And when he was actually engrossed in the subject matter in his hands, she would peek at him. Watch him, take him in until those beautiful eyes would flicker up to catch her. Their coy game had been in play for the last three months, but it was only recently she'd noticed the titles on his book covers. It seemed a little crazy to assume they were for her until it became too obvious to ignore. The title three weeks ago had been, *Suddenly Single,* then *Women Who Want,* then *Will She, Won't She,* and today, as he settled into his seat with practiced casualness, he lifted his book and she read, *Follow Where I Lead.*

He read for a few minutes, per usual, then cast a lazy glance at her over the top. She didn't notice. Her eyes traveled over his polished brown leather uppers, over his dark gray wool-clad legs, up the buttons on his deep blue shirt one by one to the pulse inside his collar, the faint stubble on his jaw, the long line of his nose, black-rimmed glasses and long dark lashes that must have grazed the lenses. He was nerdy at first glance but shockingly handsome at even a cursory closer look. She was wondering if he knew how his eyes seemed to blaze against his candy complexion, if his polished unassuming nature had been honed this way, if he knew the way these clothes were designed

to showcase with subtlety the surprising heft of muscle underneath. She wondered so long she suddenly realized she hadn't
bothered to look away. She was staring, dreamy-eyed, at him,
and he was staring back.

The game had changed. He didn't smile, just closed his
book and looked at her. He was no more than ten feet away,
but this naked review telescoped him oddly closer. She thought
she could smell his cologne, and it made her breathing invol-
untarily deepen. She was trapped in amber. Not stagnant but
liquid amber pouring over her body in waves everywhere he cast
his gaze, sticking her in place and filling her body with molten
heat from the crux of her thighs to pool in her belly and light
a fire that burned her thoughts right out of her head. Some distant voice in her mind called for her to be reasonable. But what
reason is there for those pinned by the eyes of a tiger? There was
nothing so predatory about him, but that he seemed to have
asked a question and found her answer was so strangely dangerous. She teetered on a vibrating edge, a woman who's accepted a
challenge without knowing what it is and finding the unknown
too enticing a reward not to risk. This is not how she imagined
her Tuesday unfolding.

He lifted his cup and drank deep while she imagined her
body turned to liquid and drunk from his cup just like that.
He sucked his lips clean without breaking eye contact, the light
of appreciation in his eyes making the move more boyish than
sleazy. He let the slightest grin arc his lips, and then stood to
leave. Was it some trick of the pleats that he looked slightly risen
in his trousers? An unreasonable hunger leapt up in her at the
prospect of his slipping away now. He was going to toss her into
the cold vacuum of space still steaming from a hot bath. Every
part of her was calling to him not to go, every part but her voice.

He closed his book on the table, tapped the cover, and left

it as he turned to walk back in the direction from which he'd come. She reveled in the sway of his narrow hips inside the fabric, the roll of his shoulders as he strode, hands in pockets, through the crowds of lunch goers and turned the corner. He did not look back.

Elisa stood on unreliable legs. She moved like an automaton to his abandoned table, clutched his book to her chest, and hurried down the street. God, what was she doing? She could just go home for the rest of the day, holed up in her apartment masturbating the fantasy of him away. But second guessing was for naught. She was possessed by need, not knowing or caring about how this thing might pan out. The world had narrowed to this one driving force: be near him, get close and then closer. All this time she'd been starving for him, nibbling at the scraps of their exchanges. She wanted more.

Her eyes locked on the back of his head as he made his way through and around clusters of strangers. She had his book, of course. If she could catch up to him she'd simply call out and he would turn and she would tell him he forgot his book. That had to be enough. Anything else was crazy. She'd never even spoken to this guy. But when he turned onto a quiet side street, no one else in sight, she didn't call out. Her voice stayed locked in her throat as she hurried after him. Her heels echoed a gentle tapping sound she was sure he could hear, but he didn't turn around. He made his way to the next street and turned, so quickly out of her sight she had to jog a little to keep up. She turned where he'd turned and saw him duck into a stairwell halfway up the block. Parking garage. He'd be in his car and away before she even had a chance to . . . what?

When she reached the second landing, she found a bay of parked cars neatly tucked into delineated spaces; every twenty feet or so stood a concrete pillar. He was nowhere in sight. She

stepped into the open, his book against her breasts clutched like
a shield, her breathing labored. Sweat slicked the little hairs
framing her forehead. What now, then? Wait to hear the turning
of an ignition and hurry to knock on his window? She suddenly
felt like a ridiculous high schooler with a crush.

Did she imagine the scent of lightly applied cologne drifting
to her along the trail he'd left? She walked forward, heels tapping a staccato rhythm to match the furious hammering of her
heart. This was not like her. This was actually dangerous. All
her better morals railed against this behavior. But it was clear
she was alone here. She'd lost him. She'd just keep his book and
bring it with her Tuesday, maybe finally speak to him. But the
scent of him was singing in her nostrils. The imagined closeness
of the man who bore that scent made her skin prickle. She was
warm in her clothes, warm enough to want to be free of them.
Warm enough to follow his trail even into the unknown.

It wasn't so dramatic as footsteps sounding behind her, or
lust-fevered hands reaching out to her from the dark. He was
just there, leaning against a car, waiting. Her heart skipped and
stopped her in her tracks. He slid his hands out of his pockets
to cross his arms, eyes on her as if to say, *Your move.* She didn't
move, just stood there like a sacrificial calf, his book clutched
now to her belly. It did nothing to ease the fluttering inside, the
heat that poured out across her hips and gathered in the satin
of her panties.

He stood but didn't advance. Instead he held out a hand
palm up. Like those long fingers were magnetized, she made
two steps toward him and he closed the distance. He was taller
up close, shoulders more broad, waving hair flopped over his
forehead shading those incredible eyes. He took his book, not
her hand. Close enough to touch, close enough to kiss, he stood
there reading the title on the dust jacket. *Follow Where I Lead.*

His eyes studied her as he pulled the dust jacket free to reveal another underneath. *Will She, Won't She.* He let it fall. He pulled this one free to reveal another. *Women Who Want.* He smiled revealing the next. And the next, and the next. Beyond *Suddenly Single,* the first time she'd noticed this little ruse, there was *Take A Risk. Let Me Know. Dreaming of You. Can't Help Myself. The Heat. The Hunger.* And the last cover, which would have been the first, read, *Show Me Something.*

She looked up into his face and found him burning in his skin. His shoulders and chest were visibly rising and falling. The impression of being too near a tiger returned. He licked his lips. By some trick of desire she did the same. She took the book and dropped it in its nest of discarded jackets with a flutter like settling birds. She took his hand and watched his eyes as she brought his fingertips to her lips. The idea of leaving without this was a flimsy fantasy. She would combust without the taste of him. He sucked in a breath when the pad of his index finger touched the soft flesh of her lips and uttered a soft moan when the wet bed of her tongue tasted him. He looked barely contained. She didn't want him contained.

She held his hand in both of hers and placed it on the open V of her clavicle. His palm was blazing hot over her heartbeat. His fingers splayed over her flesh, found their way inside to slide over the top of her breast, across her shoulder, up her neck. His grip was firm on the nape, his thumb caressing her jaw, her chin, her lower lip to pull at her open mouth. He leaned in. He groaned across her tongue, "Kiss me," and she received his lips with greed.

He cupped her face in both hands to hold her against his kiss. He sucked at her lips, lapped at her tongue with his own, no air lost between them. The unknown was a drug that intoxicated them both. She barely noticed when he slipped her buttons free and tugged her blouse from the waistband of her skirt. She lavished in the weight of his hands sliding around her bare flesh to cover the small of her back and pull her to him. He smelled like clean laundry. He tasted like coffee, like cake. But his body was a machine built for filth.

The long line of his cock pressed against her belly rigid as a rocket and rumbling just the same to break free. His urgency kicked up when her fingers traced the mass of his erection through sensible trousers and she squeezed. She had a breath to look in those dreamy eyes, now glassy and lit from within, to say, "Fuck me," before strong hands had her lifted off her feet, skirt hiked around her waist, and legs wrapped bodily around him.

He took two steps and had her against a concrete pillar, holding her there with the force of his pelvis and his insatiable kiss. She had his shirt undone to seek out his nipples, his impressive shoulders, the heave in his taut belly. He pulled the top of her bra down to reveal hardened nipples to draw one and then the other into his suck. He was groaning in delight. Rumbling into her mouth so deep she didn't know those nimble fingers had undone his fly and pulled his dick free until he was tugging her panties to the side and the head of his cock was waiting between sex-soaked lips.

Just a beat. One moment to wait, quivering at the tip before he drove his hips forward and impaled her. He wanted to see her. He held her around the waist in python arms and watched her face as he did his work. She gasped and the sound echoed. Musical. She couldn't look away from those eyes, that beautiful face made hard in his need. Open mouths not an inch apart, they shared breath as he dug for depth and stretched her like a glove around his insistent plunge. Resting tight against his hips, she felt his hardness against her cervix in a fit so perfect it was as if he'd been ordered and made for her. The molten rod of him slid perfectly into place only to retreat and seat himself again so deep. He was just this side of too much, but the quaking ache he produced deep in her belly was a medicine she couldn't get enough of. He rolled against her with a rhythm and reach that ignored her limits. He didn't have to know the need that brought her here, only that she did need.

He danced against her, some imagined music keeping time as he devoured her throat with open-mouthed kisses. He lapped at her lips and kicked up his pace. He covered her mouth with his own and began to fuck in earnest. His hips pinioned, unrelenting as she clutched at the fabric of his shirt. She sang her praises against the curve of his neck, his pulse which smelled like a sated Sunday morning in a stranger's tangled sheets. He whimpered nonsense against her lips and clutched at her hips to pound a message in a rapid reckless staccato so hard and so deep she felt her nerve endings all over prickle and sing and gather electricity.

She closed her eyes and sucked air to feed the fire now set to burst, hoping only that he wouldn't stop. She might have begged aloud, might only have thought it, but he complied. Don't stop. Don't stop. Don't stop. He maintained, miraculously, the rapid-fire pace he'd set and watched as her head tilted back, her mouth opened, her legs went rigid around his hips, and she broke like a dam in an earthquake.

She soaked him, the tight fit of her body spasming around him like a fist bringing him over the edge. He slipped free and pressed forward to slide his cock between her belly and the waistband of her skirt. Not on the oil-stained concrete but over the flesh of her belly he let free and covered her in a streaming pulsing jet of molten jism.

His heart was barely contained thunder in his chest that mirrored her own as he let her slowly to her unready feet. There they stayed, spent, heaving breath, quaking and wet from each other as the outside world slowly clicked piece by piece back into place. She blinked up at him, and he smiled down at her, neither wishing yet to unclutch their hands from the other's clothing. It was a sunny afternoon in the city, just past lunch time. That no one had discovered them was a wonder. He buttoned her shirt. She buttoned his.

In the weeks that followed, Elisa would both condemn and applaud her behavior after the fact. She hadn't gone back to the coffee shop in three weeks, not once. That was okay. Whatever he had been for her, it had helped massively in putting Mick in the rearview. It had invigorated her in so many ways, confirmed some things she'd hoped were still true and did away with many of her needless insecurities.

That she'd left him there in the garage with nothing but a kiss on the cheek, no contact information, no way to find her again, was something she still struggled with. She dreamed of him, often. She conjured his image in the shower, suddenly standing there in the steam with her. That magnificent cock in his fist and advancing on her. She caught phantom whiffs of his scent at the strangest times. She could go back to the coffee shop, see if he was still going there. But if he wasn't, well, it was too fragile a fantasy to risk. Clogging it up with hopes and expectations felt beside the point. But God, she did want him again. She imagined him walking up behind her at the farmers' market, scent-first. Or here in her sunny apartment some Saturday morning. Maybe she'd be in bed, reading naked, and there he'd be in her doorway. Or sliding in between the covers like no time had passed at all, no questions between them. But that was crazy. That was all in the rearview. She felt very sure if she kept saying it she would someday soon believe it.

She was close to that when she came home from work one

Wednesday and found someone at her door waiting for her. They weren't supposed to let strangers into the building like this, but if he'd signed in at the desk, they might have believed whatever story he'd spun. Mick leaned on her door looking like an admonished puppy, a massive bouquet of flowers in his hands. He smiled sheepishly at her, false humility she couldn't believe she'd never seen through before. She wasn't going to invite him in.

"Look," he finally got to the point, "McBride wants you there. He doesn't know we've had a separation and he keeps asking about you. I want you there. You were my rock while I worked on this thing and you deserve to celebrate it with the rest of the team. It's just a party. I know we've got a lot to work on before we can get back together. But these are literary folks, and I know you always said you wanted to work for publishers. Could be an opportunity for you too. What do you say? Be my plus one?"

"What about Cassandra?"

He shrugged but couldn't look in her eyes. "History. Ancient history."

His pathetic attempt to reconcile was a haphazard veil over his true intentions. *McBride wants you there.* Mick's boss had always liked her. And he could get her at a table with the publishers she wanted to work with. So it was that Friday night found her trussed up in her very best strapless red revenge dress, bending the ear of the powerful and ignoring Mick at every opportunity.

She wasn't surprised when he elbowed his way between her and McBride as a show of prowess to introduce her to the publishing house's new artistic director. But she was surprised when she turned to see the guy. Tall, broad shouldered, ridiculously handsome in a mop of floppy dark curls, bright eyes, and glasses.

Mick said, "Elisa, this is Jack Warren, he's—" But she'd already stepped in close to smell that cologne again and slipped her hand against his proffered palm to smile her recognition back at his. She felt like one of those cartoons lifted off her feet to drift nose-first along the winding pink trail of a delicious scent. Like drifting home. He cast those blazing eyes over her face, licked his lips, and smiled back.

She squeezed his hand, knowing she wouldn't be letting it go again, and said, "We've met."

HOT NEIGHBOR GUY

Kate Sloan

Another night, another masturbation session in front of my laptop. One hand down my panties, one hand scrolling—first lazily, then more insistently—through the filthiest annals of the *Brokeback Mountain* fanfiction archive. Last week it was *Fight Club*. The week before that, *Pulp Fiction*. This week? Cute cowboys with sun-worn faces and hard cocks.

But nothing's really grabbing me, except my own hand. I lounge lazily amongst my pillows and my gaze floats out the window. The neighbor guy just got home, the one whose window is up and across from mine. I see him most mornings, shrugging into a well-pressed dress shirt and carefully knotting a tie. I see him most evenings, too, when he gets home late, like this, suit jacket disheveled, dark brown hair in disarray. I flick my eyes back to the sexy prose on my screen. Then back to the hot neighbor guy. He would make a great gay cowboy. My hand in my panties agrees.

Unfortunately, I do always think of him as the Hot Neighbor

Guy. It's Tiff's fault. When she sleeps over, we like to peer out at him, giggling like fools. We dim our lights, munching cheese and crackers at midnight, and cackle about his perfect pecs as he paces the length of his living room, orating authoritatively into a cellphone or hammering out an email on his iMac. "*Goddddd,* I know it's been too long since I got laid because I want to fuck Hot Neighbor Guy *so baddddd* right now," Tiff shouted the last time we did this, and I laughed and asked if she wanted to borrow my vibrator, and one thing led to another, and . . .

My eyes are squeezed shut, holding images firm in my mind; I flit back and forth between Tiff and the Guy, Tiff and the Guy. Separately or together. Separately and *then* together. I bite my lip, eyes rolling back. Eyes opening. Eyes seeing him. Eyes meeting his eyes. What? Why am I meeting his eyes? Why is he looking at me?

I yank my duvet across my body, scramble for the light switch, try to extinguish myself in the dark. But I get wet halfway to the lamp, glancing up at that smirk. Deep brown eyes. Two stories up. Smug with amusement. With something like lust.

I think better of it, leave the lamp on. I lean back languorously in the bed again, swaddled in my purple sheets. I pick up my wand vibrator, always ready for service on the sidelines. I press it against my panties and turn it on, hoisting the lace hem of my nightgown. It whirrs through my vulva in that familiar way, immediately making me wetter. Or maybe that was his face. The way those dark eyes are still staring at me, wolfish and wanting, every time I dare to look up. I blush under his gaze and press the wand ever more firmly against me. I think about those upturned pink lips, their condescension and how they would whisper against my skin. I come, hips bucking hard, against the rumble of the wand.

All thought is banished from my head as I slowly float back

to the land of the living. And when my eyes slide open, I see him. Still sitting in his desk chair by the window. Still staring. Still smiling.

I do a theatrical little bow, like I'm a Broadway star and he's front-row center. He golf claps approvingly. I can almost hear it, through two windowpanes and twenty feet of chilly October air.

Tiff doesn't believe me when I tell her. "Stop joking around!" she says, and shoves me hard enough to nearly spill my cosmopolitan on the couch. "Hot Neighbor Guy is in his own world! His own league! He'd never fuck with plebes like us." She flops dramatically onto the floor and then asks me if I'd like a refill.

I don't invite her to stay that night, even though she's tipsy and horny the way that she gets, and even though her long braids are looking very pullable and her face very slappable. She pouts prettily, lips glossed lilac, as I put her in a cab, and I whisper against her hair, "Next time, I'll make you come so hard, you forget all about the Hot Neighbor Guy." The warm clang of her laughter echoes long after the taxi pulls away.

I journey back to my walk-up, dim the lights, drop off our cocktail glasses in the sink. A glowing form catches the corner of my eye as I return to my room. I glance up and see him. The person I've been thinking about all night, if I'm honest with myself.

His eyes are fixed on his fancy computer screen, which floods his face with pale blue light. At first I figure he's just burning the midnight oil on a work project, but then I notice a telltale throbbing in the muscles of his right arm which betray, in no uncertain terms, that his hand is wrapped around his cock and stroking it. And if the rising blush on his cheeks is any indication, he's very damn hard under that desk.

My lights low enough that I feel incognito, I slip into bed and gaze up at him, rapt. My hand drifts almost unnoticed to my clit through my jeans. I tug the seam against my most sensitive spot, in rhythm with my neighbor's steady strokes.

I study his face for clues. I notice that I'm filing information away, as if someday I will use it. *That's the face he makes when it feels really good. That's the way his triceps tighten when he starts to get close.* As if I'd ever need such information, say, from my position kneeling on the floor in front of him with his cock swelling against my tongue.

I watch him so closely during his orgasm, wonder so intently about the porn on his screen, stare so obsessively at his pleasurable grimaces, that it takes me a moment to realize my clit is coming simultaneously against the seam of my jeans. A sympathetic response, pleasure pounding so fiercely through my body that I crumple and cry out.

When I manage to look his way again, he's still in his desk chair, staring sleepily into space. Part of me wants to cuddle up beside him in my bed and drift off to dreamland. Another, more reckless part of me wishes I was riding his cock so I could see him make those faces from close up.

There comes a snowy day, the first real snow of the year. It heaps the streets. I watch it fall from my window, cup of tea in hand, thanking the wintry heavens I'm a freelancer and don't have to brace the cold to go to a gray office somewhere.

He's up there, I notice, watching the snow too. Phone in hand, talking a mile a minute. Must be working from home today. His dark jeans and gray sweater look nothing like the sharp suits he wears to whatever fancy downtown job he has. I catch myself staring at his crotch. And then *he* catches me staring at his crotch, and I nearly drop my tea.

He smirks (as ever), then waves. His pink lips are so affecting that I forget breathing is an option for a moment. I meekly wave back, embarrassed to be seen in the light of day. I must have looked hotter in the dimness of night, face flushed with pleasure. Now I'm just . . . me. Fuzzy cardigan. Fuzzy slippers. Fuzzy sense of appropriate neighborly boundaries.

But evidently not wanting to firm them up anytime soon, I splay out against my pillows and let my legs fall apart. Am I really such a salacious slut that I'm going to jerk off for this stranger *again?* I let my hand wander where it wants to go, weighing my options. Biting my lip.

He speaks sternly into his phone and then turns his milk-chocolate eyes back to me and holds up his fingers in a "V" in front of his mouth. Sticks out his tongue. Does something filthy with it that makes my clit twitch under my lacy undies. The universal signal for cunnilingus.

And then he's focused on the call again, checking the screen of his computer, checking a notebook on his desk. Amid all this checking, I take a moment to check in with myself. Do I want to be in this situation? Do I want to be in this situation *with this man?*

A smile bursts across his face as he makes some joke to who-ever he's talking to, and his enthusiasm pulses through my clit like a wave enveloping the shore.

I pick up my vibrator from its usual spot and put it, well, on its usual spot.

Letting my eyes drop closed, I fantasize about alternate reali-ties: him kissing me in my bed, fucking me roughly in a public bathroom stall, bending me over his desk and telling me to be good. I press the wand more firmly against my vulva and get swept away in sexy reverie.

As my climax approaches, I open my eyes and catch my neighbor, phone abandoned, eyes fixed on me, one large hand pressed against the glass of his window like he wants to warp through it. I'm ogling the hardness in his pants when I explode against the wand's faithful head, each orgasmic contraction stealing my breath the way I wish this man would with his kiss.

Tiff is over for another "girls' night." We're sipping rosé in my bed, her leaning against the headboard, me against the wall— our usual positions for "girl talk" sometimes followed by a "girl fuck." Except normally when we do this, we're not checking every six seconds to see whether the subject of our stakeout has shown up yet.

"You said he gets home around seven?" she asks, examining her pink rhinestone watch.

"Or a little later, yeah." I eye her slyly. "Why, are you excited?"

"Girl, of *course* I'm excited!!" Tiff shouts in my face. We burst into giggles. I was joking, naturally. I've been her best friend for twelve years and we've fucked off and on for much of that time. Obviously I can tell when she's excited.

When the clock ticks closer to eight, we start to wonder if he'll show at all. "Maybe he's out of town. Maybe he's on a date with some hot blonde," I murmur in Tiff's ear. The wine and the waiting have gotten to us; we've inched closer together like we always do, like magnets. Her honey-colored eyes are wine-hazy under her curtain of braids. "Maybe he took her straight to the bed when they got home, and that's why we haven't seen him yet."

Tiff's inner thighs are warm and slightly damp under my fingers, which I'm surprised to note have crept between her legs. It's in the moment of deciding whether to tug her panties down that I see him. Hot Neighbor Guy. Sitting in his desk chair, watching us, sidelong, as if that would keep us from noticing.

"Fuck. He's watching," I say.

"*What?!*" she exclaims and sits up straighter, throwing an urgent glance over her shoulder. But not, I notice, removing my hand from where it's landed.

Once her giggles have settled, I go back to stroking her, slow. As her head tips back against the window and her eyes slide shut with pleasure, I let my gaze drift past her, to meet his. Dramatically, I bring my fingers to my lips and suck Tiff off them, making eye contact first with him, and then with her, when she opens her eyes to insist, "Put them *back,* babe. No one told you to stop."

Inspired, I nudge her into a lying-down position so I can straddle her body and press one thigh between hers, my thumb still circling her clit. I alternate between kissing her and peeking at Hot Neighbor Guy's pervy smirk. "Does he look like he's enjoying himself?" Tiff asks.

"Mmhmm," I say with a nod. "And so do you, babe." I throw one more pointed look up at our window voyeur before kissing my way down Tiff's body, mouth en route to her arousal-swollen cunt. I bury my face in her, trying—I realize—to get them both off. I do.

One day I just get too curious. Hoping he's gone into the office, I sneak along the halls of our apartment complex and through its dim stairwells, searching for his door.

I've memorized the position of his apartment in relation to mine, theorized on possible apartment numbers. Wondered if it even mattered, if knowing would help me in any real way, or if the desire to know was just the rabid curiosity of a horny, smitten weirdo, a label I must reluctantly accept.

The right door, I'm almost certain, is 813—slightly up and over from my own humble hovel, 609. I stare at it for a moment, not sure what I was expecting to see. Him, naked, opening the door, waiting for me? No such luck.

Curiosity sated for the time being, I slink back to my nearby abode. But I haven't been back five minutes before a knock on my door distracts me from work (though let's be honest, I was already distracted).

When I fling the door open, no lingering figure appears at either end of the hallway. There is only a note, scribbled firmly in black ink on a blue index card.

If you'd like to meet as much as I would like to, come to 813 tonight at 9 p.m. No need to bring anything but you.

I laugh out loud, not because the note is funny but because I've never been so shocked, delighted, and terrified by anything in my life.

What I did not anticipate about planning a scintillating rendez-vous with one's neighbor is that they may be able to see you try-ing on the lingerie you'd planned on wowing them with.

He's taking a work call again, I infer from the set of his jaw, and so I deem it possible to do a trial run. To examine in the mirror all the colorful fabric I hope he'll claw from my body the first chance he gets.

There's the blue set, the pink set, and the yellow set. There's the white lace set and the black velvet set. There's the way I notice his distant shape in my peripheral vision, while trying to focus on my reflection and not on his reactions.

There's the set made of black mesh, and the set that's so see-through it might as well not exist. There's the black faux-leather set, the green satin set, the metallic pink set that was a Galen-tine's Day gift from Tiff.

But the set I settle on is simply red: a bloody-yet-bright red, a sexy-yet-sophisticated red, a fuck-me-but-also-fuck-you red. I allow myself the liberty of a single glance his way and catch the merest ghost of a smirk before he saunters away from the window, leaving me alone with my scantily clad reflection.

When nine rolls around, I have thrice already had the thought that I ought to change my underwear, in case the wetness of anticipation scares him off. But if he didn't know I was a horny girl from watching my nightly routines, then maybe he's not smart enough to fuck me anyway.

I arrive at his door in a short pink dress that zips all the way up the front, a sinful invitation. I considered bringing a bottle of wine, before remembering he'd asked me not to bring anything. Instead I brought my cleavage, framed to perfection, and the sweet grace of my quivering body.

He opens the door when I knock. I expected him half hard in sweatpants. I did not expect him stunning in a tailored blue suit. I did not expect the smell of his cologne to resonate in my clit like the clang of a gong, sudden and true.

"Well, hello," he says—and what else is there to say? "Would you like to come in?" His voice is as smooth and oaky as I'd hoped, like top-shelf bourbon.

I sashay into his apartment. "Great place," I say. His decor says record label executive, creative director, maybe high-end podcast producer. His body language says, "I will be unable to prevent myself from fucking you if I'm not careful, so I'm going to be careful."

He gestures at a black leather sofa and I sit. "Would you like a drink?" he asks. His presence is even more intoxicating than I'd envisioned in my wand-fueled interludes; I'm careful to sit in such a way that no wetness will mar his furniture. I say yes and he shrugs off his suit jacket, rolls up his shirtsleeves, and sets to work in the kitchen with a jigger and a cocktail shaker.

"So why did you invite me over?" I ask. Wanting to hear him talk about me. About anything.

"I liked seeing you in your bed," he responds simply as he slices a lime and slots it into his juicer.

"You wouldn't have preferred seeing me in *your* bed?" I reply, aware I'm spouting nonsense. Maybe *all* of this is nonsense. Maybe everything up until his cock inevitably sliding inside me is absolutely nonsense.

He lets out a bark of laughter that makes me feel like a bad girl in the best way. "Believe me," he says, "if I'd walked into my room and seen you in *my* bed, your clothes would've been on the floor so fast . . ."

The sentence hasn't even completely exited his lips before I've flitted to his bedroom, passing behind his back while he fusses with rum and simple syrup. I settle on the edge of his bed. Drinks at last assembled, he turns to find his living room empty, and then it's a matter of seconds before he appears in his bedroom doorway, cocktail glasses abandoned, eyes hungry and ready.

"You said my clothes would be on the floor," I murmur. And then it's on.

He bolts across the room and tugs down the zipper of my dress, like he's been thinking about it all night. Sinking to his knees on the floor, he pulls my slutty shoes from my feet and lets them tumble onto the rug. "Can I make good on that promise I made?" he asks shakily, his touch hot on my thighs, and my mind replays its tape of him demonstrating cunnilingus on his two spread fingers. I barely have time to gasp my assent before he has yanked my panties off me, spread my legs, and settled his hot mouth against my hotter cunt.

My back arches, pressing my pelvis forward as his tongue makes contact with my clit. He moans and paws my thighs farther apart so he can apply more pressure with every up-and-down stroke of his tongue.

I'm already so wet, have been wet for hours, so vulnerability rushes over me when he slides his tongue down to the opening of my cunt to lick me there. But he hums appreciatively and licks with ardor, his big hands warm and comforting on my hips.

His mouth is even wetter with my juices when he moves back up to gently suck on the tip of my clit with his pink lips. I stare down at him, grabbing his dark hair in one hand and propping myself up with the other, amazed to see up close the handsomely angular face I've stared at from afar so many nights.

The rhythm of his tongue is sending me swiftly toward an edge I won't be able to pull myself back from, so I tap his arm to stop him. I need to see the cock that's been haunting my fantasies. And preferably to have it in at least two of my holes, ASAP.

I playfully tug on his tie, pulling him to me for a deep kiss while he's still kneeling between my legs. His lips are freshly wet with me. I tug at the waistband of his suit pants and whine softly, "I want these off," and he stands and obliges.

"You're gorgeous, you know that?" he says as I pull him toward me, his half-hard cock at my eye level, and take it out of his black cotton briefs. It's an average length and thick; the walls of my pussy clench instinctively just imagining what it'll feel like inside me.

I gaze up at him innocently and stick out my tongue to twirl it around the head of his dick. "You really think so?" I say with an insolent smile. I suck on the head gently, maintaining eye contact. Unable to stop staring at this man I've never seen without two thick panes of glass and several yards of space between us before tonight.

When he's as hard as I want him, I beg him to put a condom on and fuck me. While he busies himself with the Trojans in his nightstand drawer, I notice it: the desk against the window where he always sits during our voyeuristic trysts. The expensive computer he uses to watch porn and answer emails. I scamper over to it, naked, and say, "I have an idea," before pressing the entire front side of my body against the floor-to-ceiling window. I tilt my gaze over one shoulder, catching sight of his lanky, finely muscled frame, now stripped naked and ready to fuck me.

He starts growling low in his throat before he even gets halfway across the room, and then suddenly he's pinned me to the window with all his weight and is shoving my thighs apart with his. "You want this?" he murmurs in my ear.

"Yes."

"Ask for it."

"P-please . . . please fuck me . . ."

And he does, pushing his thick cock into my sopping cunt. I tip my ass back toward him to give him a better angle and let out a whoosh of air through my gritted teeth as he shoves in deeper. "Fuck, that feels so good," I whisper, one cheek pressed flat against the cold glass.

I wonder for a moment if anyone in the other windows is watching us, the way we've watched each other. I slide my hand down between my body and the window until my middle finger lands on my clit and begins to circle it in rhythm with his progressively deeper thrusts. My eyes fall shut and I picture all kinds of strangers gazing at us, all of them stroking themselves surreptitiously, all of them thinking about how good we're gonna feel when we come . . .

And then I do, my cunt spasming around his dick, its firm girth making each contraction send a wave of intense pleasure through me. My head full of stars, I barely notice that his thrusts are speeding up like he's getting close. But when he sinks in as deeply as he can and groans low, his impossibly hard cock

twitching inside me, I squeeze my muscles appreciatively around
it to make his orgasm as satisfying as it can be. Mine certainly
was.

When we catch our breaths and separate our bodies, I peel
myself off the window and laugh softly at the sweaty imprint
we've left on the pane.

I step delicately into my panties again and slip my bra on.
"That was fun," I say, blushing despite myself.

He stretches out on the bed and sighs contentedly. "That was
transcendent," he agrees, and I smile.

The following morning, as I lie in my bed with a mug of coffee
and a head full of raucous recent memories, I watch him put on
his usual suit and tie, and realize I never even asked him what
he does for a living . . . or his name. Maybe he'll forever be the
Hot Neighbor Guy to me. Maybe I'm fine with that.

SECOND SEASON

Ash Dylan

I t had been twenty-one years, but Megan's second season already looked a lot like her first.

Of course, she wasn't Megan tonight. As far as the *ton* knew, Megan Stapleton was on a faraway estate. Mourning the unexpected loss, under whispered circumstances, of the loutish lord whom she had married after her first season. The *ton* probably wondered what she even looked like; nobody in society had seen her in years.

Poor girl.

Good thing she wasn't Megan tonight. Instead, the footman at the ballroom had announced Rebecca Lovegood and all eyes had turned to see whom that might be. Perhaps an heiress of some sort. Perhaps an American, with a name like that.

Perhaps someone's conquest.

That was the real reason Rebecca was here. She had a ticket to leave the country by ship the next day but wanted one night as a young woman. One night of what could have been her season. An acquaintance had helped cover up streaks of gray in her hair with a home mixture of wine and nuts and she knew not what else. A relative life of ease had kept her face more or less youngish. Staring into the mirror, in a dress the modiste told her was the latest fashion, she had convinced herself she could pull this off.

But whatever confidence let her concoct this scheme in the first place had faded with the light outside. Twenty-one years later and she was in another ballroom, standing against another wall. Perhaps she was still Megan after all.

"I don't recall seeing you before."

The voice was comforting, warm and deep. Hidden layers in the tone that seeped into her skin. "Pardon?"

She turned to face the man who looked like the definition of what could have been. Slightly tousled hair that she wanted to spear with her fingers, set atop a face of character—strong jaw, sensuous lips, and thick brows that focused her gaze toward his kind eyes, eyes that were focused on her.

"I remember faces, and I haven't seen yours."

"I'm new. Here. I'm new here." She could only imagine how wallflower-like she sounded. "I'm American." She was raised in America until her parents brought her over to find a match. Even though most of her forty years had been in England, she still felt American through and through.

Her companion nodded, a small smirk tilting his lips. "So I could tell you I'm a duke, or a viscount, and you . . ."

"I'm American." Confidence was coming back. "I wouldn't know the difference," she lied. Her eyes strayed from his face to take in his solid frame filling his suit. He could wrap her in his arms like a blanket. "And I wouldn't care," she added truthfully.

He nodded instead of saying who he really was. Maybe

another person keeping secrets. "And your name." He sidled closer, his next words a whisper. "It wasn't on the list."

He had checked up on her. Megan liked that.

"What are you suggesting? That I saw a real invitation, made a copy with my name, and proffered it at the door expecting to be granted entrance? Sounds excessive."

The best lies were the truth. She had seen an invitation, for her daughter, whose first season was off to a slow start since she decided to skip it and tour France. Alone for the first time in decades, Megan decided someone in the family was going to have a season, and it might as well be her.

"Not suggesting anything, Love. Good." Her name on his lips was two strong syllables that felt respectfully indecent.

"And you are?" He smiled instead of answering, so she tried to prompt him. "Sir . . ."

"Sir will do." He sipped from a cup as he drank her in. She felt his gaze like a touch. But not unwanted. Not intrusive. Like his voice and his demeanor, his attention on her felt nothing but safe. His eyes were a dark brown, like the liquid he sipped, with a glint of fire from the nearby lanterns. She guessed he was in his mid to late twenties, but the same dim lighting that protected her truth shielded his as well. "Are you familiar with our terms of address?"

"This is my second season." Again, the best lies were the truth. "Why? What are you supposed to call me?"

"You tell me, Rebecca."

"Rebecca will do."

To himself as much as her, he replied, "Yes, she will."

"Are you talking to me too much?"

"I like talking to you."

"What will the *ton* think?"

"I don't care what the *ton* thinks."

That made two of them, but she was no closer to knowing who he was. But then, his reputation would only matter if she planned on more than one night.

"Are you what they call a rake?"

"Tonight, I'll be whatever you want me to be."

She took the cup from his hand. He yielded the instant their fingers touched. "You seem too polite to be a rake." The liquor burned her throat but it was a new sensation, so tonight she loved it. "Aren't you supposed to whisper wicked things in my ear? Suggest activities that make me blush?"

"Only if that's what you want."

"Why don't you find out." A command more than a question. A challenge.

A waltz started. She wasn't swept away to a secluded bedchamber like she had hoped but found herself in his arms and moving around the ballroom. The dance lessons preparing for her first season came back to her. She could feel the stares of the *ton* but knew not whether it was for her or him. She didn't care. The night was young, and she could pretend that so was she.

"Isn't this where you sweet-talk me?"

"You have the most expressive face. Your forehead creases when you're in thought, and the lines around your eyes tighten at the first sign of emotion." She balked at the attention to her face, the thing that might betray her first. "Like right now."

"That wasn't what I had in mind."

"I meant I want to see your face when you come." His eyes were smoldering. His voice that had until now warmed only her surface was burrowing deeper, causing an ache between her legs that needed relief she wouldn't get on the dancefloor. "I bet you're even prettier when you're getting fucked, Lovegood."

She swallowed, not used to being talked to that way. Not used to liking it.

"Want me to go on?" he asked.

She also wasn't used to being asked about her boundaries. She liked that too.

"Yes," she breathed.

His firm hand on her waist guided her through the motions of the dance. She let him guide her. The dance served its purpose—she could imagine from his gentle control how he would tend to her needs if they were alone.

"How did you know to put your hair in a chignon just for me?" She felt a slight tug as her head arched back. Time stood still as he loomed over her, the only thing in the world his eyes taking her in, his breath heavy with need. "You like it when I tug."

"Yes," she said, soft as air.

He let go of her hair, his hand gripping tighter on her waist.

"I like earning your yeses, Rebecca. I want to kiss between your legs until that's the only word I hear."

"Am I blushing?"

He leaned back to check. "Not yet."

"Guess you need to try harder."

"You're no wilting flower, are you, Rebecca?"

She had lost her playfulness over the years, knowing it wasn't appreciated. But she had no reason to hide who she was anymore. And every piece of her she revealed to this man was accepted without question. Why couldn't she have met someone like him twenty-one years ago? She shrugged, playing along. "I'm American."

She still didn't have a name. He could own this place. He could work for the owner for all she knew. It didn't matter. She wasn't here to get married.

Rebecca Lovegood, née Megan Stapleton, was here to get fucked.

"Would you care for a tour? Unless you'd rather fill your dance card."

"Show me everything," she said.

He gestured toward an open door. She nodded and walked ahead of him. The firm press of his hand to her lower back urged her forward. She was walking amongst the *ton* as if she were one of the unmarried ladies seeking a match, but in her head that hand was touching, stroking, pinching, and rubbing exactly where she needed. She felt playful and shameless, exactly what she wanted out of tonight.

When they entered an antechamber—alone, it seemed—she could discern his smell. A faint cologne, woodsy and sharp. Like him, it was not overpowering, but pleasant as it crept up on her, put her at ease and made her want to breathe him in.

"May I?"

She nodded.

He raised a hand to cup her cheek as his thumb stretched to brush along her lips. A soft stroke, back and forth, as she fought the temptation to dart out her tongue and lick. His touch was reverent, a worshipping caress.

"You have the loveliest lips."

"Taste them."

Megan knew firsthand if they were caught, there would be pressure to marry. But she had money, now. She had experience. And nobody knew who she was. She would have this kiss with no regrets.

His mouth closed the distance to hers until the only thing that mattered in her world was the soft press of his lips. Feeling her, growing familiar, then tasting. She sighed into his body as their caress became a kiss, a true rake-debauching-a-wallflower kiss. His tongue tracing indecent suggestions against hers. Every stroke a promise of what he could do between her legs if only she gave him the chance.

With a kiss like that, he deserved a chance.

He pulled back, licking his lips like her taste lingered. "Fuck, you're sweet."

"Am I blushing?"

"Not yet."

"How do you know I'm not trying to trap you in a marriage? The *ton* would talk if they saw us."

"I'm not worried about it."

Neither was she. But the night was no longer young, and neither was she. It was time for what she'd come here for.

"Where's the next stop of the tour, Sir?"

Without a word, he took her hand in his and led her through the house. Up one set of stairs, then another. The people around them grew sparser until they were alone. She could hear muffled voices coming from rooms, whispers from alcoves. They weren't the only ones seeking seclusion.

"A good estate has a good library." He opened a door in a dim hallway. He knew this place well.

"I wouldn't think people read books the night of a party," she said as she walked into the room ahead of him.

The gaslit sconces against the wall came on, painting the room with soft light. The lock behind her clicked. "Precisely," he replied.

When she turned he was already there. He held her waist and pulled her close. She didn't know what to do with her hands. Had she ever hugged her husband? She settled for resting them on his chest, feeling his muscles tighten at her touch. His arms went around her but not to hug. No, his deft fingers went to work on the fastenings of her dress.

"Am I blushing?"

He took the silk of her loosened dress at her shoulder and slowly tugged it down. Down to her elbow, restraining her arm. Then he slipped his fingers between her skin and the strap of her chemise, then lowered it as well. His strong, callused hand slipped into her stays and cupped her breast, rolling her nipple between his fingers, teasing her to a sharp point, until she was nothing but short breaths, a quiver in her stomach, wet between her legs.

"Not yet."

He had to be lying. Her skin was flushed from his touch. Warmed further when he repeated his actions with her other arm and brought that breast to a pleasant, aching peak.

Like the dance, he knew the next steps. His gentle, capable hands eased her clothing down, piece by piece, until it lay pooled at her feet. Despite being stark naked before a stranger, she hadn't flinched. She knew there was no shame in getting exactly what she wanted. He guided her backward until her legs pressed against a chaise that rested against the window. She sank down on the red velvet and instinctively reclined back. He dropped to his knees before her.

"What if . . ." She gasped at the electric feel of his fingers tracing her calves. Not usually a sensitive part, but she wasn't used to being touched this way. "What if I'm not who you think I am?"

He smiled as his hands journeyed up her full thighs, coasting over her dimpled flesh, until he cupped between her legs. A finger slid inside and she sighed. "You've told me absolutely nothing about yourself." He leaned forward toward a breast and wrapped his lips around her nipple, his tight suck eliciting a gasp, ending with a lingering swipe of his tongue across the skin of her chest. "I know you're pretty." He drew her other nipple into his mouth as another finger slid inside, easing her open. "And I want to fuck you." His thumb stretched to stroke her swollen clit, and she melted at his touch. It felt so carnal, the feel of the chaise against her bare skin as her fully clothed lover dispensed attentive kisses to her breasts, her stomach, lower, his tongue darting to trace the silver stretch marks she could no longer hide and no longer cared to. "Can I fuck you?"

Simple questions deserved simple answers. "Yes."

As soon as the word was out, his shoulders were pressing her knees apart. Then the entire world narrowed to the feel of his lips on her pussy. Long, slow licks along her folds, teasing her apart until he drew her clit between his lips and sucked. She'd heard whisperings of this act. Stolen glances at ribald etchings in books she wasn't supposed to have seen. But she never imagined it would feel like this. Like every nerve in her body was alive, like the sensation was too much and not enough at the same time. Like she needed release but would fight it to her dying breath, because she never wanted this feeling to end.

She moaned like she never had in her life. Like she wanted the world to be jealous.

"There she is," he said, as two blunt fingers replaced his mouth. He pressed into her, curling to touch a bundle of nerves that sent her hips arching. "That's my girl."

His girl. He thought she was young. He thought she was his. She liked both of those things.

He guided one leg to drape over the armrest of the chaise. His thumbs spread her apart, and his mouth—his greedy fucking mouth—devoured her. She acted on instinct when she got close, pressing her palm against the back of his head. It only urged him on, lapping at her harder as she felt the heat rising within her, building, until she exploded, riding her orgasm out against his face.

She leaned back against the chaise as her breathing returned to normal. When she opened her eyes, he was there, inches away, staring back. "Fucking beautiful when you come. I knew it."

She didn't have words to express how it felt—fucking a stranger, a *younger* stranger, when for so long she'd thought exciting things would never happen to her again. She only had words for her simple demands.

"I want to see you." She wanted to see a man who was gentle and kind and gave her more pleasure in five minutes than she had had the rest of her life.

To his credit, he listened. He stood and pulled his shirt out of his trousers. His deft fingers made short work of the buttons on his placket. He teased the flap open but let his hands fall. He knew she needed to do the rest herself.

She eased his trousers down. She saw his strong thighs, dusted with fine hair, and wanted to feel him on her hands, her tongue. Such a foreign sensation, wanting to pleasure a man. She could tell from him biting his lip and his shallow breaths he was barely in control. She loved that she was the cause.

His trousers dropped to his feet. She wrapped her fingers around his jutting cock. Slowly tugging, feeling him grow in her hand. She wondered what he would look like in ten, fifteen, twenty years. When he was her age.

She closed her eyes as she slid him into her mouth. She felt the weight of him against her tongue as her lips wrapped around his cock. Flicking his crown, rubbing the salty liquid that seeped from his tip around, then caressing along his length. His hand gripped her chignon and guided her.

"Fucking gorgeous when you suck a cock, Rebecca. Prettiest thing I've ever seen."

Her life had been one of filling roles. Daughter. Wife. Mother. Always there to support others. Never deserving of someone's attention. Never feeling like something she had done was special. And yet here she was, kneeling before a young man as he said the way she sucked a cock was a sight to behold.

She loved having him in her mouth, warm and thick and perfect. She loved how he made her feel. She wanted more.

She lifted her mouth but kept him in hand. When her slow strokes weren't enough, he jerked his hips, fucking her grip. "What next, Sir?"

His voice was deeper, something between a grunt and a growl. "Turn around."

Were it earlier, she might have balked at such an order. But she knew enough to trust his intentions. She found herself crouched on all fours on the chaise, her arms resting on the window ledge. Then those hands were on her hips, squeezing her flesh. He held himself in hand and guided his hardness between her pussy lips. Resting there until she was squirming against him. She eased back, swallowing every inch with her hips. Eased back until he was sheathed inside her.

She'd never felt that full, that stretched. When she clenched her walls against his cock, a shiver shot through her body. She gasped and looked into the window, to see his reflection staring back. She knew he was gorgeous when he lost control. But that was nothing compared to how he looked when he took control. Like right now.

"Are you ready?"

She nodded, then bowed her head. Braced against the back of the chaise as he thrust. Thrust again. He was done exploring; now he was fucking her—and she fucking loved it. The clap of his hips against her ass. The steady slide of his cock inside her. He stroked along her bare back, then his fingers crept underneath, brushing against her clit as she got closer, closer.

He gripped her chignon in his fist and tugged. Her head

arched back. Their eyes met in the window and when she saw a man undone—eyes glazed, stomach tensed, forearms rippling as he gripped her hair—she came again, jerking her hips back against him and burying her screams in the crook of her arm. He pulled out with a swift jerk and then warmth striped her back.

He wiped her off with his shirt, hastily discarded it on the floor, then joined her on the chaise. He pulled her close, her back against his chest, his arm wrapped around her. She felt him against the small of her back. The intimate press of his cock that hours earlier would have been something she couldn't imagine now felt . . . normal. They were still strangers to each other, but at the same time they had become something more—partners who were naked, exposed, the only distance between them their secrets.

Noises drifted from outside the window. The clomp of hooves, the creaking wood of carriages arriving and taking off, the low ambient hum of the *ton* taking leave.

The party was over.

"If I go looking for Rebecca Lovegood, I won't find her, will I?"

She had already suggested she had forged the invitation. It wasn't too far a leap that she had used a fake name. "No. And I can't find you because I don't know your name."

"No."

She had planned on one night. He hadn't pressed. Hadn't been offended she didn't try to find out who he was. "I could find you again, though," she said. "I'd ask for the kind man with the perfect tongue whose cock I sucked so prettily."

He laughed into her back. When it came for his turn to say how he'd seek her out, she realized she didn't want him to. But his words, like everything else about that night, were exactly what she needed.

"I won't go looking for you, Rebecca, because I don't think you want to be found. And I respect that. I respect you. But if you ever wanted more." He paused. "With someone like me." Paused again with the weight of something she couldn't place— maybe regret, maybe doubt. "I don't know where that leaves us." He kissed the middle of her back, softly. The way someone who cared about her would. "But I think if something's meant to be, life has a way of giving us a second chance."

This man was much more dangerous than a rake. He could break her heart if she let him.

"Do you have to leave?" she asked.

"Not yet."

She sat up and looked into the window. Through the glass, she could see the faint outline of shapes moving in the dark on the grounds below. Then her eyes focused on her reflected form. She didn't see the same woman who had been staring into a mirror earlier as she tried on her dress. She was naked, sweat cooling on her bare skin, but that wasn't it. The woman looking back at her now was comfortable. Content. Happy. If this was Rebecca, Megan wanted to get to know her better.

"You okay?"

She didn't answer right away, still lost in thought. She was never getting married again. But an affair could last as long as she wanted. She had a ticket for America, but she could always get another.

"Rebecca?"

She looked down at the handsome, sittable face that had seen every forty-year-old inch of her and still wanted more. "Yes, I am." She straddled his chest, her pussy hovering above his mouth. "May I?"

He nodded.

She sank down onto his lips. He wrapped his arms around her thighs and settled in. His patient tongue went to work, kissing and licking until she was bracing for release, her fists white-knuckle tight on the chaise.

She was alive and on fire and riding the handsomest face in the *ton* and it had taken twenty-one years but it felt like she was just getting started.

Maybe she'd have a second season after all.

KEN'S OF
KENSINGTON

Friedrich Kreuz

It was a hot night, the kind of night on which I would have once ventured out to a club, danced myself into oblivion, pulled a guy and taken him to a sauna to have fun with before dawn. Since COVID, my pleasures are harder to find. Apps have done something to fill the absence, but real human interactions are more rewarding, especially when anonymous, when not mediated by unnecessary words. I like to work for a new partner with my body, not dial up takeaway, explaining my precise desires that can rarely be met.

Gone for now are the times spent scanning the dance floor, looking for someone who moves the way I like, who carries their body in ways I find appealing, seducing them on the spot until we are grinding into each other, kissing, not speaking, hungrier and hungrier until we have to release our lust (in the club toilets, in a hidden corner in the streets outside, back in his room). Gone are the hours spent waiting in the dark to see who approaches, reaching out to touch me, no words, silent interactions that flare up into incandescent sex.

These are the things I miss the most, when I am reduced to my body, free of thoughts, a receptacle for someone's pleasure, an outlet for my own. Now it's my room, my phone, some queer porn on my computer, paid for, of course, no one to rub up against so easily, no one to ask for consent. Sometimes people drop by, friends in my fuck-bubble, guys I meet anonymously online who are horny and vaxxed like me. But now it's all planning and protocols and talk about vaccinations and what we have lost before we start. At least there is a vaccine, not like in the last pandemic that took so many friends and lovers. Viruses mediate social interactions. I knew the PrEP and STI statuses of people whose names were unknown. Safewords, not their employment. Safe sex practices, not their social status. My phone is filled with guys called Red Uncut XXX, Trans SM XXX, Black London XXX, FFrench XXX, the list goes on. XXX is a big family.

That's what I was doing tonight. We were talking on an app, and he seemed like my kind of guy. He knew people I know. He was intelligent. His pics were hot, his banter fun, and he was into the same things as me. Not just the filthy sex that our mutual pictures exhibited, seeing my asshole before he heard my voice or smelled my skin. But like me, he liked gay history, and missed the anonymous queer spaces, the sexual heterotopias where we could become a part of ourselves that was shriveling from neglect while shut away. That connection was the real spark—we thought about sex in the same sociocultural ways, we worried about what would be left after the pandemic. That was all I wanted to know about him, although he asked me before sending a picture of his nice cock, so I knew that, too. I sent him a flurry of requested smut in reply. It's a different dance now, but it leads to the same end.

"Did you ever go to Ken's in Kensington?" he asked.

"The sauna? I wasn't living here then, but I've seen pictures. Didn't it close years ago?"

"It did, ten years ago. You know it's still accessible?"

I did not. My interest was piqued as the evening unfurled before me.

"Do you know how to get there?" I asked. He did. My heart was starting to race with each text arriving. This was the kind of hookup I wanted.

"Why don't we meet there?" he asked. "The traditional place for anonymous sex."

And then I was in a taxi. And then I was shuffling in a back street where he'd said to meet. And there he was. He pressed his finger to his thick lips, so I was silent, eyes down, mostly. He was hot. Younger than me. His dark skin merging with the shadows. His eyes were concealed under his cap, but his mouth could be seen parting into a half smile. He took off his hat. I liked how he looked at me with kind eyes. I wished I could have first seen him dancing in a club instead of meeting him on the street, prearranged, but a stranger is still a stranger. I followed him silently to a gate behind a block of flats. He jumped the fence and let me in. "Keep quiet, keep your torchlight down. Follow me," he whispered and closed the gate behind me.

Through the overgrown ferns and vines into the dark I followed him to what used to be the discreet entrance. Into a neglected garden, where I imagined naked men past, sunning themselves lazily in an urban oasis. Down some stairs to the unlocked back door. When we were inside and the door was shut, he called out for squatters and junkies, but the neighborhood was quiet and the place was empty. "I'll show you around first," he said. It was a guided tour into the archaeology of gay sex.

The back entrance opened onto a long corridor, the floor covered in dust, walls scribbled with low-grade graffiti. There were

a few empty bottles, not much broken glass, a little evidence
that people come here but not often. We walked past the old
changerooms, the showers, the toilets, just like a punter would
have, into a room that had a huge empty swimming pool below
a glass ceiling. I knew it from William Yang's photography of
the aqua drag shows that had taken place here, where all around
the pool naked men held each other, happy, smiling, now gone.
I could almost hear the music, disco-sexo sauna mixes grinding
the men together. I could almost smell the glistening sweat.

"So here we are," he said, his voice reverberating in the hollow room. Finally I could listen to the rich timbre of his voice.
Pitch darkness, except in front of our torchlights, faint sounds
of traffic from the busy road out the front. "Can you imagine
how much sex has happened in this pool?" He sounded strong
in the shadows.

"Why don't you show me around?" I asked. "Treat me like
you just rescued me from the pool." I jumped down into the
empty space.

He took my hand and led me up the dry steps, through the
labyrinth of rooms, everything existing only in the cone of
light we cast. Words sprayed on the walls would appear out of
the dark and then be lost again. "Suck my cock." "Mind the
AIDS." "I miss you." "More please." "But why?" He stopped
and pushed me up against the wall, his hand on my bearded face
as he kissed me. Such soft lips. Such strong hands on my back.
I felt myself wanting him. I felt his cock getting hard in his running shorts and brushed myself against it.

"Come here," he said. He took me by the hand into a room
with partitions, glory holes cut in place. "Stay here with your
eyes closed." He knelt me down in front of a hole to wait for his
cock. I could hear that he hadn't left the room. I waited until I
felt alone, and then, from behind me: "I miss these anonymous

encounters. I miss looking down and seeing my cock disappear into a man's throat, not knowing who it was. I miss seeing how much he wanted to give me without any return but the pure joy of giving."

"Me too," I said. "It was the purest form of pleasure. Just a cock gliding down my throat. No class. No politics. No judgment. Just giving and receiving."

"Knowing nothing about the person except for their cock, it becomes everything. The totality of the interaction."

"I miss it," I said.

"Let's do it."

I nodded into the dark.

"Open your eyes," he said, leaving the room with the flashlight until I became accustomed to the blackness. I could see from the shadows on the ceiling that he was coming around to the other side of the wall, but for the moment I sat in pitch darkness. I detached from everything and let myself open up to the space. I unbuttoned my jeans and got my cock out and found myself already leaking, slippery between my fingers, which I put in my mouth to taste the sticky, salty scent of sex. How many mouths had sat on the floor like I am now, cock in hand, waiting for a man to serve? I was playing a part that so many men had played, right here on these dirty tiles. I rolled my foreskin over my cock and back, feeling myself getting hard. Countless times I'd been in this position, waiting in the dark of some cramped room in a sauna somewhere, aroused by the anticipation of the next cock to come to me, to come to this anonymous hole, hoping for the best, long, thick, strong prick imaginable, no man attached except by how he used it. Here, I knew what was to come from the pics he'd sent. I was in for a treat. My cock swelled in my fingers. Light flooded the chamber.

He moved over to the hole and adjusted his flashlight so that only the bottom half of the room was illuminated, so he could move out of the light to disappear. He gripped his heavy cock through his shorts, looking just like one of the images he'd sent, possibly taken that evening for me. I watched him stroke himself through the fabric through the peephole, my fantasy coming to life, a private show that I would soon taste.

He came closer to the hole and pulled down his shorts. His thighs were strong. His pubic hair was in tight black curls. He leaned back a bit to move his half-hard cock into the light. "Do you want it?" he said. I moved my face to the hole.

He held his cock back, so I pushed my face to his balls, warm, sweaty from the balmy night, intoxicatingly him. I sniffed. I licked. I sucked them softly into my mouth while he let his thick cock fall onto my face, resting against my nose, the head a myopic blur that smelled so good and dripped in viscous strings onto my forehead and eyelids as he moved, smothering me. Every sense I had was wrapped around his sex, his balls feeling tight as he pulled back to stretch them in my mouth, the base of his cock pressed against my nostrils, his shaft pressed against my face with his big hand. He pulled his balls out and rubbed my saliva over me, using my tongue to lube up his dick.

He put his hand to my face, tenderly. "Open," he said, and I let him put two fingers into my throat, sliding down the groove of my tongue to where my throat becomes rough and wet and I need to think about not gagging. I'm well trained, of course. I gave him what he wanted. I was perfectly still with my mouth open and his fingers sliding into me. I barely moved as I wanked, on edge, overfilled with sensations I tried to contain. He took his wet fingers out of my mouth and rubbed his cock, gripping it at the base as he pushed it toward my face, tracing around the circle of my waiting mouth with the tip before letting me move down along his shaft.

He had a fantastic penis. That's why I was there, to serve this thick cock that plunged down deep into my throat and back, every movement deliberate, testing my reactions with precision. I became used to his girth, his length, teasing him with my tongue as I pulled back. I was in total control of his pleasure. I rocked myself into a rhythm, greedily licking his balls that I held in one hand every time I got to the base, wanking him with my throat, taking him out to let my cock-scented saliva run down my gullet. My beard was wet. My fingers were wet. I pressed myself around the base of his prick so deeply that his hairs tickled my nose. I kept up this perpetual motion, fucking him with my throat while I wanked on the floor until time seemed to stop, until I was just another mouth servicing a cock in this precise spot, a portal back into the time when the same room was filled with men watching and waiting for their turn. There were ghosts crowding around me, watching, all of the men who had spent the best moments of their lives doing what I was now doing. We all became the same entity.

His cock started to swell. I put both my hands on the wall and pushed myself down his shaft, letting him lean back and fuck my face harder as he became more aroused chasing the orgasm he wanted to spurt into me. The more vigorously he fucked me, the less the world existed for me. There was just his cock, hard, leaking, strong, pushing down my throat as he fucked an open hole in the dark, my stubbly lips grazing against his delicate skin. I was nothing but the sensations he felt. Slight moans escaped his lips. When he started to come, his cock throbbed, pulsating between my lips as he flooded my mouth. He stayed inside me as I swirled his spunk around with my tongue, tasting him, teasing his cock, feeling the last spasms of joy mingling with his hypersensitivity. When he pulled out, his cock hung, glistening, creamy white against his dark skin.

My face smelled like his sex, his spunk welled in the corners of my mouth. Some of it had escaped onto the floor, mixing with every ancient drop of come spilled before at this temple of cock. We were a part of the history of this place now. The torch went off with a click.

He came back around to my cubicle, finding me, flooding the room with light. I stood up and we kissed, my face still wet. "That was fantastic. Thank you. I haven't been sucked off like that since they closed the saunas." My smile showed him how pleased I was. "Come. I'll show you some more."

We walked around the darkness. There was a BDSM chamber behind a barred prison door, a St. Andrew's Cross fixed firmly to the wall, shackles ready to restrain the next victim. There was a sweat-scented pine box of a sauna. A Roman steam room, where he bent over to imitate how men used to fuck here, holding onto the Corinthian columns as many had before, his running shorts sliding up the crack of his round ass which he pushed back toward me. There were ghosts all around us, their pleasure still resonating in the ether, sucking on the energy of our interactions. There was a room of piss troughs and toilets, big enough for a party, places to chain the piss slaves to the steel urinals. There was the corridor of private booths, where couples and groups would once have fucked while hearing their neighbors fucking, where solitary men had closed the door and wanked to the sounds of the sex dripping from the ceiling.

We went into a booth. We kissed. There was a mirror. I looked down to see his hands gripping my ass as he ground his cock against my thigh, his stubbly chin against my skin as he sucked my neck. His strong fingers held my body. I breathed in the scent of his cock from my beard. "Fuck me," I said. He turned me around and bent me over the bench, pulled down my jeans, opened my knees, and grabbed me. My face was eye-height to the mirror. I watched as he spread my cheeks, taking his time to look at me, breathing me in slowly before he licked my ass. I couldn't hold back the sighs. His mouth was pure bliss. I ground myself onto his tongue shamelessly, getting as much of him into me as I could, rocking my perineum over his lips, giving myself to him. I could feel my cock swollen and hard. I was transfixed by the image of him eating my ass in the mirror, seeing what anyone would have seen if they had peered in the open door and decided to join us. The only sounds were his wet tongue and my moans and the ignorant traffic drifting by above us. I was lost to the rhythms of his tongue in my hole, galvanized by waves of pleasure that came with every lick.

He stood up, took his cock out of his shorts. He was already hard, so he slapped it against my hole. I saw myself move; waves of anticipation spread through my body. I pushed myself back toward him. The light of his flashlight kept his face in the dark but illuminated the long strand of lube that he drizzled onto his cock and my hole. I could tell he was watching in the mirror as he played with my ass, getting me ready, pushing just the head in, wanking himself slowly, teasing me, holding me back from impaling myself deep on him. I was concentrated entirely on this point. His fingers gripped my hips, and he pulled me back along the length of him. He pushed himself in as deep as he could, grinding his pelvis against me. His balls touched mine. We started to move. Out, slowly, not all the way, and then in again. The slower he fucked, the harder he got. He fucked me to a rhythm of long thrusts. I rocked my hips in time to get the utmost of him into me. It was bliss.

He pulled my chest back so I was standing, leaning my hands against the wall, my leg angled to better see him penetrating me. He wrapped his fingers around my pink cock and jerked me off in the same long, deliberate strokes. My hole gripped his prick as he pulled out, sucking him like a greedy pair of lips. Every time he fucked into me, his heavy balls would smash onto mine. This is what turned him on, the switch that made him fuck me like an animal, or like I was one. He fucked me hard and deep while he jerked me off, staring at the precome glistening in streams from my cock onto the dusty platform where I was being taken, raw. When I came, he came, my intense spasms clinging to his as I milked him dry. My spunk shot onto the wooden bench, flooding my nostrils, alkaline. He pulled out and his semen started to leak out of me. He turned me around, so we could both watch. He held my cheeks open, gaping dark pink and dripping in white streaks through the black hairs and down my balls. I pushed, swelling and open as he dribbled away onto the floor. He slapped my tender hole, then licked out the last of his come. It was the first time I'd seen his face the entire encounter. We both looked happy.

"That was hot," he said, as we both watched my stretched pink hole regaining a composed state. I throbbed with pleasure still. I can see why guys like taking pics of my ass, gaping after they've used it, my curls wet with their semen, the same photos I now send to guys I want to fuck. A complete reveal before meeting a stranger to use me. Setting the bar for where I want them to take me, one fuck linked to the next.

"It was. Very. It must have been years since this mirror saw that kind of action."

"It's sad, isn't it. Such a magical space lying empty."

"Can you imagine how much pleasure has been had here?"

"It's incredible. It was once a space to be free. And now it's empty."

"You know what we should do?" he asked into the darkness after a moment's pause.

"We should organize an orgy in here, before the summer is over. Anonymous."

"How would we do that? If it's our friends, it's not anonymous. My friends have probably already fucked your friends."

"What about if we invited every guy we spoke to on the app? Like, 'You want to fuck me, come here midnight next Friday. Bring a friend.'"

"Like an old rave. Give out the address an hour before. That's a brilliant idea."

"Isn't it?"

"Okay. Let's do it."

We lay there, the room buzzing with our energy having laid empty for a decade, swelling with the germ of anticipation of the fun we would bring back to this place. I could feel the presence of the men who'd been here before, lying back in this same postcoital spot, connected only by sex to the men by their sides.

"Come on, let's go," I said.

"Actually, I'm going to stay. I want to give some more thought to the orgy. I'm serious."

"Me too. We owe it to the men who used to come here."

"I'm glad we met, then."

"Yeah, you're hot."

"You too," he said and kissed me.

"I'll be in touch. I've got your number. What's your name?" I was holding my phone.

"Put Ken."

"Okay, Ken," I smiled. "I'll text you soon."

The garden air was damp; it had rained while we were inside. There were no lights on in the apartment blocks behind the trees, no planes in the starless sky. The web of a golden orb spider had stretched across the path I had to take out. I managed to crawl under her without too much disturbance, and by the low light of my phone I beat my way through the wet ferns to the gate, which I jumped and turned toward the main road where I might find a taxi. I felt a smile on my face that I had not felt for some time, the thrill of leaving a place where I'd had intense sex, which I left behind me, humming in the air like a deep moan echoing through time.

OUR REFLECTION IN THE MIRROR, MIRROR

Jessica Leigh Roode

I know you are placating me when you say, "*You're so hot.*" What you mean is that what we are doing is hot. How we look outside this mirror is not important. I am not some pale version of a quiet woman you may overlook on a normal day. You are not actually a smaller, softer version of someone I once dated. No, here in the confines of this single stall bathroom and its floor-to-ceiling mirror we are just two strangers, not seeing each other for who we are but who we could be.

You sit on the closed toilet, and I sit on your lap, legs spread, both of us facing the mirror. I have been watching you as you stroke my body and whisper beautiful words about my hair, my skin, and the color of my skirt suit, of all things. My eyes follow your hands in the mirror as they worship me and I start to believe, just for a moment, in our little fantasy. You touch each garter with the very tips of your fingers, caressing up and down the straps.

You put a finger into my panties, stroke along the seam of my pussy, back and forth, caressing the lips, teasing. As if we have all the time in the world. As if someone isn't going to knock any second to kick us out of here. No, you keep petting and smiling at me in the mirror. Stolen worship is exciting, especially when you are not the fairest in the land, and never will be.

As I look into your reflected light brown eyes, I remember where we are. I remember how we got here together, in this bathroom. I remember sitting at the bar asking for a drink. I remember you sitting down next to me. Immediately, I liked how you were dressed casually, relaxed, in a plain T-shirt and jeans. I liked your short beard, cut close to the cheek. I liked your dark hair and how it was a little ruffled, as if it'd barely seen a comb that morning. I thought I liked you most in that moment, but I had yet to feel your hands stroke me so lovingly, as if we'd known each other forever.

You asked me those typical questions. *"What's your name? What do you do for a living? Do you come here often? Where are you from? What's your favorite book?"* Not all the answers were right, but the conversation went well enough. I learned then that you are younger than me by ten years, and when I noted that to you, you laughed at me and said it didn't matter.

Here in this bathroom, the mirror we both gaze in is not a tool to show us who we really are, but a tool to tell us what movements to make next. This mirror is here to guide your hands and mine across each other's bodies. It is not going to tell me I am too fat and too old to fuck. It is simply a tool for pleasure. Our pleasure. You make the mirror this way. You transform my image into something to be desired. With your words out in the bar, with your hands now, and what I know will be your lips, mouth, and cock soon.

As you competently and gently maneuver my body from your lap to a sitting position on the top of the toilet, I remember the gentle way you touched my shoulder when my drink was empty. The way you created the silence I needed so I could fill it with my own stories. But I also remember the simple, straightforward way you told me about your life, and included me in every moment. Those moments culminate into this one, where your movements are as economical and straightforward as your storytelling. There is just a slight touch to help me out of my suit jacket, to take off my shirt, for me to help you with your jeans and your shirt. It is quick and quiet, and soon we are standing before each other, nearly naked in a bar bathroom, unfiltered by the gaze of the mirror.

This is juxtaposed to how we got here, where just minutes before, in the middle of a story, you took my hand and leaned forward. We had kept holding each other's hand from that point on. Even that felt thrilling, and I knew then that I wanted you this way, naked before me, sooner rather than later. At this thought, I just laugh at myself, discordant to the quiet nakedness I find myself in now.

"What?" you say, and I laugh again. *"Is all of this manliness overwhelming? It's all the muscles, isn't it?"* You pretend to flex, and we laugh. As our laughs die naturally, we stare at each other again, learning. As if the mirror conditioned us to just look and be with each other, in this moment, with no expectations beyond the here and now. Or perhaps this is how strangers are with each other after too many drinks on a weekday. Whatever it is, we feel completely normal doing this in a public restroom, so slowly and sensually. I panic a little at the thought of all the germs in here, then I remember how we got here.

Back at the bar, when you got up to go use the bathroom, I followed you. The single stall between the gentleman's and ladies' room was being cleaned, and I could smell the scent of lemon. I can smell it even now. When we exited our respective rooms a few minutes later, the cleaners were gone. I saw you and you smiled, I felt I must kiss you immediately. So, I did. I pushed you by the mouth, hands on your chest, into this bathroom. We saw that tall mirror and laughed but then we stood side by side, staring into it. Realizing the possibilities. *"It's just been cleaned. We can have a little fun,"* I said. But we both just stood and stared at that giant mirror for a few more silent seconds.

I feel the urgency of our location, again, but you do not seem bothered by it, so I ignore it, too. Now, I open my naked arms, and we kiss, flushed naked against each other. These are not the short, friendly kisses you give to someone on a first date. But immediately deep, wet, open-mouth kisses. You make satisfying little noises at the back of your throat, and I know this is what we were supposed to be doing from the very beginning.

You settle me back onto the toilet seat, legs spread again, and kneel between my legs. You do with your lips what your fingers did before, stroking, mouth closed, along the seam of my pussy, lightly. Teasing. You nuzzle and smell deeply. As if you have no better place to be. As if this is the only place you have ever belonged. Your hands gather one large thigh and move it over your shoulder. Your hand spreads my pussy lips open.

The first lick is tentative, and you groan at the taste. Earnestly, if such a thing is possible, you drag your tongue from my clit down and back up again, spreading all my juices around. You make little pleasure-filled humming noises. Those noises make me feel sexy, uninhibited, and I arch up. I look in the mirror and I see myself, breasts exposed, nipples hard, small and pink, my lingerie-clad legs wide open with you between them.

You lick my clit in slow circles, drawing out the tease. I am panting in short bursts. My eyes move frantically from the sight of you in the mirror, the back of your head moving in a steady rhythm, and of my own naked reflection splayed before you. My hips are moving in time with your mouth now. Your tongue is pressed hard against my clit. I hold your head to stop it, and you press your tongue to my clit even harder. I move my hips against your mouth, fucking your stiff tongue and feel the first wave of orgasm surge.

A series of sights, sounds, thoughts, and smells flood into my awareness. I see my sweat-soaked self in the mirror. I can hear my own frantic panting and your muffled moans as they vibrate against my clit. I feel the illicit nature of my exposed body, as if anyone can see me this way, my unseen life finally witnessed. As you pant heavily into my pussy, I can smell it and the whiskey you drank earlier tonight. My mind begins to blank completely and all the images, scents, and feelings from the last few moments coalesce into just a series of bright sensations. The mirror, the location, you, my thighs, my pussy, your tongue.

I am gripping your hair so hard I can feel myself start to spasm. You stick your fingers in my pussy and begin to fuck them in and out of me. My whole body clenches in orgasm. The ride down is just as fraught but slower, and wet. You are still licking and finger-fucking me. I try to push you away, but you tell me no in a short, muffled sound, "Mhm" and keep going. The impression of being caught at this point is so fleeting, I realized I've never really cared and should stop dwelling on it.

You continue to fuck me with your fingers, slow, then fast, then slow, then fast. But your tongue keeps the same hard, direct contact it has been, applying pressure and I am bucking against you. My arms and upper torso are wet with sweat, and I am barely able to hold onto the toilet seat. All I can think of is coming again, how close I am, how excited I am. I keep reaching toward the orgasm then coming back then reaching again and coming back.

Suddenly, you stop. You sit back on your legs, take a deep

breath while you feel around for something. I watch you in a daze as you stand up to put a condom on. I am barely able to remain standing without your hands on my hips holding me and nearly fall when you pull me to sit on your lap again, facing the mirror. I lift my body and watch my pussy take your cock in one sure thrust. We both watch, transfixed by the sight. After a bit, we find a rhythm and move in time together.

All the while you are saying a string of words into the mirror, watching your cock go in and out of my pussy. You become obsessed with saying "Oh, God" over and over in half breaths. Then, "Come on my cock," in excited whispers, breath blowing over my neck and the tips of my ears. The steady stream of words turns to nonsense, either because you are saying nonsense, or I cannot hear words anymore. All of this heightens my excitement, the muffled sounds and your puffed breaths, and seeing myself getting fucked. So I begin to circle my hungry clit in the mirror, reaching urgently toward orgasm. Suddenly, it's all too much again and I begin to come.

I feel the jerk of your cock releasing in my tightly clenched body. I watch all of it, in our now precious reflection. We are a kaleidoscope of panting breaths, skin against skin, and a sensual feast for the eyes.

After this, we slowly put our clothes on, and we leave the bathroom. We chat quietly over one more drink. You give me your number, and I give you mine. I am not sure if I will call you, and I am not sure if you will call me. What I know is the mirror in that bathroom set us free, and I will never forget the way you and it made me feel beautiful.

PRIVATE BEACH

A.J. Harris

The lady from customer service was all smiles and apologies when we finally connected. "I'm terribly sorry for the confusion. But it looks like there was an error and this beach was double-booked."

"So, what can we do about this?" I rubbed the bridge of my nose. Beside me, the strange woman who'd appeared on the beach not five minutes after I arrived crossed her arms. The decontamination jumpsuit's paper-like fabric crinkled and crackled, like the mangrove leaves under our booties. They'd hidden the touchscreen for reaching management in a concrete post behind the largest mangrove. Discreet, designed not to break the illusion. Like everything else here.

"I think we both spent a lot to get private beaches. Can one of us be moved to another preserve?" The woman pulled off her jumpsuit's hood. Masses of black curls rushed down her back.

I pulled down my hood. Salty breezes tickled the short blonde hairs on the back of my neck, just around my neural interface nodes.

"All the preserves are booked, unfortunately. We can try to reschedule but it would involve a rescheduling fee, and the nearest dates are two years out."

"No!" we yelped in unison. I turned to the customer service rep. "Um, can you give us a bit?"

After the screen went mute, the stranger and I conversed. We were in similar binds. Three whole days away from work, plus the rental costs on a simulated mid-twentieth-century restricted beach, plus insurance, plus supplies and built-in time for the full pre-entry decontamination—all required years of planning and saving. We couldn't afford to reschedule.

"We're adults, right? No judgments. It's not a tiny beach for one. Max occupancy is four." She swept her arms out. The simulation was based on a private cove in now sunken Florida. High stands of mangroves circled the inlet. Two bungalows flanked the beach, in view but separated. In the center sat a traditional set of showers, a small bar and restaurant (fully automated), and restrooms. We'd see each other but never have to interact.

"No judgments?" The beach's terms of service focused on damaging the environment and other patrons. We could do whatever we wanted so long as we harmed no one, and nothing, in the preserve.

"No judgments. I didn't go through all those probes just to go back to work." She rubbed her left shoulder. The decontamination process included a full medical check: UV skin peels, vaccinations, internal gastrointestinal purge, full updates on birth control, and neural link cleaning. It was the first preventative care I'd been able to afford in over five years.

"All right. I'm in."

"Great! We have an accord, sir. I'm Marla." She peeled the glove off her hand and offered it to me. I did the same. Bright blue metallic paint tipped the nails on her ivory fingers. I was almost tan in comparison, and my purple nail polish felt restrained.

"Hi, Marla. I'm Del." I shook her hand. "Pleasure to meet you."

"Nice to meet you, too. Now, let's talk to the management and see if we can ignore each other for the next few days."

The "ignore each other" plan lasted about two hours.

After twenty minutes of time with customer service, we headed to our cabanas and unpacked. Our small huts were well stocked with simulation-friendly sundries. I boggled at the idea of *only* needing SPF 100 protection against the sun. My street clothes remained outside the sim, in a decontamination locker. Only essentials were taken into the beach. Spoiling the well-curated preserve generated harsh fines.

I didn't need anything special. A few clothes for the cool evenings, fresh port protectors for my neural links, and the largest memory cards I could afford. Management provided sandals, sunscreen, beach mats, and towels. On the sand, umbrellas and wooden reclining chairs awaited us. I stripped, gave myself a quick covering of coconut suntan lotion, and made the briefest of stops at my beach chair before diving into the ocean.

Salt spray. A cold rush around my ankles and legs. Chills running up my belly and back as the oncoming waves engulfed me. Roaring as water smashed into the beach, followed by a slow hiss as the sand drank in the surf. It was everything the memories promised and more. I fell into a slow, easy swim, following the current. The swim tanks at my condo complex, with the heavy haptic suits and water chlorinated into oblivion, felt like coffins compared to swimming naked and free through the raw ocean.

I dove. The song of the waves changed under the surface. High, airy crashes became low rumbles and deep gurgling. Silt tickled my hands as I paddled with the waves, letting them carry me. When my lungs complained, I surfaced.

"Whoa. Hi." Marla swam beside me, curls wet and gleaming in the sun.

"Oh, hi. Sorry. Current pulls everything here, I guess." The water drew back. My toes grazed the soft sand beneath us.

"Yeah. Nice form. Where did you learn how to swim?"

"Memories inherited from my grandmother. She used to go to beaches like this before the coastlines shifted. Think that's why I found my job." I touched my neural ports. "I work with submersible drones and dive exo-armor. Keeps me swimming. Sort of. What about you?"

"I'm a sense-net aerialist. And dancer. And underwater dancer." She touched her neural ports. "If I'm not flying, I'm swimming. Spend lots of time in dive tanks, recording sensations for immersive movies. Or hooked into arial rigs."

"What brought you to the beach?"

"Photos." She flashed a surprisingly wicked grin. First time I realized her eyes were the same jade green as the ocean. "My grandmother and grandfather were art students in England, back in the day. They spent all this time on beaches, or in beach houses, naked as the sun. Took thousands of pictures. I got ahold of them when my mom passed and just envied them. Can you imagine? No filter masks? Intact coastlines? Water you can swim in without heavy gear?"

"I should get you a copy of my grandmother's memories." I kicked, riding a wave up into the air for the briefest of moments. "She was Croatian. Lived there before the '22 war. Thought swimming in suits was unnatural. Have a memory of her admonishing tourists for wearing thongs. Different world, huh?"

"I'd love to see the memories. Thank you." Marla pointed to the shore. "Race you in?"

"Next wave. One-two-three!"

We surfed into shore, riding the froth and foam until the shallows caught up with us. Looking back, Marla let herself loose. She seemed to stay in the water while I stepped out. When I turned, wondering if she was okay, she startled and leaped out of the receding waves. It wasn't until much later I realized she was watching me step from the surf, naked, wicking sea foam from my arms and belly.

Not like I could claim purity and innocence. Marla rising from the surf sent a surge of heat right into my cheeks. Water beaded on her ivory skin. Tiny goosebumps dotted her arms, belly, and breasts. Her gumdrop nipples were shell pink under the sun. She wrung water from her hair, sun catching her muscular form. I lingered at the dark curls between her legs. They matched the coal-black waves on her head.

We motioned at our umbrellas, made noises about a good swim, and retreated to the showers. A quick rinse and I sat on my wood and cloth reclining chair. The umbrella cast thick, spiky shadows over the tiny dunes left by my footprints. Sun tickled my skin. I reached for the coconut oil.

At least, it said coconut oil. "All natural. Non-toxic." It flowed from the bottle in a thick, clear ribbon. I spread it with my hands and applied it to my shoulders. An errant glance across the sand showed Marla doing the same. She dribbled oil across her clavicle, set the bottle down, and rubbed until her upper arms and chest gleamed. Cupping her breasts, she splayed her fingers over her nipples before running her slippery hands down her belly.

I turned away and focused on myself. Before my vacation, I researched beaches and sunbathing. Even in the days before UV warnings, people burned easily. And everywhere. Thorough application of skincare products was essential. So, I was methodical. I oiled up my arms, my legs, the back of my neck. Even my toes and ankles.

And my cock. I did not want to burn there.

The oil felt cool at first, but when I rubbed it into my skin, it grew warm and welcoming. I closed a fist around my stiffening length and let out a small moan. Blushing, I checked on Marla. Did she see me stroking myself?

No. She was similarly occupied. One hand lay across her breast, nipple pinched between thumb and forefinger. The other hand dove between her legs. Tufts of pubic hair puffed between her fingers. She worked her pussy in wide circles. When she spread her legs, I saw the briefest flash of pink.

I watched her, capturing the image of her in my mind: this stunning stranger, pleasuring herself on a blue and white beach chair under a bright red umbrella. Another dollop of oil flowed onto my purpling glans. I rubbed, slowly. At home, jacking off was a quick deal. A dopamine release in the shower before a long day. It had been ages since I'd taken my time, enjoyed myself. But here, away from the world—if I couldn't take my time now, when could I?

Eyes closed, I ran my fingers up and down the underside of my cock. Oil trickled through my pubic hair, collecting under my balls. With my other hand, I cupped myself, warming the oil against my skin. I guided the warmth up my belly, across my chest, and over my nipples. It mingled with the heat rising from the sun-warmed sands. The wind tickled me. Stray grains from the dunes picked at my skin. Every sensation became a kiss and a bite from an invisible lover.

I opened my eyes. Hypnagogic red and yellow flares faded. Marla stood above me. Blue sky stretched behind her. She gleamed like a newly harvested pearl. Her labia peeked from her thick pubic hair, pearlescent and wet. She licked her lips and said, "God, I want to touch you. Can I touch you?"

"Yes." I sat up. "Please."

Marla spread her palm across my chest. My heart jumped. She splayed her hand across my pectoral muscles. My nipple stiffened under her palm. She didn't trail her fingers downward. Instead, she traced my clavicle, my neck, and my jawline. I shuddered. How many years had it been since another human being cupped my chin? Marla brought me close and kissed me.

Tentative, nervous kisses. We were out of practice, trying not to bump teeth or pinch lips. I scooted back, making room on the chair for her. She straddled the leg rest and embraced me. Her hands kneaded my back. I slipped my arms around her, running my fingers up into her hair. The slow kisses dissolved into a torrent of hunger. I devoured her mouth. I lapped at her tongue.

"Wait. Stop." Marla pulled away. "You don't have to do this. I don't want to make you do anything you don't want to—oh!" She caught the tears rolling from my eyes with her thumbs. "I'm sorry!"

"No, it's not that at all." I pressed her hand against my cheek. "You feel so wonderful. And you taste amazing."

"So do you." She laughed, tears forming, and licked my nose. "Coconut oil suits you."

"Thanks."

"What do you want to do?" Marla rested her arms on my shoulders. Goose pimples pricked up along her arms. I kissed the inside of her elbow.

"I just want to enjoy this—whatever this is." I kissed her. "I haven't felt this human in ages. You?"

"I want to enjoy this, too." She bit her lip. "Also, I really want you to eat my pussy. And jerk you off until you come on me. And then I want you to fuck me in the beach shower."

I blinked. "Wow. In that order?"

"Now that you mention it." She stood up. "Come on me first. Then, lick it off my tits and pussy before you eat me out."

"And after that?"

"And after that, you'd better well fuck me."

We switched places. She moved the chair's back until it became a fully reclined bed. Legs spread, knees bent, feet dug into the sand, she watched me drizzle oil onto my stiff cock. I straddled the edge of the chair, nearly burying the canvas in the sand, and stroked myself. I made sure she could see me cupping my balls and running my fingers along the veiny surface of my shaft.

She played with her tits as I toyed with my nipples. Her finger slipped between her labia. Mine stroked up and down. My gleaming head appeared and disappeared into my fist. Precome drizzled down my knuckles. My toes curled. I dug my feet in, forcing myself to slow every stroke.

Marla noticed my ragged breath and the strings of pent-up jizz now dribbling from my fingers. She cupped her breasts, licked her lips, and said, "Come on. I want to feel it. Spurt all over me."

I didn't need more encouragement. My hand became a blur. I spasmed and moaned. A surge of thick, white semen flew from my cock. It took all my attention to direct the streams onto Marla. Creamy dollops spattered on her chest, belly, and pussy. Jizz dripped from her pubic hair onto her open labia. She took a drop and rubbed it across her tumescent clit.

"Let me get that for you," I said, before bending down and tasting her. She was the ocean: salty, sharp, and all enveloping. I spread her folds apart with my tongue, licking all around, luxuriating in her deliciousness. Where I could taste myself, it added a little musk to the flavor palate. I used the tip of my tongue to write out the sensations on her clit in large block letters.

Marla writhed. She grabbed my hair and pulled me closer. "Fingers. Please."

I drizzled more oil over my hand. Two fingers at first, massaging the roof of her pussy. She clenched, twitching and spasming as my tongue continued writing sonnets on her clit. I added a third finger, tenting them, spreading her wide. She gyrated against me, against my hand—and stopped.

"I can't wait. Cock. Please."

I looked up. "But the shower?"

"Don't need it." She grabbed my shoulders. "Please say you're hard again."

I didn't need to say it. She could see me, erect and eager once more. Marla lay back and curled her legs up, folding in on herself, baring her gleaming pussy. I ran my glans over her labia, wetting us both, before sliding in. Muscular legs, trained in acrobatics, snapped around me like a coiled spring. She wasn't letting go. I didn't want to be anywhere else.

I thought I'd forgotten how to fuck anything beside a pussy-shaped sleeve tied to a sim-sense rig. But my body remembered. We moved together, sliding, gliding, fucking. She kissed me, lightly biting my lip. All my weight fell against her. My legs quaked, shuddering with each thrust. All the while, I teased and pulled at her tits.

"That's it. Right there," she whispered in my ear as I dove her depths. "I can feel you. Oh, you're so warm."

I kept my core and groin muscles tight, focusing on my thrusts, on the rhythmic slap of our bodies against each other. She moved with me, following my lead like a practiced dance partner. We swam together, in sync, stroke for stroke. The jizz I'd spattered across her seemed like a drizzle of rain compared to what built up within me.

Marla must have sensed me fighting. Again. Breathless, she growled, "Come inside me. Please."

Her "please" broke me. My cock swelled and pumped, over and over, until my balls ached. Seeing me orgasm, all uninhibited moans and quivering muscles, triggered Marla. Even spent I kept fucking her, rubbing myself against her clit, until she dug her fingernails into my back. Sweat, salt, and coconut oil filled the air. Marla's hair covered my eyes. When she relaxed, last of her orgasms complete, I tried to slip out.

"No." She held onto me fast, acrobat's legs tight around my waist. "No, stay. Want to feel you dripping out."

"Okay." I rolled us onto our sides, doing my best to stay within her. Eventually, my erection slackened. I slipped free. The breeze from the ocean cooled us. We shivered.

"Now what?" I brushed hair from her eyes.

"Now, I think, the shower." Marla chuckled. "Then maybe dinner? Try the robot chef?"

"And after that?" I brushed curls from her eyes. "After this? What now?"

"I don't know." Marla kissed me. No soft kiss. Intense, deep, and almost painful. "I don't care. This, whatever this is? I want to enjoy it for as long as I can. Is that okay with you, Del?"

I spent a moment listening to the ocean. Two more nights— three more days—on a secluded beach with a stranger. No rules. No bosses. No breather masks or algae blooms in the water. No storm warnings. Nothing but Marla and whatever we wanted to do with each other that day.

"Okay?" I grinned. "We have an accord, sir."

Together, we headed for the shower, and did our best to not think about the future.

CHARLOTTE THE PIRATE QUEEN

Dr. J.

Had I found him? Today's inspiration?

His name jumped off the page beside an incredible picture of manliness the likes of which I'd never witnessed before.

A draft of cool air ruffled my stack of papers on the dark wooden desk in the musty upstairs corner of the museum. Quick footsteps followed. I grasped the seat of my chair and turned toward the sound.

As I glimpsed the man entering the room, the hair on the back of my neck stood. I glanced back at the page and then back again to the intruder.

A gravelly voice boomed through the air. "Oh, I'm sorry. I didn't know anyone was working here today."

I knew reading history created pictures in my head. It was my point of being here. Yet I never imagined I'd be able to summon up the people from the past and have them materialize in front of me.

Here stood a man from another time in all his period garb. It was as if he'd stepped off the page of this historical book. My body vibrated.

"No worries."

As I slid my gaze from the top of his scarf-knotted forehead, down to his vest, which offered a glimpse of his bare chest, his body tightened. A sash spanned across his hard body, from broad shoulder to trim waist. At the juncture of the cloth on his hip, my gaze drew downward to his tight pants with the outline of his muscular thighs and a full crotch. The black cavalier boots completed the sexy ensemble. I retraced this incredible landscape upward and when I reached his face, he smirked.

"Aye, never see a pirate before?"

The sexy rumble of his voice called my lady parts to attention. Heat crept across my face. *OMG I'm gawking.* I swiveled my chair toward the desk and my work. That didn't help. There he was, staring back at me from the opened book. He'd already reached stardom as my fantasy material, and now it was happening in real life.

I cleared my throat. "Of course I have, just not one during my research time."

"Ah, family genealogy or historical research?"

Metal jangled behind me.

"Historical research," I sort of lied. I used history for two things: to become part of a family and to capture my fantasy material. Sitting taller in the chair, I twirled around.

"I understand. My presence seems to surprise."

And definitely arouse.

"Well, you, Captain Hernandez, are in context. Just unexpected."

He chuckled. "Great way to frame it. My name is Vincent,

otherwise known as Captain Hernandez. I'm doing my docent
shift for the museum tour today. My locker is here."

Vincent placed a backpack in a bin and attached a set of
old metal keys to his belt at his very sexy waist. His demeanor,
height, muscles—well, everything about him—spoke to me. As
he sauntered closer to the desk, lemon and sandalwood floated
off him.

Can this man get any more attractive?

"Do all the docents dress the part for enacting history?"

"We dress up the week of the Shrimp Festival. It's tradition."

"Hmm. Interesting. My name is Charlotte." I glanced down
at his sturdy hands, clutching the large key ring. In an instant, I
imagined nimble fingers caressing my skin and then holding me.
I shook off that arousing mental video so I could speak. "Do
tell, what are the keys for?"

"If anyone gets unruly, I can throw them in the old jail. It's
the highlight of the museum." He leaned over the desk.

"Hmm. You're doing historical research on my family?"

My hand smoothed the page. "Your family? Ah, no. This was
generic historical research. Finding you was serendipity, I guess."

"What do you do with your research?"

His warm eyes pulled me under his pirate spell.

Suck it up, Charlotte, be bold, say it.

"I use history to create fantasy." As I licked my lips, his gaze
centered there, and he shifted his stance.

"Hmm. Fantasy as in a bold new world or fantasy as in
something naughty and fun?"

"Both." I swallowed hard. "But today, the second one."

I watched him tilt his head, bite his lip, and adjust his sash
across his mighty fine chest. As I sat in the cool museum, the
temperature rose in me and the moments stalled as he took his
sweet time responding.

"I'm a competent and detailed reenactor. Would you like a collaborator in your fantasy creation?"

I had invited no one into my private fantasy world and no one had ever offered. The creation process had always been my solitary endeavor, but then I'd never had the muse of my research show up. I ogled him as I mulled over his offer. I may not have known this man, but everything in me called out, yes. Maybe it was the fact that this setting and his presence not only went to my head but also settled between my legs. I seemed primed for anything.

"What did you have in mind?"

He turned and pointed to an old trunk. "The local pirate's club keeps their clothes in there. You could pick out something." He jingled the keys and cocked his head. "And at five p.m., meet me at the jail, wench."

The tone of the word "wench" sucked me in. "How far do your reenactments go, Vincent?"

"You mean, what can I provide, Charlotte?"

I nodded.

"Off the top of my head, the pirate's favorite wench of the bordello comes to get him out of jail and they have a smoldering reunion or I could lock up the wench and have her beg me to let her out by offering sexual favors."

OMG. *This man could be my soul mate. How could I have found him?*

"What do you get out of doing this?"

"Maybe my fantasy is someone coming into the museum looking for something I can offer."

Could we be any more in sync?

"Charlotte, I can be your full-service collaborator. You could direct the scene, creating what you want." I blinked as I continued to think. "And if you want, take me for a test drive?" His sexy wink sealed the deal.

Vincent offered me fantasy heaven, the way I wanted it. I wiggled in the chair and drank him in. My body betrayed me in so many ways: wet panties, erect nipples, and a dry mouth.

If I attempted to stand, would my legs hold me up?

He must have sensed my dilemma because he stepped in front of my chair and bent down almost nose to nose. I inhaled his arousal's unique sea-salt scent, wrapped in the aroma of old books and the damp mildew of history. As it washed over me, I felt empowered.

I leaned forward, focusing on his lush lips. I pictured a reunion of the wench and her pirate man. *What would it be like?* I had to know.

I launched myself upward at Vincent, my lips aimed for his. When they connected, electricity shot through my body as if he had shocked me and I him. His arms wrapped tight around me, grasping in a familiar hold as if he couldn't believe I was real or here again with him. The taste of lust pushed through me. I grabbed onto his vest, trying to get closer to him. Our bodies responded in mutual desire, tongues speaking a common language. I broke off the kiss, my chest pounding, and looked up at him.

"Oh, my. You're a pretty good reenactor."

"You're a pretty talented director. I guess the lingering question is, what more do you want from me?"

"Hmm. Well, Captain, maybe you'll find out at five."

He stood tall and looked me over. "Now my fantasy is working. I'm up for anything." Smiling, he touched his lips and headed out of the room, clanking.

Ah, the fantasy, the history. The man left me alone to conjure a plan.

In front of me, the trunk he mentioned beckoned, and I answered the call. After I unlatched the antique fastener with a click, I flipped the lid and there it was. The outfit I wanted.

Forget the wench. He was getting a real woman.

When I pulled on the boots, it grounded me into my role. I was Charlotte, the pirate captain, the queen. I turned and glimpsed my reflection in the glass map door. *Did I recognize myself?* The leather bustier with intricate leather buckles did wonders for my breasts, hiking them in a pert fashion as the underlying chemise dipped low, highlighting my cleavage. I radiated desire.

For years now, this is how I'd created my family of origin history, pretending I was part of something. That's what being an orphan did to me. But today was the first time I discovered a sexual component and acted on it. It riveted me.

A real history enactment with Vincent Hernandez, descendant of the Hernandez family, brought to the new world by the infamous Turnbull Menorcan flotilla to farm indigo. He represented strength in conviction, as his family had broken from indentured work and fled to create a better life.

But Vincent chose a different path. He maintained his connection to the sea and captained his own ship. That's what I'd read, anyway. I'll take that kind of strength with me.

I was ready to direct and enact.

As I traipsed down the stairs, I followed the distant voices. A door opened and shut, signaling the close of the museum day. At the entrance, I spied the closed sign hanging on the front door. Clanging metal alerted me to the jail's direction, so I made my way down a hallway.

At the doorway to the jail room, I watched Vincent reset the chains and their attachments on the wall.

"You think you can sneak up on me, wench?"

I froze.

He was in character. In this place, filled with history and

lore, his stature and character brought it all to life. But I wanted to find out if he'd play. I wanted to see if I would.

"I don't know who you think you're calling a wench, sir. I've earned my place and status in the world."

Vincent straightened and pivoted. His eyes narrowed and his teeth pulled on his bottom lip. As his gaze floated over my breasts and tight waist, I held my breath. I knew the minute it registered who I was playing.

"Ah, the pirate queen, Charlotte, returns from her voyage. Am I your first stop or did you hit the Palace Saloon for some fortification?"

I lifted my chin. "You were the one who couldn't meet my demands."

"If you believe that, then what are you doing here?" He stared me down. I squirmed in my skin as this repartee heated me up.

"Sea changes you. I've had time to think."

He meandered toward me. Holy crap, his pants strained with his arousal. A hint of the pine scent, no doubt from the nearby mill, wafted in the air. It was but one part of the magnetic force pulling me to him.

"And your thoughts, my queen."

He traced my jawline to my chin and dropped his finger onto the skin of my chest. My breath hitched. The color of his irises changed as his pupils dilated. He was a predator, worse than I'd encountered on the sea because I allowed him to bypass all my defenses and strip me emotionally bare, and we were so close. My nipples ached and my vagina clenched rhythmically. Together, with our eyes locked into that moment, we became lost in the singular delight of a lustful connection.

"You were right, Vincent. I need to be handled and handled well."

I looked around him to the wall with chains.

"And you can start now."

He leaned in and ran his nose and mouth along my forehead. His tongue dabbed my skin, reminding me of insane chemical influences. I quivered in response.

"So now you're able to tell me what you want?"

"I am."

He nodded. "How may I serve you, my queen?"

I raised my hands to lower the chemise and stopped, knowing I was breaking character. I leaned in. "No one is coming in here, right?"

"Nope, not tonight. It's Friday," he whispered.

"Okay. Hey, do you have condoms?"

He patted his pocket. "Yes, right here."

"Okay, good." I nodded.

Vincent cleared his throat. "How may I serve you, my queen?"

I pulled down the chemise, and my breasts popped out over the top of the bustier. Vincent licked his lips.

"Touch them, Vincent, however you want."

With a firm hand, he clasped one, then bent down and swirled his tongue on its nipple as he pinched the other one. He smiled at me. I wanted to give, and I was ready to take.

"I'm going to punish you for having me wait so long to give you what you deserve, Charlotte."

"Yes, punish me, Vincent."

"Take off your belt and unfasten the trousers."

I dropped the belt to the floor and unbuttoned the pants. The intensity of his gaze summoned a place of power in me.

"Now slide them down as if we have all the time in the world."

Inch by inch, the scratchy fabric worked down my legs. I

imagined his view of me, with my breasts popped out for feasting, held up with the bustier and my lower nakedness on display.

"Come closer to the wall."

With my pants bunched over my boots, I stutter stepped forward. Vincent squeezed both breasts and seared me with a kiss like earlier. *This guy was good.* He reached between my legs and cupped me. "I will bring you to it, Charlotte." He circled behind me and palmed each asscheek, massaging and pulling them apart. My scent filled the room.

"Place your hands on the wall."

When I complied, he fastened the leather cuffs on each wrist, which forced my knees against the wooden bench.

"Vincent." My breathless utterance rolled around the room and I shuddered in sheer delight.

Vincent nudged my feet apart and dropped to his knees. His hot breath skated across my ass and then his warm lips planted light kisses over both cheeks.

"How did you come to your decision, Charlotte, to give yourself over to me?"

I bowed my head, thinking how to phrase my thoughts.

"There is no trust for me on the seas. I'm always looking over my shoulder for who will seize my cargo, my ship, my reign. I need one place for trust and solace and . . ." I shivered. Vincent squeezed my asscheeks.

"And . . ." he said.

"And pleasure. Give me pleasure, Vincent."

Vincent pressed his hand on my back, which pushed my chest down, and straightened my dangling arms over my head. My butt tilted up so my sex became his playground. Bent over, I focused on the carved-up bench below me. For a fleeting second, I wondered who had been here before me and then his hot tongue ran through my drenched seam. I snapped my eyes shut, falling into bliss. He licked and sucked, unleashing loud noises from me I didn't know I was capable of, accompanied by his very sexy sounds of pleasure. My wrists accepted the sweet torment of pain laced in.

Captured. I was captured.

Vincent used every part of his mouth, lips, tongue, and face as tools to work my clit and female flesh and left me yearning for more. He awakened something inside me, deep and mysterious. I wanted to let it out. When I heard the tearing of the thin plastic condom foil ricocheting across the room, I was ready.

"Charlotte, this is my claiming. You are mine."

"Yes, Vincent Hernandez, I'm yours."

He rubbed his cock between my vulva lips. My brain registered his length and girth. I rocked back, and he met me with each motion. Our dance made me wetter. And after he positioned his tip at my entrance, he curved his body around mine. With his hands on my breasts, he anchored my body onto him. How he made me feel safe and powerless at the same time mystified me, but I wanted what he was giving me.

"Charlotte, my pirate queen."

His first thrust engulfed me. It was otherworldly. He transported me to another place, history or heaven, I didn't know. Over and over, he stirred the pleasurable waves in me, to heights I'd never known. One hand pinched my nipple, the other stroked my clit. As he hammered into me, my fingers and palms sank into the bricks, abrading my skin. I didn't care. This was what I wanted, what I'd missed.

I floated in the afterglow. Vincent completed my historical research journey with his North Star but it wasn't enough.

"Vincent, I want to see you. Sit on the bench. I want to be on your lap."

Vincent cradled my breasts and squeezed lightly. "Is that an order, my pirate queen?"

I managed a giggle. We could barely stay in role.

"I want to see that handsome face of yours when you come next, by my command."

"So demanding, my queen. We have a predicament. Your pants are stuck on top of your boots."

"That's never stopped you before, Captain Hernandez."

"Hold still."

I looked over my shoulder as Vincent pulled a knife from his boot. My heart soared. With lightning speed, he cut the leather laces holding the sides of the pant legs together and pulled them over my boots. I straightened my body, relaxing the pull on my wrists, as he pushed down his pants and slid onto the bench under me. He took the time to remove the condom and tie it off before he placed another one beside him on the bench. I laughed.

"What's so funny?"

"A condom in history." He shook his head.

"Now what were you commanding me to do, Queen Charlotte?"

"Free me."

Vincent grinned as he reached up and unfastened the cuffs from my wrists. In a quick motion, I placed one knee on the bench beside his thigh and then the other one as I settled myself on his lap.

My hand dropped to his shoulder, and I slid it up his neck, clutching his hair as I settled my other hand on his cock. "You have brought me much pleasure tonight, sir." I massaged him and cupped his balls while I gazed into his eyes.

"Aye, Charlotte. You honor me with your trust."

He snaked his arm around my waist, pulled me flush against

his warm body and kissed me. I spiraled back to the kiss upstairs. I imagined kisses we had had over time. Built-up passion seared us both. Never had I experienced this in my lifetime.

Maybe our connection is timeless.

With my hand trapped between us, I felt his cock stiffen. Our heat and energy mingled with intensity. I pulled back to look at him and saw it reflected in his eyes and the tenseness of his face. My nails scraped his scalp, and he leaned over and kissed my wrist.

"You honor me with your touch, Charlotte."

"What do you want, Vincent?"

He chuckled. "You've given me what I wanted."

I cocked my head. "What was that?"

"You came."

"Yes, I came."

"No, Charlotte, *you* came. Ancient lore said you would return."

"What?"

"Before you leave, there's another page you need to read in the book." Vincent nuzzled my cheek. "I'm happy it was with me."

His eyes dragged me into another world, another time, and I went willingly. He rolled on the condom and I eased down on him. With every inch of him I took, it cemented our connection.

Delight and joy washed over me. I rose on him and crashed back down like I was the boat and he was the sea. He provided the pace, and I stoked my fire, my clit burning me up with another eruption. There in the jail, we merged again.

I was the sail of my ship, taut against the wind, stretched for best use, and I expanded to take all I could. Vincent was giving me an out-of-body experience.

I collapsed on Vincent and his easy caressing motion on my

back lulled me back into the present. With my nose buried in his chest, the lemon and sandalwood brought me back to the damp space of the museum jail. I lost all sense of time as we sat there, joined.

I looked up at him. He smiled down at me with a knowing look.

"Vincent, thank you for such a memorable reenactment."

"It was my pleasure, Charlotte. I'll never look at the jail the same way."

"I hope I'm not keeping you from other duties."

He pulled out a pocket watch. "I am needed for the pirates' landing soon. We better get you dressed."

Gathering up clothes and the evidence of our coupling, we moved back upstairs to the research area and the pirate trunk. As Vincent collected his backpack, I dressed, then wrote a note about the pants needing new laces and stowed it away with the pirate clothes.

"Thank you again, Vincent."

"Yes, Charlotte, my pleasure. Oh, I left the information for you on the desk. I need to run, but read it before you go. Don't worry about locking up, the door automatically locks behind you."

"Vincent. One last kiss."

When I tasted his reverent warm lips again, I sighed. Then he kissed my forehead and left.

I walked to the desk to gather my research belongings. The book was open to a new page.

Charlotte Dubois, Queen of the Pirates.

Destiny.

A map outlined Pirate Queen Charlotte's routes and her ports of call. This island was her starting point and Vincent was her first port of call.

Vincent gifted me with this life and a new family.

I gazed over at the trunk. Never underestimate that history and the universe, when combined with a powerful want of connection, provide a path.

I tapped the page.

Savannah.

What waits for me there?

UNTAMED: A MODERN PRIMAL LOVE STORY

Nikki Rae

The rules were simple:

1. Find the lion
2. Do as he says
3. Wait

At the very end of the typed list was delicate handwriting:

Say the word and it stops.
I'm proud of you, rabbit. I look forward to devouring
you.
—X

Four months ago, I would have never considered showing up to a strange place I didn't know to meet a man whose voice I'd only heard a handful of times—let alone wearing a lace dress better suited for sleeping, heels that made me a foot taller, and a large plastic bunny mask that covered everything but the lower half of my face.

Still, he could accomplish quite a lot from thousands of miles away. Perhaps that was the reason I'd agreed to meet. I needed to know for myself if he was real or like every other self-professed "dominant" man: all talk.

I'd been to the events, I'd seen the parties, and I had dabbled with most of the lifestyle offerings. However, the encounters always left me disappointed, in need. Something was lacking and it wasn't until I'd encountered "X" that I'd had a name for it.

The cold made my nipples harden under the garment, which made me gasp with sharp pain. Then I sank into the warm aftermath like a bath at the end of a long day.

Send a picture of you wearing the clamps.

I blushed at imagining his deep voice even though it had only been a text. The tiny metal appeared unassuming, but the more time that passed, the more eager I became to remove them.

No, he'd said when I asked immediately after sending him proof. *They come off when I say.*

My mystery guy was private—he didn't have social media aside from the app we met on, and he even told me he'd deleted it once we'd become exclusive. He lived in Europe and based on his slight accent, I'd guessed the UK.

Normally, I was not the relationship type, but X made it . . . fun. Like a game. He gave me tasks I completed every day. Sometimes they were mundane like "wear a blue top" while others required heading to a bodega at three in the morning and purchasing a lighter, condoms, a candle, and a single ginger root. This was purely so he could see if I followed direction, and it gave me purpose throughout the week while I was busy organizing schedules or filing paperwork.

X had provided me with photographs, videos, phone calls, and even a FaceTime or two. In the months we'd been talking, I'd seen the man completely naked except for a copy of that day's newspaper. However, as far as his face went, I'd only been given glimpses of an angled jawline. The rest of him was just like his words: beautiful with the promise of something dark beneath. Likewise, he'd seen every inch of me except my face. I preferred it that way. Anonymous. No judgment, no expectations. Just instinct.

Music was the first thing that greeted me. After that, a low-lit room cast in a bright shade of violet. There was a lobby with a bar, couches, and pillows amongst the tables and stools.

Hyperaware of my surroundings, I was convinced that one of the men in the sea of disguises was mine. I spotted masks of all kinds on people in various states of dress and undress, but none of them matched the descriptions I'd been given.

I chose a seat away from all the action in the corner as I stalked the area with just my eyes.

In a matter of minutes, the cushion dipped to my left. I stared up at a man in a gold lion mask that covered his entire face so not even his lips were visible. In his simple black shirt and leather suspenders, he'd rolled up his sleeves to reveal tattoos across every inch of the roped muscles and olive skin.

"You're here for Mr. X?" His voice was light and airy, a pair of dark brown eyes smiling back.

"Y-yes," I stuttered, managing to straighten my posture.

"Here." Reaching into his back pocket, he produced a black strap of leather. I only got a glance of the shiny letters spelling out the name X had given me before it was around my neck.

It will keep you safe. Tell others you're mine.

"And . . ." From the opposite pocket, he removed a strip of red silk fabric, which he fastened around my eyes so I couldn't see. "Ready?"

I nodded.

He tugged me to my feet and my mouth went dry. The chase was about to begin.

As soon as we were outside, my feet stalled, but I was shoved into motion until I was pressed against cold metal. A lock disengaged and it registered we were getting into a vehicle, and that was when I started to fight.

"Uh, uh, uh, little rabbit." The lion easily overpowered me, pinning my wrists behind my back in one large palm. "No running yet."

I calmed myself, hardly aware of him lifting me into the back of what I assumed was a van and plopping me onto a seat. In no time, we were in motion.

"Do you talk?" he asked after a while.

Releasing a breath, I said, "I-I'm just shy. Sorry."

That was true. I'd suffered from anxiety for as long as I could remember and the only way I'd found to overcome it was to insert myself into situations where that feeling was confronted. I preferred to forgo the pleasantries altogether, which was partly why this evening sounded so appealing to me when X had broached the subject.

"That's all right," he assured me. "Scared?"

My knee had begun to bounce with nerves and he stilled it. "A little."

His chest vibrated with a chuckle. "Also okay. Desired, even."

We hit a bump and a strong arm spanned across my front so I didn't fall. He was right; fear was part of the experience—what I'd asked for—and I'd be lying to myself if I said I didn't already feel the heat flooding my belly at what was to come.

"Just so I know you remember," said the lion, "what's the special word?"

X had given it to me to use if things were taken too far,
but I'd insisted that wasn't possible. Not in my fantasies. Then
again, he'd informed me that reality was quite different.

"Beetlejuice."

"Hand signal?"

In case your mouth is . . . busy.

I held up three fingers.

"Good girl." The praise made me clench my thighs and he
must have noticed, rubbing a palm over the lace that ended
above my knee. "Now we can start."

A sharp breath threatened to choke me, but I sat still as
he proceeded to expose my breasts, revealing what I'd been
required to wear underneath. He brushed past one nipple and I
gasped, more surprised than in pain.

"So nice and pink." The other nipple was flicked, eliciting a cry
from deep within my chest. He laughed quietly. "I wonder if you're
the same here." Without warning, his hand was up my skirt, out-
lining the hem of my panties before he withdrew. Half relieved
and half disappointed, another strangled whimper left me.

"Patience, baby." His voice was no longer muffled so he must
have taken off his mask. In the next instant his mouth was at my
throat, teeth unrelenting but sending warmth throughout my
spine. He laughed again when he pulled away. "You're going to
make this too easy."

Sore nipples exposed to the air, he tied my wrists in front of
me and removed my shoes.

The car came to an abrupt halt no less than twenty minutes
later, and then the back door was open and he was hauling me
to my feet.

"I will give you a five-minute head start." Feet on hard
ground, he removed the blindfold—not that I could see more
than a few inches in front of me in the blackness.

"Off you go," said the lion, treating my ass to a smack that made me jump. "And rabbit?"

I tilted my head toward his voice and it was no surprise that I only saw the faintest outline of his large figure.

"Don't let me find you first."

We must have been far from the city. It was so silent that not even cars passed, and it wasn't until I moved that any noise was made. Adrenaline kept me warm as I aimlessly sprinted into the trees. The clamps had been tampered with: the lion had secured bells to them. Bound hands in front of me, I used my upper arms to keep the bells from ringing. The cold bit at my exposed skin, creating more urgency.

I'd been training for tonight for weeks, lifting weights and using the treadmill, but the uneven ground made speed difficult. With every passing second, I knew the hunters were closing in.

Footsteps reached my ears, but they were distant; I still had time.

I felt my way through dead leaves and fallen twigs, scraping my knees on rocks. The pain made me more aware, and my pumping heart kept me on edge.

Needing to catch my breath, I curled around the thick trunk of a redwood like the husky bark could hide me from the inevitable. As I slowed my senses, I couldn't help but replay X's voice.

He'd called me this morning, which was a rare occurrence—we usually stuck to texts and pictures. His deep yet soft words had caressed the shell of my ear through the receiver as though he was there, right beside me.

Are you ready, little rabbit, to be devoured by the things that go bump in the night?

Are you ready to abandon your human shell?

Become prey?

Just as vividly, I remembered my answer: *Yes, sir.*

I was drawn back to the moment when I spotted a glow peeking between branches. They were heading toward me.

Without thinking twice, I dashed further into the forest to put more space between me and my pursuers, but my foot lost purchase on new terrain and I landed on my knees. This made the bells go off, effectively giving away my position.

I hissed at the failure as well as the sharp need that raced through my nipples, wishing more than anything I could take off the clamps so I could better concentrate. There was a hiking trail I knew well that cut through the park near my apartment, but I couldn't be sure they'd driven me there.

Through my frantic pulse mashing through my ears, an indiscernible shout came from where the light was quickly approaching. They knew where they were going. They knew how to find me.

Disoriented and already tiring, I was desperate to flee, so without hesitating a moment more, I dragged myself to my feet. I darted into softer grass, feeling my way toward a trail I wasn't certain existed.

From another place I couldn't see came a howl—human—followed by more intermittent yelling from one hunter to another. They were loud because they could be; they had no predators here.

Just a lost little bunny rabbit.

Eventually, I landed in some brush where the moon illuminated a small clearing. Here was where I started to crawl, legs aching and mud soaking my dress. When I was able, I scrambled to my feet and broke into a sprint, following the line of trees.

I wasn't fast enough and all too soon, I smacked headfirst into a solid wall of muscle. I bucked and fought, but it was no use. In an instant my back was against the ground and he was panting on top of me.

Something cool and sharp pressed against my throat and I
felt the tiniest droplet of blood bubble to the surface. I stilled
as he straddled my waist, one palm in the center of my chest.
With every breath, I felt the cold wind, the throbbing need
between his legs. Between *us*. Though instinct told me to run
and hide, a different, simpler side of me thought differently. It
wanted more.

"I told you, baby bunny," said the rough voice of the lion.
"You shouldn't have let me find you before him." Leaning close,
I felt his tongue against my cheek. "Now you're all mine."

He sucked at the small wound, sending searing needles
through my system as well as white-hot heat through my core.
We'd all been thoroughly tested and I was on the pill. That
way, we didn't need to worry about such human things as
blood-borne illness or hindered by human inhibitions. He
pressed his hardness into me, seeking friction. Marking his
territory. Before I let him get too carried away, I brought
up my hands and dug my nails into his forearms until he
released me.

With a grunt, he tried to grab my ankle as I bolted, but I
was too fast. I could hear him laughing and then he shone the
beam of his flashlight on me, whistling into the dark to alert his
packmate.

Another set of footsteps joined his, sprinting ahead. I was
torn as to whether I should give in, surrender to the beasts, but
something kept my legs moving.

Unfortunately, predators who ran in packs often made their
kills.

From the side, I was tackled into the dirt and a pair of hands
wrapped around my wrists, lifting my arms over my head. Chest
heaving, I was too exhausted to throw him off me. The lion set
down his flashlight so it was directly in my face.

I squinted to see a naked chest, glittering eyes staring at me through the mask. "Let's call Mr. X, shall we?"

A strangled cry escaped me as he toyed with one of the bells, keeping me in place as I squirmed beneath him. When that didn't satisfy him, he closed his mouth around my nipple and sucked until I had no other choice but to scream. In pain or pleasure, I wasn't sure, but the need coursing through me was impossible to ignore.

"That's it, rabbit," said the lion, encouraging me with what I now recognized was a knife between my breasts. "Don't hold back."

A scrape of the tip and he let the fine trickle of blood flow between my breasts to my belly button. I gasped and he wrenched my head backward, exposing my neck to him as he raked strong fingers across my ribcage. I shrieked again, unsure if it was from bliss or fear yet unable to deny the liquid mercury flooding my core.

As far as I could tell from the lantern he carried, the pack leader wore a fitted white button-up with a leather strap across each shoulder. This was tucked into navy slacks, and he shed a matching jacket, hanging it on a nearby branch like we were in a hotel lobby.

"Finally," I heard the lion sigh, letting up the tension on my bonds just a fraction.

Our visitor bent before me, tugging at the cuffs of his shirt so he could undo them. "There's my pretty rabbit."

That was his voice. Deep, soft, dark.

Meeting his eyes, I found the fox mask I'd been searching for all night. In the lantern's glow, it was black with gold-and-white accents, a smile poking out from the open bottom and his familiar aqua eyes beneath.

He lined up his shoes and then pants like we were in his

personal closet. Even in the dimness, I could make out the tight muscles of his thighs and back—what lay between.

As he turned around, he nodded to his friend and before I could see the complete view, the lion had pulled off both clamps at once. Rather than instant relief, it was far more painful than when they'd been attached. Incoherent sounds fell from my lips while he lapped at the sensitive buds, enjoying my struggle as he held me down.

Suddenly, the lion's fist was in my hair, tugging back my head so all I could see were stars. His hands groped and prodded as the fox lowered himself to the ground, light fingers traveling across my thigh where the stockings had been torn. The fox made the hole wider and wider until the fabric was shredded, and the lion did the same with my dress.

All the while, I fought with them and myself, wanting and not wanting, needing and rejecting. The person I was forced to be every day and the primitive part of my brain battled for control, but all of this had been arranged so I could quiet my mind.

Abandon my human shell.

Become prey.

Naked and writhing in the dirt, the fox brought my knees to my chest. Meanwhile, the lion propped me against him with his fingers around my neck, forcing me to watch as X's tongue made contact with the tight bundle of nerves between my legs.

I cried out, but he pulled away before I could chase my release, mouths and fingers shoving me toward the brink and yanking me back.

"Just as pink," the lion cooed into my ear, swatting my exposed buttock and making me clench.

On his feet, the lion kept my legs spread with one arm, stroking himself through his pants with the other. I opened my lips obediently, the way my fox had taught me during our many long-distance sessions. X used his fingers first, drawing saliva from my mouth, down my chin, chest, and abdomen. My saliva and blood combined as he circled my clit, and for some reason this drove me closer to the edge of no return.

With his free hand, the fox clawed at my ribcage, heightening every sensation as the lion guided my head down his velvety length. When I came up for air, my underwear was ripped away, the material leaving a trail of arousal across my skin.

Blue eyes shining up at me through thick, dark lashes, the fox's teeth scraped my breast and then he was filling me with every inch of him.

For a short instant, everything was silent. Nature took over my senses and I was at peace.

Then he angled his hips, thrusting into me until I was unable to restrain myself any longer. Tossing my arms over his shoulders, the fox let me cling to him as my climax threatened to shatter my lungs.

Something so small wasn't meant to be at the mercy of such creatures.

The lion suddenly groaned under his breath and backed away, his release spilling on the ground. Almost unfazed, he leaned me backward so the fox was hovering over me, deeper than I could have imagined.

After that, someone extinguished all the lights and the night poured back in.

Tomorrow, I would have time to think about what I'd done in the dark. I would go back to my normal life and normal job, and no one would be the wiser. But I would know. Deep down, I'd had my own beast within me, and it had been starving.

So I fed it. I became part of the evening along with the insects and all manner of night dwellers. I was held by the very hunters

I'd been running from, at their mercy as the three of us morphed into a mass of teeming life. Part of the earth. In the cool breeze, surrounded by the scent of soil, the moon shone down on the things that went bump in the night.

LIFE'S
TOO SHORT

Sienna Merit

I walked into Benny Luc's, and to my horror, she was right there at the bar.

Just as gorgeous as she was every time I saw her, all that flame-red hair loose and free over her tattooed shoulders. She was pulling beer for some old man, posed like a pin-up at the tap as she flashed him a pretty smile through black-painted lips. Like nothing had changed.

It had been nineteen days since I'd been to Benny Luc's. A lot had happened in those nineteen days.

I steeled myself by the pool tables, deliberately turning away from the bar, trying to think. Just seeing her had ruined all my carefully plotted fantasies, all my wildest dreams. All I'd ever been able to manage around her was a drink order, if that. Her deep brown eyes would cut to me, and I was lucky if I remembered my own name.

"Seriously, next time, you've gotta shoot your shot with her."

I cringed as Bryn's loud, no-nonsense voice cut into my thoughts again. It was thick with laughter and cigarette smoke. If I closed my eyes, I could picture her, brassy blonde curls bouncing, full lips still sparkling with whatever remained of her glitter gloss. She had embraced the Y2K trend and was wearing a full throwback, belly top and cargos . . . last time I saw her.

"I mean it. Make a move! Life's too short to be shy!"

Life's too short.

"S'cuse me."

A man jostled past me as he moved around his pool table, trying to find the right angle for his cue. I had been standing there too long. I looked toward the bar and realized the red-headed bartender was gone. Something in me deflated, even if the rest of me was relieved.

I went to the last stool at the mahogany curve of the bartop and hopped on. I had agonized over what to wear, and in the end I'd gone with my only pair of jeans and a low-necked top in a green that brought out my eyes. My hair was a blonde bob, and I tucked it behind my ears every time I fiddled with it. I wasn't Bryn—I didn't know how to put myself together for a night out. But she'd always said I had the sort of rack people paid surgeons for, so I'd shown it off tonight, hoping maybe . . .

What? That the redhead at the bar would look at my tits and fall under my spell?

The thought was ridiculous. I shouldn't be here. My throat felt hot and tight and I could feel my eyes stinging. This just wasn't possible without Bryn.

"Hey, whiskey-ginger, right?"

I had to go home. I don't know why I even bothered to—

"Hey, you okay?"

When I looked up, she was there. Looking at me.

She was prettier this close. A little shorter than I'd thought. I could see her nose had a little stud, and she had the tiniest scar beneath her bottom lip. It was white with age. It was easier to look at than her eyes, which were the brown of leather.

"I'm good, yeah," I heard myself say, a little choked.

"Whiskey-ginger, right?" she asked, her head tilting to the side quizzically. I nodded a little, and she turned away to go make it.

My heart hammered, but I could almost hear Bryn's teasing laughter, her, "See? Was that so hard?" I wanted to tell her to shut up, but she was in my head, so I had problems a "shut up" couldn't fix. Instead, I watched as the bartender I had come to see made me the drink I drank every time I came and wondered why I still felt like I didn't belong here.

Maybe because I had never gone without Bryn? This was our traditional haunt, once a week if we could manage it. We had made a point of it, just to catch up, since our personal and professional lives had become all-consuming and we no longer had time to spend hours on the phone every night like we did in high school. We'd tried all sorts of places before Benny Luc's, but the drinks were good here. And once the hot bartender showed up, I'll admit, the idea of switching venues lost all appeal.

The drink landed in front of me, bitten-off purple nails landing on the bar next to it. For a second I could feel those nails on me, their rough edges dragging redness into my skin, and a shiver ran through me with the thought of it.

"So where's your friend? Did you beat her here this time?"

I looked up, and those brown eyes pinned me there, a little bit of mischief in them. My mind was blank for a second, and then things came crashing back. Sixteen days ago, a foggy Monday morning. That call from Bryn's brother, his voice hoarse and barely audible. No one knew she had a bad heart—not even her. Next thing I knew, I was in a black dress at a cemetery, putting a bouquet of daisies on a coffin. And that was the last time I saw Bryn.

I opened my mouth to answer her, but what could I say? Anything but "She's dead" seemed like a lie, but I sure as hell didn't want to break the ice on my best friend's headstone. Before I could even think of the right words, a bunch of women in light-up penis necklaces and bachelorette party sashes came to the bar and started pounding their hands to it.

"Shots, shots, shots!"

"Hold that thought," the bartender said, her black lips quirking in faint amusement. She pressed her finger to the bar, as though sticking a pin in this conversation, and then she was gone, striding across the bar and bending low to grab shot glasses. "All right, all right, what're we drinking, ladies?"

Fuck, her ass was a dream in those tight black jeans. I tried not to stare like a complete creep, but it was hard not to. That denim was practically painted on, and she was perfectly comfortable stretching it to its limit. The party all ordered tequila shots, and that opened up an entirely different view. I could spend all night watching her reach up to the top shelf to get a desired bottle, her body stretching in that little crop top. The hem gaped over her belly and bare waist, and when she leaned, I could see the perfect place to put my hands when—

As if I'd ever get the chance to touch her.

I bit my lower lip, willing the stupid voice in my head to shut up. She'd talked to me. She knew my drink order. That was a good sign, right?

Her eyes darted my way, making my cheeks warm. I knew I'd been caught. I looked away quickly, but when I looked back she seemed to be concentrating on pouring. Stupid. I should've kept my eyes to myself.

"Hey, while I'm over here, do you need a top-up?" she called, and it took me a second to realize she was talking to me.

I blinked and looked down at my completely full high-ball glass.

"Uh, I'm okay. Taking it slow tonight."

"Sounds like I've got you all night," she purred, her lips curving in a smirk that hit my heart and went straight down. "Lucky me."

I flushed. I felt my heart pound, her attention entirely unexpected. My *God,* was she really looking at me like *that?*

"Make a move! Life's too short to be shy!"

Bryn's voice, the last things she ever said to me, rang in my ears. I took a breath and then another. "Hey, um."

Yeah. That was good. *Hey, um.* Poetic.

She started back toward me. I thought maybe she'd heard me, but before she got close, I felt a shove and nearly fell off my stool.

Some guy in a football jersey about three sizes too big for him was squeezing between me and the bar, looking red-faced and annoyed. He was close enough that I could smell the cheap beer on him. "Hey, we've been waiting on nachos for twenty minutes!"

She gave the guy a cool look. "They'll be out soon. Why don't you go back to your table and I'll send over some more beers, okay?"

"Well, hurry it up," the guy said, and moved to turn away. But as he turned, he swayed a bit and elbowed my almost-full whiskey-ginger off the bar. Onto me.

I gasped as the cold hit me, jumping to my feet. Now my low-cut top was a fucking ice catcher, and I was covered in booze and ginger ale. Even my bra was soaked. There went my perfect eye-catching outfit. There went all my cool.

He didn't even notice. Hell, he was already halfway across the bar, sitting down with his buddies. If Bryn had been here, she would've marched over there, told the guy off, and made him buy us another round. If Bryn had been here, I might've laughed it off and said it wasn't so bad. But she wasn't here. And I just wanted to cry.

A hand grabbed my wrist.

"Awe, fuck, babe, let's get you cleaned up."

It was her. Of course it was her.

She all but dragged me to a room marked "Staff Only," which turned out to be a bathroom. The fluorescent lights inside were powerfully bright after the dimness of the bar. Her hair was still wild, that fire red, and her skin was still vampire pale. But she was just as sexy here as she was tending that bar, her crop top still showing off the dip of her waist and the swell of her hips. She turned her head, looking down at the already sticky mess on my body, and I looked away, embarrassed by the intense way she was staring.

"What a dick," she muttered, grabbing some paper towels and turning on the hot water tap. She soaked them and turned back to me. I thought she was going to offer them to me, but instead, she began carefully wiping the mess from my skin.

Her fingers were gentle. The water was warm but not scalding. She moved slowly, starting at my collarbone and working her way down. I found myself pressed to the sink counter, my heart hammering as she stepped between my legs and looked up into my eyes. Her touch moved low, brushing into my shirt, and I couldn't hide the sharp intake of breath that accompanied her bare skin against the dark skin around my right nipple.

Her lips curled into the most wicked smirk I'd ever seen.

"So, I . . ." I tried, my hand reaching up to stall hers in its path down my shirt. She started laughing at me before I could even finish the sentence. I'm sure my face was red as a stop light. "What?"

She leaned close. Hell, she was pretty. And the way she was leaning in, I felt exactly how she'd feel if I were to hold her. "I'm Angie."

"Angie." I said, nodding as though this made sense.

And then she kissed me.

A soft little peck of her lips on mine was all it was. At first.

But I could almost hear Bryn squealing in my head, telling me to go for it, to grab this chance and not waste it. I couldn't just stand there. My hands came up to hold her face, to grip her by the hair, and I kissed her, *really* kissed her.

She gasped. I don't think she was expecting what she got, not from the way she moaned against my lips, sagging a little into my hold as I tugged her in. Her hands dropped the wet, sticky paper towels she was holding, and she moved to grip my waist. She could feel my nipples perking through my cold, wet shirt. I could feel her body melting into my touch. This fantasy, this wild-haired beauty I'd been dreaming of for fuck knows how long, was real and right here.

I think I may have lost my mind a little.

She pulled back for a second to look at me. Her eyes . . . they were melted brown sugar, bubbling with energy, with heat. Her lipstick was a mess, all over her face—and probably mine. She grinned a little, reaching up to touch the corner of my mouth. "This is a really good look for you."

"You're funny," I said, probably flushed and messy.

"I'm serious, I've been trying to figure out how to get my lipstick on you for months."

I think I forgot how to speak when she said that. I choked. It didn't matter, though, because she was pulling me in for another kiss, one that crushed her body to mine. Her tongue coaxed me into it, hands moving from my waist up into my drenched shirt. Her hands on my skin were warm and playful, moving over my curves and up to my bra.

I yanked back when she cupped my breasts in her hands, making an embarrassed noise. Not only were my tits highly aroused, they were currently drenched. She looked at me with a mischievous sort of grin and pulled her touch down to grip the hem of my shirt, then pull it up over my head, revealing my only good bra—the one that made me feel my hottest. It was basic and black, but it made my breasts look fantastic. She saw them and let out a little groan.

"Hell, you're hot."

"Actually, I'm fucking freezing," I deadpanned, because I didn't know what to fucking say to that. I'm hot? *I'm* hot?

She grinned at me, reaching up to unclasp my bra. Instantly, the cups fell apart, exposing my pebbled tits and freeing all the ice from my drink. She tossed my bra to the counter and pressed against me, her touch skimming those purple nails up my back. That alone was enough to make me groan, and I tugged her long, wild hair, dragging her in and pressing kisses to her throat. She was getting more and more breathless every time I tugged her hair, and when I started kissing her neck, she made a sharp little sound. I was going to pull back, but she clenched her arms around me, keeping me there for a second as she whispered, "More. Bite."

"Here?" I whispered, and let my teeth graze the spot. She sucked in a breath and clung to me tighter. "Yeah. Here," I said, now more confident. I bit down, careful not to create a mark, and she moaned louder than she had before, her fingers digging into my bare back as she trembled for me.

She was sensitive. Or really turned on.

I pulled back and she kissed me again, her hands dragging

around front to feel my breasts. She started kissing her way down to them, spreading the remnants of her lipstick over my pale skin, and when she got to the sticky mess on my chest, she lapped at it, her eyes peering up at me through her lashes.

Heat flooded me. I watched her with no small amount of need as she licked whiskey and ginger ale from my skin, lips kissed free of black lipstick, eyes sparking with some wicked dare. I tugged at her hair, and she grinned up at me as if she was glad I'd caught onto her weakness. She moved where I guided her, and soon her lips were wrapped around my stiff right nipple. I let out a groan, my head tipping back. She bit down, and I felt everything in me go taut, my need throbbing. "Angie!" I gasped to her, my voice strained.

She tugged hard at my nipple, looking up at me with those mischievous dark eyes, and I shifted closer at her urging, only to feel myself pressed back against the counter. Her hands were on my jeans, pulling them open and shoving them down my thighs before I ever realized what her plan was. When my jeans hit the floor, I pulled her harshly off my nipple and shivered hard with the way that loss went through me.

"Counter. Now."

She was a hungry, merciless wildfire when she got going. I was breathless looking at her. I followed her urging, shoving myself onto the counter, and she went low, dropping to her knees on the bathroom floor. Oh, God, when she touched me she was going to know—

Her fingers dragged up between my thighs, and a wolfish grin lit her face as she felt my panties. And then those were being peeled off, wet as my bra was, but for an entirely different reason.

"Fuck, you get so wet, don't you?" she murmured, her fingers dragging up to spread me. I could only let out a stream of noises, no words, as I was exposed, and she laughed, leaning in and tasting what she'd already done to me.

I really was wet for her. Had been getting there since the moment she bent over to get those stupid shot glasses. She seemed to revel in it, making her own loud noises as she spread me wider and dipped her tongue against my vulnerable clit. The touch sent sparks through me, and I gripped the counter, spreading myself wider as she got comfortable. Her tongue rolled over me, taking me higher, and my head fell back against the mirror as she made a point of sucking at me to make me shiver. Like she knew me already. Like she'd been thinking about it forever.

She wasn't done. She reached up and pressed one, then two fingers inside me. I bucked a little, squirming. It'd been so long since I'd done anything with anyone, the feel of her fingers was pooling heat in me fast and thick. I'd come here thinking I was ready to try; I never expected to succeed like this. She smirked against my clit as her touch reached deep, feeling how wet I was, how absolutely wild I was for her. She clearly knew she had me just as surely as I had her with a tug of her hair.

Then she hit the spot she was looking for.

I slapped my hand over my mouth as I felt her, just barely muffling the sound I couldn't stop. My body squeezed around her, I felt her rock her fingers against that place inside me, and my toes curled tight as I felt my release nearing. I tried to breathe, tried to stop myself from coming.

I tried. I really did.

But she could feel me squirming, clenching, close, and she only sped up, her fingers intensifying their urging, hitting that sweet spot over and over again until I was over the edge, my thighs clenching around her face, my need tightening with my breaking point.

She didn't stop until I was a trembling, spent mess, my over-sensitive need squirming under her tongue as her fingers left me. When she pulled back, her face was messy with my juices, and she grinned up at me like she'd won something.

"Fuck, I thought you would tear my fingers off there," she said through a grin.

"Oh! I, fuck, I'm sorry, are you—?"

She laughed at me, wiggling her wet fingers, making me flush. "They're still attached."

I grinned back at her, dragging her face up for a long, trembling kiss. It'd been a damn long time since I'd come like that. And in a bar bathroom! This woman was absolutely lethal.

She pulled back, resting her forehead against mine. "God, I've been wanting you for *ages*. Can I take you back to mine tonight when my damn shift is over?"

"Hell yes," I agreed, kissing her again. Her hands went to my breasts again, and I laughed, catching them before they got too fresh. "Hey, how am I supposed to go back out there, anyway? My shirt and bra are soaked."

"I'll get you a Benny Luc crop top." She smirked, reluctantly pulling away. "You'll look cute. What size are you, large? XL?"

"What, without a bra?" I asked, my arms covering my breasts. They weren't exactly unnoticeable when they weren't reined in.

She laughed. "Babe, you've got a hickey on your chest and black lipstick in places you haven't even noticed yet."

Oh, she was trouble. "That's a little different than suddenly going free bird."

"Oh, my God, you're fucking adorable. C'mon, life's too short to be shy," she said, laughing as she left the words hanging in the air.

I felt myself choke.

I could practically feel Bryn squeezing my shoulder as I pulled on my pants, hear her laughing as I tried in vain to dry my bra under the bathroom hand dryer. I had been missing her all night, but suddenly it was painful, bittersweet.

Somewhere, she was raising a glass to me, telling everyone who'd gone before her that her best friend had just landed the girl of her dreams. Somewhere, she was really fucking proud of me.

Maybe that somewhere wasn't here. But I felt it, just the same.

PARC-AUX-CERFS

Jordan Monroe

Alexander Kulas, one of the owners of the DC area's premier pleasure palace, Parc-aux-Cerfs, hadn't had an intentional orgasm for a full calendar year. Not since he'd seen the hearse pull away, the headstone unveiled, the life insurance payout finalized, the last hospital bill settled. It hadn't been his first funeral, not by a longshot; being in his midfifties, he was of that age where he used more bereavement leave than vacation time. What made that last burial so different was that the deceased wasn't a parent, a colleague, a distant great-aunt.

Burying Selena, his wife and soulmate, had sapped him of his vitality.

In a bittersweet twist, the cancer had been aggressive, thus cutting her suffering short. Selena, never wanting to sit still, wrung out every minute of her life, cashing out her retirement to buy ludicrously expensive bottles of wine for them to share. She'd insisted on the two of them having erotic portraits taken, which he now kept hidden in their closet, tucked away behind her collection of vintage Hermès scarves. He couldn't bear to let them go, and he also couldn't bear to look at them.

That was all last spring. Now, with the annual Festival of Priapus kicking off tonight, he was needed back at the club. His partner, Adrian Rochester, sent him his standard payouts each month, despite his extended absence from the establishment. Rochester owned another club within the city, Piacere, but the two of them recognized the demand for a larger, more discreet space.

Navigating the wooded, winding road in his nondescript Lexus, Alexander struggled to summon any amount of virility. Mourning Selena, while certainly painful, had not been made more difficult by exasperating any other addictions because, both fortunately and unfortunately, his wife was his addiction. He neither dove into the bottle not sought relief in the thrill of losing money at cards, and the last thing he needed was to partake of the entheogens offered to him by the more eccentric members of Parc-aux-Cerfs, who zealously insisted that he needed to break down the barriers of his mind. Alexander didn't need to drink mushroom tea to understand completely that his magnetic, sensual, beautiful wife was forever out of his reach.

The enormous stone house loomed before him as he drove up the hill and around to the back, parking in one of the two spaces in the garage. Adrian's Mercedes was in its spot. Alexander sighed and turned off his car, then leaned back in his seat and stretched his legs.

I'm not ready, he thought. *I can't do this.*

A sharp knock on his window startled him. He turned and saw Adrian standing there, a carefully plucked eyebrow raised quizzically. Though the glass muffled his voice, Alexander heard him say, "Sitting in the car doesn't count as being here, you know."

Alexander grunted and opened the door, swinging his long legs out and standing on the concrete. If he kept his mind on the present, like his therapist taught him, he just might finish the night of festivities without breaking out into gut-wrenching sobs. "You and Marian have been holding things down fine without me, from the looks of the place."

Adrian shrugged. "Members have been asking after you, hoping for your return."

"And what have you been telling them?"

Adrian opened the door into the servants' quarters, which had been converted to a dull office space. He opened the white refrigerator and pulled out a water bottle, tossing it to Alexander. Adrian got one for himself, took a sip, and then answered, "The party line. You've taken a leave of absence for personal reasons but remain a vital and valued member of the Parc-aux-Cerfs family."

Alexander cleared his throat and mumbled his gratitude. Adrian, being a slightly more emotionally free man, swung an arm over his shoulders, not saying anything. Instead of recoiling, Alexander relaxed and sank into the gesture. He hadn't had human contact, aside from the occasional handshake, in months. Lowering his head, he allowed a solitary tear to leak from his eye and trickle down his cheek, disappearing into his closely cropped gray beard.

"I'm glad you're back, Alex. But if you need to leave tonight, go on and do that. No hard feelings."

Alexander sniffed and straightened up, squaring his shoulders and swiping his finger across his eyes. Dammit, Selena would hate to see him like this. The Festival of Priapus was her favorite event they hosted. Held on the night of the vernal equinox, Parc-aux-Cerfs opened its doors to both members and their guests, debuting the latest sculpture installation in the garden. Adrian had informed Alexander of this year's selection: an enormous steel umbrella with fairy lights dangling from the frame. The piece was titled *Shelter in the Storm;* it would have been perfect for Instagram influencers, were it not for Parc-aux-Cerfs' strict no-camera policy.

"You go kick things off. I want a look at the sculpture before the yard gets crowded."

Adrian nodded and made his way to the front entrance of the mansion to greet guests. After Alexander collected himself, he left the garage and trudged along the stone path, trying to remember why he'd come. He knew he needed to feel alive again, needed to sense his blood flowing like a river of vitality through him, as opposed to the sludge of despair he'd experienced these past months.

Parc-aux-Cerfs was built with woods surrounding the stone mansion, as though the building had grown among the trees. The stone path led to a clearing where the sculpture stood. Flicking the strands of lights out of his way, Alexander walked to the center of the sculpture and stood beneath the umbrella. He inhaled the crisp early spring air, letting it fill his lungs completely. The barest hint of decaying leaves and rich soil danced in his nostrils, reminding him that time continued to tick on, whether he wanted it to or not.

I shouldn't be here, he thought, clenching his fist around the cold umbrella handle. *I'll just drag everyone down.*

"Oh, I didn't know someone was already back here," a warm, alto voice washed over him.

Alexander turned and saw that a party guest had joined him. If it weren't for her piercing green eyes, he would have mistaken her for Selena: thick, dark hair, lips the color of pomegranate, ghostly pale skin, curves to make a man weep, all contained in a whisper-thin black lace robe.

He cleared his throat. "I've heard the speech before and I wanted to experience the art before everyone else."

"Ah, so you're a member of the club."

"So to speak," he answered. *What does your hair smell like? How does your skin taste? Do you like having your nipples pinched?*

Alexander tightened his grip on the steel handle, wondering where in the hell those thoughts had come from. Turning away from her, he shut his eyes and heard his pulse in his ears, both pleased and surprised by its elevated rate. Taking a couple of deep breaths, he let relief wash over him.

He released the handle and shoved his hands in his pockets. Facing the woman, Alexander allowed himself an overtly lascivious scan of her body. Instead of a retort, his guest thrust her shoulders back just slightly, lifting her breasts. The interplay of light and shadow let him see the contours of her pointed nipples. He swallowed, suddenly nervous.

"Do you have a name?" she inquired, taking a tentative step toward him.

"Alexander," he replied, not moving. For some irrational reason, he believed if he moved an inch, he would wake up from this dreamscape.

"A kingly name," she said quietly. "Is there a queen in your life?"

He clenched his jaw. "There was," he muttered.

"I'm sorry," she replied in that understanding tone. Alexander was grateful he didn't have to explain himself. She turned away from him but before she could take another step, he reached out and gently clasped her wrist.

"Please don't go," he whispered.

"I won't," she said, walking closer to him. He could smell her perfume: lilies pressed between cedar planks, both a masculine and feminine scent.

Alexander didn't release her hand, instead rubbing his thumb along her wrist. "How should I address you?"

She lifted her lips into a smile. "For tonight, I'm Siren."

"And for tomorrow night?"

The woman pulled their hands to her mouth, her lips hovering over his fingers. "I'd prefer to focus on tonight."

Tonight? Alexander gulped. It had been so long since he'd left in the morning with a thank you and a grin. With Selena, there was always a tomorrow, a next time, a chance to improve and draw out her pleasure.

"And what if I'd want more than tonight?" he blurted, staring at his shoes in shame.

Delicate toes covered the tips of his boots and a slender finger twined in his beard, tilting his chin up. Alexander met Siren's green eyes, marveling at their depths. He dug his fingernails into his palms, resisting the overwhelming urge to weave his fingers through her hair and pull her mouth to his. His pulse thundered in his ears, reminding him that he was, in fact, alive and awake.

"What you need is tonight. Tomorrow can wait." She wet her lower lip and his eyes locked onto the small tip of her tongue.

In a ragged voice, he asked, "Any limits I need to know?"

Siren leaned closer and he could feel her body's warmth beneath the lace. "My safeword is 'steel.' Take whatever you need from me."

Alexander reached for her shoulders and gathered her closer to his body. Gently, he hooked his thumbs around the fabric edges and pulled it from her, tossing it over one of the umbrella spokes like a flag signaling his surrender. Beneath the sparkling lights, he noticed a little scar on her collarbone, her rosy nipples, the wild curls at the juncture of her legs. Groaning, Alexander clasped his hands to her waist and pulled her to him, pressing his lips to her neck.

Siren laughed in surprise, then sighed and coiled her fingers in his hair. He licked and bit at her neck, proceeding up to her ear and drawing her earlobe between his teeth. She gasped and he whispered, "If you're not careful, I'll take everything from you."

Planting a featherlight kiss on his temple, Siren answered, "Good. I don't want you to stop."

Alexander grunted and ran his tongue along her jaw, feeling her quiver beneath his hands. As he skimmed his hands up her waist and brushed his knuckles along the undersides of her breasts, his lips found hers and he thrust his tongue into her warm, eager mouth. She tasted like sweet, earthy wine, a taste in which he was happy to drown. Her fingers traveled from his beard to the buttons of his dress shirt, making quick work of them. He wore no undershirt, and the cool night air sent tingles along his belly.

Siren wasted no time and ran her fingers along the field of black and gray hair along his chest. She pinched and pulled at his nipples, causing Alexander to groan and throw his head back. Refocusing, he gripped her waist tightly and lifted her up, turning her so her back was pressed against the steel pole supporting the sculpture.

"Hold onto the spokes," he commanded, stepping away from her.

With a defiant grin across her face, Siren reached up with both hands and did as he instructed. Alexander stood back and admired all of her: full breasts thrust upward and outward, thick thighs he would be happy to die strangled between, dark hair getting caught in the spring breeze and fluttering across her languid face.

"Don't let go of them," he told her, his voice ragged.

"I won't," she responded, her chest rising and falling rapidly as her breath became shallow.

Alexander approached her and knelt at her feet, his lips closing over her right nipple. She moaned as he sucked hard, flicking his tongue over the taut peak. In one hand, he lifted the other breast and pulled at its nipple; with the other, he trailed his fingers along her inner thigh before stopping at the joint where her leg met her hip. He rubbed his thumb along the delicate skin, carefully avoiding her plump lips, prolonging her exquisite torture. Siren rolled her body, dutifully not removing her hands from the spokes yet shaking beneath his hands and tilting her core toward him, demanding relief.

Relief he'd give her in due time; he wasn't done savoring the gift of her.

Releasing the nipple from his lips, Alexander asked, "What do you want from me, Siren?"

"Everything," she cried. "God, I want everything."

For the first time in who knew how long, Alexander smiled. He pushed her legs wider and picked up one of her ankles, placing it on his knee. Pressing his face to her belly, he inhaled the scent of her wanton need. He moved the hand that had been caressing the line along her hip to her center, running his knuckle between the seam of her inner lips, pulling away just before grazing her clit. Siren groaned and tilted her body further forward, silently begging him to let her collapse with pleasure.

Alexander spread her lips apart and flexed his middle finger along her opening, delving into her slick, warm cunt. Siren squeezed her inner muscles around his finger and he growled with delight, knowing she'd soon do the same around his cock, if she'd allow him that pleasure. He looked up and watched her breasts rise and fall rapidly, her eyes closed and her hands still clasped around the umbrella spokes. He pressed a gentle kiss to her mound and quietly asked, "May I?"

"Please do. Fuck, please lick me," Siren exhaled.

Without removing his finger, Alexander lowered his head and lazily licked her inner folds, savoring the fact that Siren was teetering on the edge of oblivion. In this moment, the world around him faded away; his singular focus honed in on this woman's ecstasy and his duty to fulfill it. After several sweeps of his tongue, Alexander found the delicate bud and pressed on it while curling his finger deep inside her. He heard Siren moan and he followed her rolling hips, not stopping his movements but continuing his pursuit. Swirling his tongue over her clit, he rotated his finger in the opposite direction.

"Oh, please, don't stop. Fuck, please don't stop," she whimpered, opening her legs wider and leaning back against the pole.

Alexander pulled out his finger and she released a cry of protestation, which transitioned into a sigh of pleasure as he inserted another finger into her. Her inner muscles stretched around his fingers and he fluttered his tongue over her clit. Her moans became higher and higher in pitch until finally she broke and pleasure washed over her. Siren cried his name over and over again as he pressed and licked until she begged him to stop. He slowly pulled his face away from her and gently pulled his hand away from her soaking cunt. Alexander rained gentle kisses along her inner leg and let her settle. When her breathing normalized, he placed her foot back on the ground and rose.

"Look at me, Siren," he said.

She opened her enormous green eyes and looked not at his face but at the rigid outline of his erection beneath his trousers. Siren bit her lower lip and still did not remove her hands from the spokes.

"Do you want this?" he asked hoarsely.

"Condom?" she answered.

"Vasectomy, plus testing required for membership."

"Good, because I've never wanted anything as much as I want you right now."

Wordlessly, Alexander unbuckled his belt, unbuttoned and unzipped his fly, and opened his trousers. Siren licked her lips as he pulled out his cock and stroked it. Relishing in her wanton perusal, he muttered, "If there'll be a tomorrow, I'll let you touch this."

Siren hummed and rested her head on one of her arms. "You're quite persuasive," she said, her lips curling into a grin.

Alexander, while holding his cock steady, wrapped his other arm around her thigh and lifted her, angling her cunt over him. He savored her wet folds, pressing himself into her inch by inch. She gasped into his neck and in one brutal motion, he plunged all the way into her, her leg flexing around his waist.

Sight, sound, and scent blurred into one sensation as he rocked into her. Cologne and perfume, spritzed on earlier in the evening, faded and gave way to those more primitive smells of salt and earth. What had earlier been whispers and words of comfort were replaced with a conversation spoken in grunts and shallow exhales. When she'd first approached him, he'd noticed the magnificence of her hair; now, with his face buried in her neck, he counted each individual strand, noting some were deep brown and others a rich wine red.

Siren lifted her other leg and he caught it, holding it around his middle, her hips cradling his. He pulled his body away from her so he could see how she looked suspended between him and the sculpture. Her skin was flushed and her jaw was slack, the picture of sensuality. Alexander, not slowing down, bent over her and bit on her nipple. She clenched around him and he straightened, his cock buried to the hilt inside her.

Sharp tingles shattered at the base of his spine and Alexander couldn't stop himself. His thrusts became rougher, his hold on her tighter, and a tiny bead of sweat trickled down his temple. With a final devastating push, he threw his head back and groaned, spilling everything he had into her. She clenched around him again, absorbing his spurts. He shuddered and slowly slipped from her hold, gently placing her feet back on solid ground. Before setting himself to rights, he reached up and unwound her fingers from the spokes, massaging the sore palms.

Siren purred and he gathered her into his arms, kissing her temple. He didn't know how else to thank her; he chose instead to stroke the crown of her head. She sighed and looked up at him before placing a kiss on his cheek. Before he could respond, she moved away from him and pulled down her robe from the sculpture, wrapping herself back in the sheer fabric.

She walked to the edge of the field of lights and looked at him from over her shoulder. Alexander knew he appeared stupefied, as though if he blinked, she would disappear. He dared not look away as she said, "Until next time, Alexander."

He swallowed and leaned against the pole, utterly satisfied and content for the first time in months.

Siren left Alexander, their commingled fluids dripping down her leg as she walked along the stone path. Passing other guests taking part in the festivities, she smiled to herself, content with what she'd provided for the co-owner of Parc-aux-Cerfs. Entering the mansion, she searched for the other co-owner. Finding him cleaning wax from one of his knives, she sauntered up to him.

"Good evening, Adrian," she said, pressing her body into his arm.

She heard his sharp intake of breath. "You smell like you've been busy. Is it done?"

Siren pulled back the plackets of her robe and presented the inside of her right leg to Adrian. "Yes, he should be back to himself soon."

Adrian raised his eyebrow at her. "Good. Thank you for this. You'll get your due in the morning."

"Leave it. His wife was a fortunate woman. Getting a taste for what he's capable of is payment enough."

"Suit yourself. Same time next week?"

Siren squeezed his shoulder. "If he asks for me, I'll be available. But only if he asks. We cannot push him."

She didn't see Adrian nod in agreement, choosing instead to leave the mansion in her robe. True to her namesake, Siren knew she was meant for temporary relief, a marker on someone else's journey. That suited her perfectly.

HALF ANGEL

Kiki DeLovely

The group was nearly finished with warm-up when the heavy metal door swung open, rays of midday sun streaming in all around a form Freya didn't recognize. She thought she knew every acrobat in town. *And I certainly wouldn't forget one who looks like that!* She giggled to herself upon getting a better look. Then half the class practically jumped out of their seated stretches when the door slammed shut as if in explanation. *Ah, a newbie.* The bang of that damn door was so tooth rattling, it was a mistake one only made once.

"Sorry! Sorry . . ." Apologizing first for the door then for being late. "I signed up online and my GPS took me to the wrong warehouse."

"No worries, glad you made it! You can drop your stuff in a locker and then join us." Freya carried on, attempting to not be distracted. "Everyone pair up! Since it's open studio today, feel free to work on whatever skills you like. Just holler if you need a hand."

Then, extending hers, she greeted their late arrival. "Welcome! My name is Freya and my pronouns are she/her. Don't worry about the door—it's a rite of passage for all newcomers."

"I'm Matías. They/them." Grateful for her warm demeanor and that she had offered her pronouns first. "I'm very much that—a newcomer—but I had been learning acro for a few years before moving so I was excited to find this space." Matías began stretching their calves.

"Glad you found us . . . eventually," she teased with a wink. "Looks like you're stuck with me since everyone else is paired off."

"*¡Qué suerte tengo!*" Matías let the flirt hang in the air only momentarily before chivalrously changing the subject and freeing Freya from her burning cheeks. "I'm plenty warmed up from jogging over here but could use a little stretching if you don't mind."

"Be my guest." She gestured at the floor in front of her, shifting into butterfly pose and fluttering her legs. And perhaps her eyelashes a bit as well.

They plopped down on the mat and Matías quickly discovered Freya was a base as well. The pair decided they could each take turns flying, working on new skills for both of them. It was awkward at first, naturally. Clumsy in their beginning attempts at the most basic poses. Inelegant through each transition. Falling over and over again. Laughing at each misstep and thoroughly reveling in every touch, painful as they may have been at times.

They were similarly proportioned—thick and tall—though Freya was all hips, ass, belly, and tatas whereas Matías was more muscular and stocky. Because they were both of significant size and strength, playing the role of base in acro just made sense. Freya enjoyed feeling her power as she hoisted another's body into the air and Matías delighted in supporting others in their creative expressions, this being the rare artistic outlet in their life. Though neither could deny newfound pleasures in their attempts at flying.

As the last of their fellow classmates trickled out, Freya and Matías were both stubbornly unwilling to call it quits until they figured out how to progress from flag up to two high. Their proprioceptive awarenesses as bases were well developed after so many years of training, but as neither had flying experience, this was where they needed some fine tuning. That was how they found themselves alone in the circus space, Freya almost feeling faint at the pheromones wafting off this gorgeous genderqueer, Matías marveling at an instant chemistry so palpable.

"So, besides masochistic acrobatic practices, what do you like to do for fun?"

Freya could've mentioned any number of hobbies but instead, just as they had locked forearms and with Matías still atop her thighs, she blurted out, "I write erotica."

Matías fumbled out of the pose and over their words. "Oh, wow . . . I-I'd love to read your stuff sometime." Trying to regain a sense of composure. "What's your most recent story about?"

"Well, it's not finished yet." Emboldened by all their physical contact, Freya took a leap outside her comfort zone. "Perhaps you could help me out . . ."

Catching on quickly, Matías furthered their flirtation. "I imagine you're searching for something like a thickening plot, yes?"

Freya grinned and nodded, her shyness swooping back in.

"And any story worth its weight in words deserves a climax, no?"

Blushing hard, Freya couldn't even begin to formulate a response.

Entirely captivated, Matías's face turned serious. "You are so fucking sexy, Freya. The things I want to do to you, with you . . ." Inching closer until Freya could feel the heat radiating off Matías's body, mingling with her own in the space between them.

"I *think* I'm familiar with the feeling . . ." Freya closed the gap, unable to bear the distance any longer, and wrapped her arms around Matías's neck.

Even though her body language seemed clear, Matías was never one to make a move without consent. "*¿Puedo besarte?*"

"Fuck, yes! Please . . ." Freya was already out of breath. The tension between the two for the past hour had been building by the second. They had come face-to-face so many times, so close to this first kiss, and each time their eyes locked but their lips didn't, just led to juicier delayed gratification. By this point Freya was dripping.

Matías grabbed her by the hips, kissing her slowly at first, taking their time, sucking on her bottom lip, testing the waters by giving it a little nip before wrapping their tongue around hers. Freya's moan vibrated down the back of their throat, the effect of which turned Matías on so much that it caught them by surprise and the pair tumbled down onto the mat below. They rolled around playfully, pressing and pulling against one another. Every last cell in their bodies thrummed with electricity as they continued to make out, reveling in finally getting their hands on one another, soft and squishy parts giving way to the firmness of others.

At one point they just stopped and looked into each other's eyes, their lust intensifying all the more. Matías intuitively read something in that gaze, something that Freya communicated with just a look, and in an instant flipped Freya over, pinning her hands above her head.

"What are your safewords, *guapa?*" Matías's question came out almost as a growl.

"Red, yellow, green." Freya could hardly believe it. Now who was the lucky one?

"And if I were to tell you to do some things for me, how would you respond?"

"*Sí! Sí . . . porfis!*" Her enthusiasm was beyond containment.

"Perfecto. That's what I thought." Matías led Freya by the hand. "Why don't you show off some of your aerial skills for me? *Desnuda.*"

With the addition of that final command, Freya's face flushed hard and her clit pounded even harder. Had she not been submissive to her very core, she wouldn't have been able to bring herself to do it. But their charming dominance really did it for her. And so Freya stripped down naked quickly before she could lose her courage, took hold of the nearest fabric that hung from the rafters, and gracefully pulled herself up the red silks. Freya quickly wrapped both ankles into secure footlocks, then slowly lowered herself down into the splits and onto Matías's eagerly awaiting fingertips. She gasped at their touch, never having experienced such an overwhelming combination of sensations before. The fabric wrapped around her feet suddenly conjured the feeling of being bound, her muscles straining to suspend her body midair and simultaneously pleading for more of Matías's touch.

Freya found herself more inspired than ever before to ease deeper into the splits, Matías's fingers working her pussy as their voice encouraged and exalted Freya, her glorious body, her magnificent movements. "You're so hot, especially with your thick thighs splayed out like that. And I love how wet you are for me. Mmmmmm . . ." Matías audibly inhaled her musky scent that penetrated the air, then slipped their free hand around her back to support Freya as much as possible, hugging her body snugly against their own while fucking her with their generous fingers. Glistening with her come, they slid in and out a few more times before Matías felt her begin to shudder. Unable to endure the impossible pose any longer, Freya hoisted herself up once more and as she twirled her legs, the silks fell away.

Holding her waist firmly, Matías helped her lower down and pulled her in for a kiss but was far from finished. "I think this story of yours needs a few more twists and turns, no?" They eyed the trapeze suggestively.

Freya, equally amused and enticed, walked over and grabbed onto the bar. Tucking her knees into her chest, she piked them overhead and draped her legs over the trapeze, gripping her calves into the backs of her thighs. Freya hung there for a few seconds, Matías thoroughly enjoying the view, before swinging her chest up and grasping the ropes in order to pull herself into a sitting position. Matías was mesmerized as Freya contorted herself into a series of poses, calling out their curious yet fitting names—Amazon, gazelle, half angel—before righting herself once again to sit upon the bar. Each movement called Freya's attention to her nudity. Her breasts hanging heavily, the jiggle of her belly, a whoosh of air across her bare skin—they all kept her keenly aware that she was putting on a show just for them. And she was surprised at how freeing it felt.

"Spread those legs apart for me one more time, my little half angel."

Freya, having relished the feel of Matías's eyes roaming all over her body in their own private performance, obeyed readily and scooted toward the edge of the bar. Matías grabbed two fistfuls of her plump ass and shoved their tongue into Freya's pussy.

"Ohhhhh, ffffffuuuuuuuck . . ." Freya wrapped her legs around Matías's muscled shoulders, pulling them in even deeper while clutching the ropes for dear life, subtly aware of the pattern of tiny fibers imprinting on the palms of her hands.

Sucking on her swollen labia, teasing her hole with their tongue, licking up all around her clit and then back down again to taunt her some more, Matías savored Freya's every drop, every squirm, every pleasure. Each flick of their tongue elicited a new, provocative noise that spurred Matías's enthusiasm. They penetrated her with the entire length of their tongue, sweat dripping off Freya's legs and down their back, her moans reverberating off the high ceilings.

Feeling Freya's legs begin to tense up and tighten around them like a vice grip, Matías focused hard on keeping up a constant pace, repeating the same motions. The flat of their tongue applied ample pressure just above her clit as she came hard against their mouth, juices drizzling down Matías's chin. They knew it would be beyond cruel to keep the poor angelic Amazon up there for too much longer but Matías was curious if Freya could endure one last trick on the trapeze. So after giving her a moment to catch her breath they asked, "Do you think you can hang from your knees for me while I give you a few spankings?"

¡A poco! Freya couldn't believe the precision with which Matías's desires mirrored her own wildest fantasies. "Have you been reading my diary . . . or just my thoughts?" she quipped. Freya wasn't sure how long she'd be able to hold the pose, but she was highly motivated by the challenge.

She inverted herself once again and Matías steadied her by pressing their left forearm firmly against the tops of Freya's thighs, just shy of her cunt yet close enough to torment her some more. They immediately put their other arm to good use, starting off with a rapid series of quick slaps to warm Freya's ass before striking her slower with increasing force. Freya had always viewed circus equipment in a sexy light, so she was delighted to find someone whose mind was just as filthy as her own.

She rejoiced in every moment. Freya's cries echoed throughout the open space and her blood rushed to her head. All the while, Matías did their best to coax the blood back up to Freya's ass and evoke even more divine noises from her throat. Before landing their final blow, Matías removed their stabilizing arm from Freya's thighs, stretched their right arm far back, and then swung it through the air with a *whoosh*. The smack landed with a heavy thud and quite a bit of follow-through, setting the trapeze in motion. Freya let out one last shriek as she swung through the air back and forth a few times before dismounting.

Matías caught the dizzy trapeze artist in their arms, steadying her and squeezing her tightly, murmuring into her neck, "You were perfect, *mi media angelita*. Come lie down with me. You must be exhausted after that impressive display."

Freya nuzzled against Matías's neck, curling her body around her new lover. She allowed herself a glance down at their entwined legs, the weight of Matías's thigh atop hers persuading her shaky muscles to quiet. They were covered in the beginnings of bruises—most notably from their fumbling first attempts at flying with one another—other parts of Freya's body which escaped her view undoubtedly empurpled as well. Both more than a bit awestruck at this development, Matías simply held her for a while before breaking their contented silence.

"So, half angel, how's that story of yours coming along now?"

Freya rolled over on top of them. "Beautifully. But, um, I think we need another climax." A glimmer in her eyes as she worked her knee between their thighs, pleased to find their shorts more than a little damp. "Or at the very least some falling action."

IN THE
ZINE LIBRARY

Em Farris

I was not in the mood to host drop-in hours at the zine library that Wednesday evening. I sighed as I plodded from the bus stop to the library's artist studio between a thrift store and an e-bike repair shop, both closed for the night. It was still early enough in the spring that it was fully dark by 6:45, it was raining, and I wanted to be home with a cup of tea, trying to play video games while my cat, Bugfairy, blocked the screen. Instead I stood dripping in the entrance of the library, fumbling for a light switch that never seemed to be where I expected it. No one had been there since the weekend and it felt like the damp cold had settled into the walls and furniture.

I moved through the small space, turning on more lights, turning up the heat, switching on the electric kettle, firing up the computer. I didn't know if anyone would come tonight, but I'd volunteered, we'd advertised it, and I was here for the next two and a half hours so that people could browse the zine collection, use our photocopier and long-arm stapler, or request a tutorial on zine-making.

I started to feel a little better as it warmed up and I could take off the bulky cardigan I was wearing over my plaid shirt and leggings. I really did like showing people how to take a bit of paper and a writing instrument and turn it into a self-published booklet with just a few snips, folds, and whatever inspiration they could bring to the pages. I loved all the weird and informative zines our library had collected over the years, from a guide to the herbs that could support recovery from gender affirmation surgery to an ode to one author's favorite vegetable, the rutabaga. I breathed in and let the smell of toner and pencil shavings ground me.

If no one comes tonight, I told myself as I set up a folding table and laid out clipart sheets, pencils, and markers, *I'll have time to make my own zine.* My day job is coding, moving commands around on a screen, thousands of characters that sometimes feel like they add up to nothing tangible. It can be hard to shift into making something with my hands, but zines give me a tangible product in only a few hours. Something I can send to friends across the country, keep on display in my living room, leave for someone to discover in the library.

I put out the donation jar, name tags, mailing list sign-up sheet, and hand sanitizer. It was 7:10. I poured some almond rooibos I'd found in the cupboard, left the selection of tea bags out, and the kettle on the "keep warm" setting. I checked to make sure the door was unlocked and sat down with a pile of magazines. When I don't come with a topic in mind, I play a game of bibliomancy, flipping through pages with my eyes closed then pointing to a random spot. I'd use the words or images there to come up with a concept and build around it.

At 7:30, PK, a regular, came in. PK is an avid supporter of

the library, a typewriter enthusiast, and, when I'm in a bad mood, extremely annoying in a way that is completely harmless and therefore even harder to bear. I always feel bad when she starts to get to me, which makes me even more irritated with her. I wondered if I could handle the rest of the night if she was the only one who showed up.

We said hello and I resolved not to let her get under my skin. I visualized a protective sphere keeping bad energy out and letting good energy in and asked her if she needed help. She didn't answer directly but started telling me about her quest for a certain kind of self-correcting typewriter ribbon. I listened for a bit, but it was more of a monologue than a conversation, so after a while I excused myself to check on supplies and returned to my magazines. My divination exercise had given me an eel in a *National Geographic,* and I was contemplating a theme of swimming upriver after a season in the open sea.

PK was using the computer to look for wholesale typewriter supplies on eBay and I was discovering how many teeth freshwater eels could have (too many) when the door opened again. I felt the energy in the space change like a bell had rung, and I looked up to see a very cute, slightly nervous-looking person of gender to be disclosed, pink skin flushed from the chill and brown wavy hair plastered to their forehead and sides of their head.

"Is this, uh . . . is this where zines happen?" the person asked, then looked embarrassed. Cute.

"This is where zines happen!" I said. "There are zines happening right now!" I spread my hand to indicate my collage-in-process somehow covering half the table already. They didn't have a response and I felt a little embarrassed for leaning in too hard. I dialed it back. "First time here? Can I give you a tour?"

I set them up at the name tag station and tried to straighten

my piles of magazines. They wrote "Harlow" in block print letters and then "they/them" in the spot for pronouns underneath.

"I'm Kat," I said, gesturing to my own name tag with she/
they on it. I'd been debating whether today was a she/her, she/
they or they/she day when I filled it out and now I was glad I'd
gone for a bit of genderqueer visibility. I was also glad I'd put
on some mascara to try to trick myself into feeling like I could
leave the house. My blonde hair was in a loose bun and I hadn't
accessorized but at least my leggings matched my shirt.

I showed them the shelves crammed with boxes and gave
them a spiel about how to find different categories. I explained
how photocopier access worked and then took them over to
the tables and supplies. "Are you here to browse or to work on
something?"

"I think I want to make a zine. I mean . . . I don't know how,
but I have this idea, and it's not working out as a story or a
poem or comic so I thought maybe I should try something new."

"A zine might do the trick! They're good for weird little
things that don't fit into neat categories. Once I made a zine
about three lost mittens I found on the sidewalk on the same
day."

"I'd read that," they said. "Maybe I'll finally learn what happened to my favorite yellow mitt a few years ago."

"I think there's a copy in the library, I'll see if I can find it
later. But first, I can show you the best zine format for beginners
if you want."

We settled in and they faced me across the table, squaring
their flat chest toward me and spreading their arms open. They
seemed a little less nervous and genuinely curious.

I took two 8.5 x 11-inch pieces of paper and passed one to
them so they could follow along as I showed them how to make
a few folds and snips that would turn into a booklet an eighth

of the size. I penciled the numbers one through sixteen on each page and unfolded it.

"Now you can see the order the pages will be in when you reassemble it. You can either erase the numbers before you photocopy or you can make pages that you glue on top and it becomes your master copy. That way's good if you're not sure what order you want your pages in."

I let them test it out on their own, trying not to watch too closely and make them self-conscious. They had beautiful hands, tending to the task deliberately. I looked away and sharpened a pencil that didn't really need it, letting the scratching sound fill the air between us.

I'd fantasized about where I could fuck someone in here many times over the years, during slow shifts when the only thing to do was look through the boxes to see if anything had been mis-shelved. A lot of cuties come through the doors, and I sometimes go home and imagine how I could have flirted, asked them out, hell, how I could have made eye contact for more than two excruciating milliseconds or chatted without retreating to the safety of the reading nook. In my twenties, I'd been the queer cliche who never knew whether she was on a date or a friend hang. In my thirties, I wanted to be someone who actually got laid.

Harlow was on the second-to-last step where you hold the sheet, folded lengthwise, at either end and find the right tension as you push so that the slits you made earlier allow it to pop out into a four-pointed star. They gasped as everything fell into place. "Magic!" they said.

And then I knew it. Today I *would* flirt. I would notice in the moment if it was reciprocated instead of going home and realizing that the interest someone showed in every stapler I displayed might not be entirely out of a fondness for office supplies. I would be forward.

My stomach dropped. Was I doing this?

I was doing this.

I smiled and held their gaze. Usually at this point I'd chicken out, worried that the other person could tell I was into them, the worst possible thing another human could know about me. This time I let myself stay. It only felt a little scary, and for the first time the thrill of excitement outweighed the nervousness. "Magic," I repeated, and didn't look away. They didn't either, and we grinned at each other.

PK brought a stack of zines over and started chattering about vintage pens. Suddenly, she wasn't nearly as irritating as she had been a few minutes ago. Her enthusiasm? Inspiring. Her single-mindedness? Impressive. PK was a beautiful shining soul, and best of all, Harlow had a good effect on her. We all chatted easily in between periods of concentration where PK read silently and Harlow rearranged loose pages. I snipped at my collage, grateful for something to do with my hands, chiming in occasionally.

At 9:25, PK left her pile of zines on the table, rushing for a bus she was almost missing. I stood up and stretched. Harlow was bent over her pages, gluing intently. "We're officially closing, but I'll be here for another half hour at least," I said. "You can stay if you like. Almost done?"

"I am!" said Harlow, pleased.

"Did your idea work?" I hadn't seen exactly what they were making, only that it looked like a combination of writing and comic-like illustrations, simple characters drawn with thought bubbles.

"I think so," said Harlow. "This is the closest it's felt, anyway. I'll have to let it sit for a few days to know for sure, but it's nice to get it out of my head into something I don't want to tear up immediately."

Harlow used the photocopier while I put away supplies and cleaned teacups. I brought in the ramp I'd put out at the beginning of the night. A community member had built it to get around the fact that the sidewalks were too narrow to install a permanent one but the building had a step up to get in. I stashed it behind the door along with the A-frame sign advertising drop-in hours and locked up. When I returned, Harlow was folding a few copies of their finished zine already in front of them. I sat back down.

"Your tattoos are so cool," I said, looking at the black line drawings of flowers on one upper arm.

"Thanks. At my next sitting I'm going to get the color done."

"Do you know what colors?"

"For a long time I imagined yellow, purple, and blue, but now I'm not sure. I might make my artist decide."

I leaned in to trace the flowers, noting that they relaxed into my touch. "The lines are so striking. Have you ever colored them in just to see what it looks like?"

"Ha! My nibling thinks they look like the pages in her coloring books, so I let her try it once. She was excited to draw on me but her interpretation was . . . more abstract than I'm going for. She ended up drawing on her own legs and I got in trouble when my sister got home."

"That's hilarious. You've never tried it yourself?"

"It's hard to reach. Even more awkward than doing the liner on my left eye."

A few minutes later I was on their side of the table, their elbow resting on a pillow I'd snagged from the nook's beat-up couch. I had laid out an array of colored markers: yellow, purple, and blue but also red, orange, pink, and green for the leaves.

I picked up the orange one in my right hand and touched my left hand next to the spot on their arm where I was going to start. Goose bumps sprung up on their skin and I felt them tense and hold their breath, then breathe out forcefully, as if reminding themselves that they could.

"Is this still okay? I'm not an actual tattoo artist, you know. No needles, I promise."

"No, yeah. I'm good. Are you an *artist* artist? Your hands feel like they know what they're doing."

I felt a thrill. "Sort of. You're probably picking up on the hours I spent in my adult coloring book phase." I laughed.

Their skin was soft. I wanted to go slowly so I could keep touching them, but it was also so intimate. The sharp scent of marker filled the air and the silence circled cozily around us. I chattered away to keep the intensity at bay. Had they grown up here? No, came for school and never left. Job? A mishmash of delivery driving, dog-walking, and freelance writing. Partners? This last question asked as casually as possible; I was quick to say "Me neither," when they said they didn't have anyone serious in their life right now.

I'd made them promise not to look until I was done. When I sat back, trailing my fingers down to their forearm before I broke contact, they didn't look down right away. They hadn't moved their arm away either, and they squeezed my fingers as I ran them past their hand. I found their gaze again.

"How does it look?" they asked, keeping mine.

"Incredible," I said, not at all looking at their arm. Then, before I could overthink it, "Can I kiss you?"

"Hell yes," they said and I leaned in. It was a soft kiss, slightly awkward as my knees bumped against the side of their thigh. We were still perpendicular to each other and we couldn't get our bodies lined up. I pulled back and smiled. I was proud that I'd made this happen, that I hadn't just gone home and wished it. And then they one-upped me.

"Have you ever had sex with anyone in here?" they asked. I laughed and said no, darting a look at the bathroom. They followed my gaze. "But you've thought about it. I can tell."

"Well . . . I've always thought the bathroom had the perfect setup. It's a small space, so it's easy to brace yourself against the opposite wall. And there's lots of grab bars, you know, for accessibility."

"Accessibility, eh?"

"Yes," I deadpanned. "You can access all kinds of things with them."

"Show me."

"Let me get something first." I went to the shelf that had the naloxone and the box of safer sex packages that the sexual health center stocks monthly. I held one up to show them, then took their hand and led them into the small space, which, thank goddex, had been cleaned recently. Sometimes in my slow day fantasies I imagined sex in the reading nook but in real life the bathroom felt much more palatable. That couch has . . . seen some things.

I set the package of gloves, lube, condoms, and dams down and held up my marker-colored hands. "I feel like I should wash these," I said, and moved to the sink. They came up behind me and put their hands on my shoulders, kissing the side of my face. I watched in the mirror, hardly believing this was happening. Then I turned around, my hands still wet. I held them awkwardly away from my sides and they laughed, pulling some paper towels from the wall behind me and slowly drying them for me, attending to each finger.

Then they stood back and pulled off their T-shirt, revealing a vine tattoo with leaves that matched the ones on their arms, curling around from their back to wind down both sides of their torso. They had an adorable plump belly and faded top surgery scars. I inhaled, started to reach out a hand, and then asked, "Do you like having your chest touched?"

"Oh, yeah," they replied, then paused. "As long as you don't act like there's supposed to be breasts there, that can make me dysphoric. But I get a lot of sensation and I like the way it feels." I nodded and moved in, one hand behind their head to protect it from the wall, the other palming their chest as I pushed them back toward it, pressing my lower body up against them. I stroked their chest, then drew my hand down their torso slowly, moving it away to press my full body into theirs as I kissed again, flailing a little with my hands as I realized my self-assuredness was running out and I wasn't sure what to do next.

But they were. Kissing me back and moving against me, they caught my hand and brought it to the front of their jeans. "Can you feel my packer?" they asked as they cupped their hand around mine and encouraged me to squeeze. I felt the soft silicone bulge and groaned yes.

"For some reason, when I was leaving the house today I didn't think I'd need anything harder."

"What a shame."

"Somehow I don't think it will be a problem."

"Not likely. How can I help you come?"

"Kiss me. I can use my fingers."

I kissed hungrily, pressing my body against them, moving back to let them maneuver their hand under the waistband of their pants when they were ready. "What else can I do to make you feel good?"

"Put your mouth on my chest. I want to feel your tongue on my nipple."

When I glanced at the mirror again I loved what I saw. They had their head back, eyes closed, their hips moving against their hand. The pencil holding my bun had fallen out. I had one leg in between theirs, a hand on their chest, my lips at their ear. We were flushed and bright. "We look incredible together," I said and they opened their eyes, smiled in agreement, and closed them again, moving faster.

As they came, I cradled their head with one hand and took as much of their weight as I could with the other arm so they could let go. I held them tightly, kissing them on the temple, listening to their breath come fast and then in a sigh as they returned to themself. I absolutely love holding someone as they come, being right there with them. We couldn't stay long in the afterglow because they were starting to slip down the wall, so we untangled and stood upright.

I was still wearing my plaid and I unbuttoned it so that my tank top underneath showed off my tits while they washed their hands. I ran my fingers down the flowers on their arm, touching more deliberately than just a few minutes ago when we'd been sitting out at the table, but I still saw goose bumps come up. "This turned out really well, if I do say so myself," I said, and they turned to finally admire my work, nodding. "I'll have to take a picture for my artist," they said. We caught each other's gaze in the mirror again, and I saw their eyes go down to my breasts. I beat them to it.

"I really like having my tits touched," I said, and shrugged the plaid off.

Their hands were just as tender and diligent on my body as they had been with pencil and paper. I leaned back against the wall, enjoying their work, moving my leg up to rest on one of the grab bars when I wanted to encourage them between my legs, where they met me with glove-clad fingers. My orgasm was fluttery and fleeting, the best I could conjure without being on hands and knees in a soft bed, but it was tender and exciting all the same. I knew I'd come back to this moment again that night, where I could take my time. We pressed our foreheads together until we cooled down and were forced to get dressed.

Later, on the bus, I took out the zine Harlow had slipped me before they disappeared down the street to their own bus stop. I planned to wait until I got home to read it, but I looked at the back page and gasped when I saw it was dedicated to "Kat, the person who showed me the magic of zine-making." Below that, in fresh orange marker, was a phone number. I sighed happily as the bus sped me home.

THE BOY TOY

Lynx Canon

It was time for my first sex toy. Cody and I had broken up two weeks ago—for the best. He was a nice guy, just not the guy for me. But the breakup had left me with a big gap in the sexual satisfaction department. I did miss his lovemaking.

I'd been making do pleasuring myself. Come home from work, shrug off my clothes, take a cool shower, and spend a little me time in my bed. When I do this, I make it sensual. I put on some R&B, pour a glass of wine, and relax into it. I light a candle and use creamy soft lube.

But my poor pussy was missing the sensations that only come from a good fucking. I was definitely on the hunt for someone new, but in the meantime, a toy would fill that gap.

"You mean you don't have *any* toys?" my best friend Charmaine asked me.

"Nope. I'm just a low-tech girl."

"I always use toys—even when I'm with Rich. It just *adds* to the experience, if you know what I mean." She gave a wicked chuckle.

I didn't know what she meant, and I wanted to find out.

So, one Friday evening, instead of hitting the wine bar or creeping home for another pussy-pleasure session, I went to The Toy Box. It was the most upscale sex emporium in town; it had even been written up in the local city magazine for being woman friendly.

The windows were heavily curtained with pink satin, with only the store's name written in gold. Taking a deep breath, I pushed open the door and paused right inside to look around.

A rainbow of dildos on glass shelves lined one wall. I'd never imagined there would be so many sizes and colors. The back wall held a variety of electrical devices. It was obvious how some of them were to be used, but others seemed completely mysterious.

I was a bit overwhelmed. I didn't know where to begin.

"Can I help you?"

I'd been gaping so hard at all the toys that I hadn't noticed the sales clerk until now. I gulped when I heard his voice. I'd been expecting a woman. I could feel the blush rising to my cheeks and warming my chest.

"Um, I'm just looking." Now, I looked at him. And he was worth looking at. It started with lustrous dark hair, just long enough to curl in tendrils at the back of his neck. He had deep brown eyes fringed with long lashes, a straight nose, and full lips that curved up at the corners.

My gaze stopped at broad shoulders; I realized I was staring. He was gorgeous. The smile he gave me almost melted my nervousness.

"My name's Michael," he said. "I'll let you look around. Just let me know if I can answer any questions."

"I'm Holly. Thanks." I reluctantly turned away from this beautiful hunk of manhood and again contemplated the rows of plastic penises on the back wall. In the clear light of the store, it was hard to get a sense of their sizes relative to the real men I'd been with.

I turned to the wall of electrical devices. They were all plugged into power strips so that you could try them out on your hand—or elsewhere, I supposed, if you were bold enough.

I picked up one that was clearly a vibrator and turned it on. I placed my hand over the tip, enjoying the way it sent a tingle up my arm. There were also plenty of vibrators shaped like cocks. Should I start with a plain dildo or get fancy right away?

Maybe I should have done some online research, I thought. Maybe I'd come back another day.

I sensed Michael next to me. In fact, his sexual charge was so strong that I felt an answering buzz in my pussy. Between his living body and all the dicks on display, I was suddenly getting very warm, and very turned on.

He said, "There's a lot to choose from, isn't there?" His voice was kind, with a bit of a chuckle to it that put me at ease.

"I don't know where to begin," I admitted.

"Are you a virgin?"

"What?!?" I sputtered.

He laughed again. "I meant, a newbie with sex toys."

"Well, yes, I am." This man was so charming, I was quickly losing any embarrassment. "I was thinking about a . . . dildo. Maybe this one?" I randomly pulled a largish, chocolate brown cock from the shelf.

Michael looked back and forth from me to the cock I was holding a couple of times. I knew he was thinking about that cock inside me, and heat rushed through my body so hard I thought I might keel over. Suddenly, I was thinking about it too. And thinking about Michael's cock. I was too horny to feel any shame.

Musingly, he said, "You want to be sure you get one big enough." My pussy gushed, soaking my panties. "I hope I'm not embarrassing you," he added. "This is a place where you can talk freely about sex."

I looked him in the eyes. "This must be an interesting place to work." *And I bet your expertise isn't just theoretical,* I didn't say.

But I could tell he saw it in my eyes.

"I love working here," he said. "And I love the people I meet here."

"I can imagine," I managed to pant, trying to control myself.

He took the brown dildo out of my hand and picked up an even bigger purple one. "Many women find they can take a lot more cock than they thought. For example, I think this one might be right for you."

I was shaking, mesmerized by those brown eyes—and by my thoughts about what I wanted Michael to do to me. "How do they find out?" I whispered.

His smile made my knees quiver. "The only way is to try it, really." He handed me the giant purple cock, keeping hold of it so our hands were touching. Chills ran up my arm from the contact.

The dildo was heavy and long, so thick my hand went only halfway around it. I didn't see how I could get it into my cunt.

Michael leaned closer. "We have a room in the back where the staff tries out new products. Since it's almost closing time, I could let you use it. If you like the dildo, you buy it. If not, I'll sanitize it and use it as a demo for classes. How's that for a deal?"

I'd love to make a deal with you, I thought, wishing I were bolder.

"Okay," I gasped. I was so on fire that I couldn't wait to feel something big and hard filling me up. "But I think I'll take a smaller one."

Michael put his hand over mine on the dildo and his other hand on my waist. "Trust me," he said. "This one is right for you."

He locked the front door and turned the sign around to say "Closed." Then, with that warm hand on my waist again, he guided me around the counter and through a door. I was expecting a dim and dirty stockroom, but we entered an attractive space with a large bed in the center. The bed was made up with crisp white sheets, a white duvet, and four fluffy pillows. Everything looked spotless. A lamp on a table by the bed cast a soft glow. I briefly wondered exactly how the staff tested the products—but I was in a haze of lust.

I turned to Michael. "Thank you. Shall I just come out when I'm done?"

This time his smile was downright seductive. "Oh, sorry, but I'm staying."

I could actually feel my pussy lips swelling. "But. Uh." I was speechless and confused. I wanted him to take me right now on that plush bed. But another part of me was chiding me, reminding myself that you just didn't have sex in the back of a store with a stranger.

"It's company policy," Michael said in a voice like melted chocolate. "We wouldn't want you to hurt yourself."

I was melting, myself. Dizzy with desire. "That's so . . . nice of you. But—"

This man was a crazy mixture of nice and sexy, with a dollop of dominance that made him all the more intriguing.

"Why don't you take your clothes off now? I'll be right here, ready to answer your questions and help you in any way you need."

I wanted to do this. I needed to. My mouth was dry, my pussy was throbbing. I turned away and quickly unbuttoned my blouse, unhooked my bra, and threw them both on the bed. I began to fumble with the zipper on my skirt.

"Turn around," Michael said gently. "Let me see your breasts." I slowly complied, feeling so vulnerable and yet so willing. His pupils dilated as he took in my tits and the tight nipples standing up, aching to be sucked. "Now take off the rest of your clothes," he said. "You'll feel more relaxed once you've gotten over having me see you naked."

Locking eyes with him, I got my zipper open and dropped my skirt. I kicked off my stilettos, pulled down my panties and stepped out of them. I was now completely naked, quivering with desire. I felt my wetness dripping down the insides of my thighs.

Michael moved to the table at the side of the bed and pulled a bottle of lube and a condom out of the drawer. "I can see you're very aroused already. But to take a toy this size, you're going to need to use a lot of lubrication."

He handed the bottle to me and motioned me to pick up the dildo. I sat on the side of the bed and hefted the humongous thing. I was sitting stripped naked in front of a man I didn't know, holding a purple phallus that I was about to fuck myself with while he watched. I had never done anything this dirty. And I was so ready to.

I spread my legs and propped the dildo between them to hold it upright, letting its base push against my engorged clit. I rolled the condom down, flipped the cap on the lube and squirted out a generous amount. Then, watching Michael's face, I stroked the lube up and down the purple cock, making sure it was nice and slippery. I saw his eyes narrow and his mouth open. I looked down and saw that he was big and hard underneath his dress pants.

Being watched was something new for me. I was pleasuring myself and pleasuring another person at the same time. It doubled my excitement.

"Go ahead," he said, short of breath.

I lay back on the bed and spread my legs, bringing the blunt head of the toy up against my sex. It felt immense. There was no way I was going to penetrate myself with this monster.

"It takes time," Michael said. "Just go slow."

I moved the head of the dildo all over my pussy lips and then ran it up against my clit, rhythmically pushing it, nuzzling my clit. I already felt the first tremors of orgasm. I desperately wanted something inside me, but now I needed to come. I thrust the dildo harder and harder against my clit until I felt my entire pussy rock and clench and then release.

I lay back, panting for breath, my arms open wide, my legs spread, completely open to Michael. Would he fuck me now? I wanted it.

"That was beautiful," he said, one hand gently rubbing his crotch. "Now that you've had your first orgasm, this is the perfect time to begin getting that purple cock inside you."

"I can't," I said. "I'm exhausted."

"Trust me," Michael said. "You'll be sorry later on if you don't take this opportunity. Go ahead. Start to fuck yourself."

His words sent a new wave of lust through me. I didn't care about choosing a dildo, I just wanted to come again. I scooted up on the bed so my back was supported on the pillows and picked up the toy. I pushed firmly, and this time my lips opened to receive the blunt tip. I spread my legs wider and pushed harder—and the head of the dildo pushed through my tight opening and slid inside me.

I gasped. The stretching and the friction of the huge purple cock were more intense than a man's cock. When I fucked a man, it was a dance. I followed his desire as well as my own. When I masturbated, I focused on my clit and all the sensations that filled my pelvis. Fucking myself with this huge purple instrument was almost intolerably exciting.

I lay back, still panting. I was on fire, practically swooning, and I didn't have the strength to keep pushing the dildo. I looked up at Michael.

"Please," I said.

His smile was an intriguing mix of warmth and wickedness. "No, Holly. Fuck yourself." He put his hand on his crotch. "Fuck yourself for me."

Heat flashed through me. My pussy spasmed, tightening against the immense dick and then loosening to receive it deeper. I pushed and then slowly pulled it out part way, leaving just the knob keeping me open. I took one hand off and rubbed my clit, then used both hands to push the shaft even deeper.

My pussy and belly were full, full of cock. I was fucking myself shamelessly, taking it deeper and deeper with each thrust until I went over the edge of a waterfall of fire.

I withdrew the dildo and luxuriated in the soft bed for delicious minutes. When I opened my eyes, I saw Michael, hot and flushed.

"Please, Michael?"

He unzipped his pants and took out his cock. It was thick and standing proud, glistening at the tip. But he made no move toward me.

"I love watching you," he said.

"I loved having you watch. But now I need you."

He stroked himself. "You need me?"

"Yes. Yes."

"What do you want me to do?"

"I want you to fuck me. Fuck me, please." In a couple of

quick motions, he stripped off his clothes to reveal well-muscled shoulders tapering to a thin waist and a rippling abdomen. But it was his cock I fixated on. After the intense fucking I'd just given myself, it looked like exactly the right size to give me a longer, gentler finish.

Michael knelt on the bed and regarded my aching pussy. He took tissues from the drawer and tenderly mopped up the lube mixed with my juices.

Instead of entering me, he bent and licked my pussy like he was licking an ice cream cone. Then he raised himself up and looked at me. "You have a beautiful pussy. It tastes so good. I want more. Okay?"

"Yes, yes," I breathed.

He bent again and ran his tongue around the entrance to my cunt, taking my labia between his lips and sucking gently. Waves of heat and pleasure radiated outward; my clit stood up and begged for attention. It wasn't long before Michael found it. His warm breath made it expand even more, as though it were reaching for his mouth.

"Oh, God," I groaned.

One of his hands reached up and cupped my breast as his mouth covered my clit and he began to suck. His warm hands roving over my body and his hot mouth against my pussy gave my hard clit exactly what it needed. So many different experiences had swept through me, from him telling me what to do and watching me do it to fucking myself hard with the toy. This was still another kind of pleasure. I orgasmed instantly, the sweet waves making me dizzy.

Before my pussy was done contracting, Michael rose up over me, pulled on a condom, and buried his cock deep inside me. The sudden fullness and his thrusts sent me over the edge still again. He rode me, timing his thrusts to the waves of my orgasm until finally, as my body was rocked with one final jolt of delight, he plunged his cock in to the hilt and came himself.

As I lay so deliriously satisfied, he gently lowered himself down on top of me, supporting himself on one elbow. I felt his lips graze my forehead and cheek before he moved down to nuzzle my neck.

I don't know how long we lay like that. I was in a dream state, enjoying the afterglow. Eventually, I came awake again— and remembered where I was and who I was with. What now?

"Michael?" I said tentatively.

"Mmmm?" He sounded like he was still in that dreamy place.

"Is this how you . . . always demonstrate your products?"

He laughed. "Actually, I've never done this before. When I saw you walk in, I instantly hatched this plan."

"Um, I guess I should be flattered?"

He looked into my eyes. "I hope you'll be more than flattered," he murmured. "I hope you'll want to do it again. And again and again—and somewhere a lot more private."

I ran my hand down his back and over his tight buns, realizing that I was being offered a lot more than I'd expected. "I'd like that."

HUNGER

Lydia Loomis

The little neighborhood of Manhattan that Tinsyss found herself in tonight should have been familiar to her. Tucked between Chinatown and Little Italy, the places around here catered to the creatures of a paranormal persuasion. Much like the other two neighborhoods, this community developed out of necessity as more creatures looked for a better life on the other side of the veil.

Her mother had traveled through the New York portal years ago to give her two daughters, Tinsyss and Risola, better lives. Risola, ever the model succubus, was doing a better job of it then Tinsyss. During the day Risola was a high-powered lawyer; after hours she frequently fed on Manhattan's elite. Often, Risola chided her younger sister for being too caught up in the modern world, for straying too far from the traditional ways. Now, Tinsyss would have to admit her sister was right. If Tinsyss was a better succubus she wouldn't be in this position, nearly unconscious from starvation, lost in an alley. If she was a better succubus she would have been able to find The Thirsty Pub and an easy one-night stand to quench her hunger. If she was a better succubus she wouldn't need to because she wouldn't be starving to death.

These thoughts blinked through Tinsyss's head as she propped herself against the alley wall, the world starting to fade out as she lost strength. She should have been a better succubus but she was a hopeless romantic. She wasn't a prude by any means but she liked the idea of finding "The One," of being devoted and loyal to each other. She thought she had. Jas was a satyr, which meant his sexual appetite was nearly as strong as hers, and the sex had been great. It wasn't just about sex though, he had also been kind and genial, at least at first, and she saw them building a life together. After a time, he got more and more controlling, and separated her from her family and friends.

It had been months since she'd talked to her sister; they hadn't spoken since they got into a heated fight about Jas and how he was treating her. It wasn't long after the fight with her sister that Jas began using sex as a way to control her, withholding it from her when he didn't get his way. He'd claim he wasn't in the mood because of the way she acted, the way she dressed, or because she was too friendly to the waiter at the restaurant. If she was also a satyr or even a human, this denial wouldn't have been a big deal, but she was a succubus. Withholding sex was not simply spiteful, it was like withholding food, water, or air. She didn't want to cheat so she would do her best to hold out and then feel so grateful when he finally came around. However, after a particularly bad fight and several days of withheld sustenance, Tinsyss finally decided to break up with him and move out.

Now, over a week later, she still hadn't fed. Sex with another still felt too much like cheating, or unromantic, or maybe part of her was waiting for Jas to come and win her back. All of it felt incredibly stupid as she crumpled in the alley with no strength. Why couldn't she be a better succubus?

"You all right there, ma'am?" a deep voice with a rich southern accent called to her from the end of the alley. Tinsyss pushed herself off the building she was leaning on and tried to answer the man, but her voice was still weak. She had started to fall back when strong arms wrapped around her waist. How did he get to her so fast?

"Whoa, there little lady. You don't look so good."

Tinsyss felt the strong arms holding her, the sultry voice, the strange earthy smell, and her mouth watered with hunger and lust.

"Help me," she managed to whisper.

"Yes, ma'am. I'm going to do my best to get you help. Are you drunk? Hurt? You need me to call a friend to come get you?"

"You . . . I need you. Please, help me."

Tinsyss snaked her hands under the man's shirt. His stomach was flat, hard, and cold, telling her he probably wasn't human but she didn't have the wherewithal to think more about what or who he was. She curled her fingers into the muscles on his waist and tried to drag him to her, her lips finding his neck. She licked up his Adam's apple, taking in a taste that was both musky and sweet; she felt the vibrations under her lips as he let out a low groan. She was starving and this man, or creature, was prime rib; she needed him. He pulled back, holding her shoulders firmly as he put distance between them. Tinsyss let out a weak little whimper at the loss of contact.

"Please, so hungry."

The man's honey-colored eyes examined her carefully.

"*Succubus.*" It was more of a statement than a question, like he was putting the pieces of their encounter together. Tinsyss started to panic, worried he would be disgusted by a sex demon and leave her to starve.

"Please." She tried to reach out to him again, but he held her firm by the shoulders.

"Is there someone I can call for you? A friend? Lover? Fuck buddy? Someone safe who can take care of your needs."

His southern drawl held no notes of disdain but sounded like concern and care.

"Please, no time, I need you."

Jackson looked down at the pleading woman in his arms. Part of him was worried about getting her help but another part was thrilled at his luck. It was hard to believe this wasn't a dream, only vampires didn't dream, so this had to be real. This woman, this demon, was the goddamned sexiest thing he had ever seen. She was petite but curvy, her curly red hair was damp with sweat and falling into her face, which could only be described as adorable. He would already be inside her if he had let his base instincts take over, but he managed, barely, to control himself. A woman like this was not one that you fucked in the back alley of a club on your way to suck a stranger's neck dry. This was a good girl; it didn't matter if she was a succubus, she was the kind of girl you took home to mom. Surprisingly, the instinct to protect her was almost stronger than his desire to fuck her, and both were telling him the same thing.

"Okay, darling, I'm going to do my best to take care of you."

He pulled her back into his arms and dropped his mouth to hers. Both of them uttered a small moan. She tasted like sunshine and sweet tea. Somehow, he had known she would. He wrapped one arm firmly around her waist, pinning her to him.

He cupped her breast, slowly rubbing a nipple until it was pert through her cotton sundress. He could feel that she didn't have a bra on and he leaned down, licking and sucking her through the light fabric. Idly, he wondered whether the dress would survive what he wanted to do to this exquisite creature.

The little demon was still weak from hunger, her eyes were heavy with fatigue, but the energy she drew from their heavy make-out session was enough for her to stand on her own. Quickly checking that they were still alone in the alley, Jackson pressed her back into the wall of the building and dropped to his knees in front of her. Slowly dragging his hand under her dress and up her thigh, he followed the path with his tongue. He ran his mouth up her inner thigh until he found her small panties, delighting in running his tongue across the lace covering her mound.

Tinsyss let out a shuddery breath as the stranger hooked one finger into her panties and moved them aside so his mouth had better access to her. For a moment, she wondered whether he was the starving one, the way he devoured her, his tongue thrusting inside, his thumb pressing firm circles around her clit. Raw, pure, lustful energy rained down over her and she felt like she had found an oasis in the desert. As her orgasm shattered through her so did a sense of relief; she had never been so close to fading away before. The stranger stood up, wrapped his arms around her, and brought her safely into his steady chest.

"There we go, darling. Feeling a little better now?"

A sudden embarrassment swept through Tinsyss as she realized what she had just done, with a stranger, in a city alley of all places. She tried to straighten up and pull away but the stranger kept a firm hand on her back, not letting her get too far.

"I am so sorry, I, I . . ."

"Stop that now, sweetheart, you ain't got nothing to be sorry for. I'm just happy I could oblige. Now, you're still weak. I reckon you have to feed some more before you're back to full health again. Is there someone I can take you to?"

Tinsyss ran a hand down her face, which she was sure was bright red by this point, and avoided eye contact with the smoldering stranger.

"Um, no, bad breakup. If you could point me in the direction of The Thirsty Pub, I should be fine there."

He looked at her for a long beat, his brow wrinkled, not letting go of her. Finally, he issued a strangled sigh.

"Look, darling, how about I take you back to my place? I can get you fed and healthy unless you feel you'd rather find someone . . . ?"

"I'd love that. I mean, if you don't mind?"

"Are you kidding? It would be my pleasure to help a beautiful woman out. It isn't every day a man like me gets to play the white knight and help out the distressed damsel."

He flashed her a dazzling smile complete with a slim set of fangs, the sight of which sent heat straight through her. Maybe she was finally becoming the succubus her mom and sister wanted her to be, fucking strangers in an alley, turned on by vampire fangs. She knew that wasn't true; what was really getting to her was how safe he made her feel, how he treated her like someone special. She spent the entire cab ride uptown trying to get to know him better and finding that she liked him more and more. She realized that she would probably end up starving to death again; there was no getting away from the truth that she was a hopeless romantic.

"Are you sure you're all right coming back to my place? I don't want you to feel unsafe."

"You forget that I'm a demon. I think if anyone is in danger here, it might be you."

"Good thing you can't kill what's already dead." He gave her a teasing smile before leaning in. "Though if you'd like to fuck me to death, you're more than welcome to try."

When the cab stopped near 84th and 5th Avenue, Jackson led her up to a ridiculously grand penthouse apartment. An open floor plan showed off all of the apartment's luxuries at once, large windows in the living room looked out over Central Park. Tinsyss felt like she had stepped into another world.

"Wow, this is a long way from starving in an alley," she joked.

"Don't be too impressed. Generational wealth. Any vampire should be able to show you the same. Between living as long as we do and the unwritten code that you provide something for those you sire, let's just say that vampire wealth is nothing to be impressed by. Very little of it came from a hard day's work."

"Oh, really? You seemed pretty hardworking and industrious back in that alley." Tinsyss turned and gave him a smile. His eyes were boring into her. She knew that lustful look. She'd seen it on many people, but this time it felt different, sending a shiver of thrill and excitement through her.

"Baby girl, I have not even begun to work for you."

Tinsyss's breath caught as he stalked over to her, swept her up, and proceeded to carry her to the bedroom. He set her on her knees on the bed, quickly pulling her dress over her head before standing back to admire her body.

"You really are perfect, you know?"

He didn't wait for her to answer, which was good because her head was spinning from the compliment. He quickly removed his own clothing as well and she got a full look at him. He was pale, lean, and broad; being a vampire definitely agreed with this man. She didn't have much time to enjoy the view as he grabbed the backs of her knees, tipping her backward. As he climbed on top of her, he pressed her back onto the bed.

"Tell me you want this. Tell me what you need," his husky drawl whispered into her hair, sending a shiver of desire down her spine.

"Oh, yes, please, more, all of it, please." She knew she was babbling but she didn't know what else to say other than to beg.

"That's my girl."

Those three words went straight to her clit as his lips wrapped around her nipple. He took his time kissing, licking, caressing her body, all showering her with praise.

"Look at you, so perfect. Beautiful. Are you ready for me?"

His hard cock pressed up against her, making his meaning clear.

Barely finding the breath for words, she panted, "Fuck yes."

Her back arched and her hips bucked; her body was desperate to get him inside her. As he pushed into her, slow and deep, she couldn't help the loud sounds that escaped her. He filled her and his energy spilled over, making him the best thing she had ever felt. She moaned again, softer this time, as her eyes closed and her head lolled back.

"Hey now, where're you going?" His fangs nipped at her jaw, bringing her attention back to him.

"You be a good girl and keep your attention right here on me."

Tinsyss's breath was unsteady as she stared into his dark honey-colored eyes. Her mother's voice rose up in her mind, reminding her that love wasn't real, that sex was just to feed, that men would only leave her, that she had just been dumped and this man was a stranger, that she should feed from him and leave, that this didn't mean anything. But Tinsyss had a hard time hearing those inner warnings over his throaty words telling her how good she was, that she was beautiful, that she was his.

Arching against him, meeting every one of his thrusts with a feverish hunger, Tinsyss raced to the edge of a lust-filled oblivion. She was barely aware that he chased her over that edge and fell with her. There was a moment of stillness, punctuated by heavy breathing, and sweat, as the shattered world reformed around them. Jackson shifted them so she was resting on his chest, cradling her and rubbing small circles on her back.

"How was that? Feeling better now, darling?"

"Hmm." She lazily nodded before smiling up at him.

His eyes had grown darker and she realized he probably needed to feed soon as well.

"You're hungry?" She shifted and pulled her hair away from her neck.

"You helped me, let me help you."

"You don't need to do that, sweetheart. I have some bags in the fridge that'll tide me over just fine."

"Come on, now, bagged stale blood can't be as good as what I've got." She gave him a teasing little smile.

He growled and grabbed her ass with both hands, pulling her close.

"Nothing is as good as what you've got. You do know how succubus blood affects vampires, right? That if I feed on you, I won't let that perfect little cunt of yours rest for the whole night?"

"Promise?"

He let out a pained grunt. He grasped the back of her head, bringing his nose along the pulse of her neck and breathing her in.

"Are you sure?" His voice was strained and she could tell he was holding himself back. She felt sexy and powerful; it was more than just the fact that she could return the favor. She was excited that he wanted it, wanted her. She nodded, presenting her neck to him again.

"If you want to stop. If any of this gets to be too much . . ." He caressed her thigh but didn't let go of the hard grip he had on her neck. "Say the word and we stop."

"I know."

She couldn't explain it, she had just met him, but she knew he would stop, knew that she was safe here. It had not been long ago, just a few hours, that she had been close to death but now she was the safest she'd ever felt.

Jackson leaned into her neck, licking across her pulse, taking a moment to enjoy the quickening beat of her heart. Already, he knew that getting over this little stray demon he'd brought home wasn't going to be easy. He was pushing a century and he had never felt like this—lost, completed, in control, empty and careening into chaos, all at once. He sank his fangs into her as she straddled his lap. She let out a little cry and jerked, rubbing her nipples across his chest. He fed, sucking her warm blood into him. The heady fluid filled him, fed him, and, true to her nature, amplified his lust. He gently licked her neck where he'd made a small puncture mark; he liked seeing his mark on her and decided to add more. Sucking, kissing, bruising, he left marks up and down her neck and chest.

"Mine, all mine," he whispered possessively. "I might not be able to let you go, darling."

He saw a small tremble in her lashes as she lifted her hips and positioned herself over his hard again cock. He held his breath as she lowered herself down onto him.

Jackson lost track of how many times they fucked that night. She was hungry and he was spinning with the aphrodisiac effect of her blood. He kept enough sense about him to make sure she was cared for, to get her water, bathe her, talk to her, and just hold her. Holding her was quickly becoming his favorite thing, right after fucking her. At some point, they wore themselves out and fell asleep.

He was woken up by the itchy feeling of the sun streaming into the room and came to the sudden realization that he was alone in the bed. A panicked sense of loss crashed over him; did she just leave? Hearing her voice in the kitchen, he let out a breath of relief, but the panic rose again as she let out a small stream of curse words.

Jackson rushed into the kitchen only to find Tinsyss having words with his espresso machine.

"Listen here, you little bitch, I need caffeine so work with me!"

She hit a button but it only caused a stream of steam to shoot out as she jumped back with a little scream. He couldn't help but chuckle; the sound made her turn around and scowl at him. It was the cutest little scowl he'd ever seen.

"You had to have the fancy gourmet shit, right? Not just a simple drip coffee machine that regular people could use?"

He walked over, grabbed her, and easily sat her on the counter. Without acknowledging her ire, he kissed her, then went about making coffee for them both.

Once she had a cup of rich black coffee in her hands, he said, "I promise, next time I will have whatever kind of coffee you like."

"So . . . there's going to be a next time?" Tinsyss's voice was soft and she didn't look up from her cup.

"I hope so, darlin'. Only next time instead of finding you starving in an alley, I thought I could take you on a proper date."

He watched, enamored, as her cheeks flushed slightly. Who would have thought a succubus demon would turn out to be such an adorable, sweet girl?

"I guess that could work," Tinsyss replied with a shrug, trying to act like it wouldn't matter to her if there was a next time.

Jackson let out another chuckle as he saw through her act. Shaking his head, he ordered breakfast for her and, once it was delivered, they talked while she ate. As they chatted, he reveled over how easily she fit into his normally isolated, empty home. She didn't feel like a stranger he'd met yesterday; she felt like she was always meant to be there.

THE DOCTOR

Bartholomew Maxwell

"And so, my final conclusions from this study are . . ." He finished his last bullet points and looked out over the conference crowd, as he got moderate applause for his talk. He felt good about his research.

A woman he'd noticed in the audience when he'd started the talk raised her hand. She was hard to miss—she was tall, big, broad-shouldered, and had lustrous terra-cotta skin not unlike his own. Her hair was in thin braids, tied neatly behind her head. She exuded confidence and radiated strength. His kind of woman. He'd heard research that showed that more women asked questions during talks when the first person who was called on was a woman, and his practice was to always call on a woman first. Calling on her as she raised her hand seemed almost automatic.

"Thank you, Dr. Keystone, for that very interesting model. I have one question. Have you thought about your initial assumption regarding the consistency of the thermohaline circulation in the South Atlantic? There have been some studies suggesting it can change much more than you are assuming."

The question was a good one, and he did his best at answering, even though he felt a little muddled as he was noticing how his body was reacting to her. Questions from others and his responses almost faded into the background as his eyes seemed to return to her face without his volition.

After the talk, David sat at the hotel bar, whiskey sour in front of him, brooding. He thought the talk went well, but that first question rattled him. He knew she was right, after all—part of his basic premise was potentially flawed. There wasn't much he could do about it, really, except go back, relook at his models, and figure out how to rework them. But as he thought more about it, he realized that most of the reason he was rattled was the questioner herself, not the questions.

She seemed to be well known in the crowd, but he didn't know who she was. He was new to the field: he'd gotten his PhD in a different field and had entered this one late, and a bit by surprise. He'd gotten a post-doc offer he couldn't possibly refuse. He was getting to use his expertise in one field to mine some of the more interesting conundrums of another.

He shook his head and decided to let her go from his mind, for now, returning to thinking about his own work. As he finished his drink, he decided against having another. He swiveled his body on the stool, preparing to rise, when he saw that same woman a few stools away, looking quite intently at him. Her look glued him to his stool. He didn't move an inch, although his cock was doing something interesting.

He watched, helpless, as she got up and walked the few steps to sit on the stool beside his. Because his knees were turned toward her, she brushed them as she sat down.

"You look like a deer caught in headlights, David."

He shook himself and turned his body back toward the bar, while still looking at her, his mind roiling, and his body responding to her presence.

"You know my name, but I . . . I don't know yours."

She smiled, and he noted a mischievous twinkle in her brown eyes.

"Diana. Diana Roberton."

The woman was *Diana Roberton?* Of course, he should have figured that out! She was very prominent, taught at Princeton, and was probably the first Black woman in the field. He remembered reading an interview with her about how hard graduate school had been for her. She was likely fifteen or twenty years older than he was.

"Um, hello, Dr. Roberton." He stuck out his hand awkwardly.

She laughed but took his hand anyway and shook it firmly. She then returned to regarding him with her inscrutable look that locked his body to the stool and made his cock hard again. She smiled and then waved the bartender over.

"Give the man what he was drinking, and I'll have another gin and tonic. Put it all on my tab."

The bartender nodded and then started to prepare the drinks. As he watched the bartender, his mind was in turmoil. She was irresistibly alluring. He could feel the yearning to submit to her—to let her have his way with him. She was just the kind of woman he loved to submit to. The more he remembered other encounters and thought about it, the harder his cock got. But then he thought again about who she was, and that he hardly knew her.

The bartender finally finished the drinks, and he set them both down with a flourish.

Diana said, "You seem a bit troubled, David. Tell me about it."

He turned toward her and opened his mouth to speak, but nothing came out. He closed it for a moment, then tried again. Nothing emerged. He was both deeply embarrassed and somehow excited at the same time.

She smiled, then continued her body-locking look. His cock got even harder, which he didn't think was possible.

"Okay, I'll make this a lot easier for you, David. I *do* know what kind of man you are, and I'm pretty sure I know what you want from me."

She slid a hotel key in front of him.

"Room 925. Come up at nine o'clock. If you're not there, no harm, no foul. You'll make a good climatologist, and we'll run into each other at conferences and be friendly. If you do show up, be prepared to tell me your hard boundaries."

She drained her drink, got up, and walked away.

He still couldn't quite believe it. His mind was in turmoil. Did she *really* know? In any event, he certainly knew what he was going to be doing tonight. He finished his drink more slowly and went up to his room to shower and change.

At precisely nine, he slid the key into the door. He walked in and didn't immediately see Diana. But then he felt a hand move over his eyes.

She said quietly, "I knew you'd be here." A blindfold slid into place.

She led him forward, turned him around, and said, "Sit." He sat.

"Tell me your hard boundaries."

"No blood, urine, or feces. My safeword is 'strawberries.' I don't like humiliation. And, um, do you *really* know . . ."

He felt her hand on his shoulder. "Yes, I *really* know. Martin and I are close friends. Thank you, David."

He felt relief. Martin was his good friend and past mentor

and knew pretty much everything about him. They'd even had long conversations about D/S, as Martin was involved in a few D/S relationships of his own.

"What should I call you?"

"Call me Doctor, of course."

"Yes, Doctor."

"Stand up."

He stood.

"Take off your shirt. Slowly."

He unbuttoned his sleeves, pulled the shirt from inside his pants, and started to unbutton his shirt. He purposely slowed his motions down, as he wanted to please her more than anything. As he pulled his arms out from his sleeves, he felt her take the shirt from him.

He then felt her hands caressing his chest, spending time on his scars. He yelped, then moaned when she twisted a nipple. He was having a hard time standing up.

"Take off your socks and shoes, then your pants."

He pulled off his shoes and socks, then unbuttoned his pants. As he unzipped his pants, he felt exposed. He let the pants drop, and he pulled his legs out of them. He felt and heard her take his pants, as well.

It was quiet for a long, uncomfortable moment. Then, her quiet voice said, "Now take off your underwear." His vulnerability went through the roof, but he wanted to please her more than anything, so he obeyed her. It seemed like forever until he felt her hands on parts of his body. She slowly caressed his chest, then his stomach. He felt her hands moving down both sides of his legs. As they moved up, she moved her hands over his pubic hair and lightly teased his cock. He felt a jolt of energy move from his cock to his chest as her finger probed deeper between his legs.

She said, "The bed is right behind you. Turn around, kneel down, and put your stomach on the bed."

He turned around and kneeled, moving forward to where the bed was, then bent over, stomach down. He heard sounds he couldn't recognize, followed by her tugging his arm, and then felt a cuff get buckled onto his right wrist. There was a slight pull as she moved his left wrist and buckled it to the other cuff. He tried to lift his arms slightly but was unable to.

He felt a slight breath in his ear. "Tonight, David, you are not a scientist. You are nothing but my plaything. I own you. I own your body. You are mine. Is that entirely clear?"

He nodded. He knew he wanted this more than anything but didn't know how to say it.

"Use your words, David."

"Yes, Doctor. Yes, I understand."

"Good."

He couldn't move much. There was silence for another very long time. He had no idea what was coming next.

He felt a caress on one of his asscheeks. "Such a nice ass, David. So nice. I'm so looking forward to ruining it."

He didn't really have a lot of time to consider what she meant. He heard a slapping sound that made him jerk, but he didn't feel anything. Before he had any more time to wonder exactly what was about to happen, the cool wood of what probably was a paddle landed hard on his ass. She thumped him lightly with it on both sides of his ass a few times, then slowly increased the intensity. The anticipation of what was coming next was moving through his body, to land solidly between his legs.

Thwack. That last slap on the right side of his ass stung. A lot. Tears ran down his face at the same time as his cock throbbed. *Thwack.* Another slap on the left side. That one stung even more. With each slap, he wasn't sure he was going to be able to stand another, but somehow, he was able to. He eventually lost track of how many times she hit him, as he floated into that familiar space of submission, pain, and pleasure.

She stopped suddenly, and he felt a cold cloth on his ass, which soothed the burn he was feeling.

"You did very well, David."

Somehow, hearing that from her brought out so much emotion in him. He wanted to please her, wanted to know that she felt him acceptable.

"And now, I'm really going to ruin that ass."

He felt a frisson of fear move through him. He wondered what she had in mind. He didn't know how much more pain he could take.

She opened up his asscheeks, and he felt a cool liquid feeling around his hole and dripping down his legs. Lube, he thought. But then nothing happened, for what seemed like forever. He then felt her hands again spread his cheeks and felt something lightly probe his asshole. Suddenly, without much warning, he felt a shove inside his ass, and felt the slapping of her body against his. He grunted, then moaned, helpless to do much of anything as she fucked him roughly. She was silent, but he could do nothing but moan and cry, as she kept fucking him. The pleasure of it was almost overwhelming—he was in a space he craved. He loved his desire for submission and his ability to bear whatever she wanted to dish out.

It seemed like both a long time, and no time at all, before she pulled out of his ass, and moved away from him. He felt another cool cloth caressing his ass and asshole, wiping up lube and anything else. He was somewhat embarrassed by how messy it might have been. He hoped it wasn't.

"You are such a good boy, David."

"Thank you, Doctor."

He felt her unhook the cuffs on his wrist, but she didn't unbuckle them.

"Move up onto the bed, face up."

He did his best, as he was still blindfolded.

She refastened the cuffs and then buckled cuffs onto his ankles. His legs were slightly apart. He heard more sounds that he could not identify, then he felt the weight of her body on the bed near his head, but he couldn't pinpoint exactly where she was. His ass was still throbbing from what she'd done.

There was some movement over his head, then he felt the warmth of her body as it hovered above his face. He could smell her scent—a musky smell mixed with something fruity.

"You have made me very horny, David. You are going to make me come, is that clear?"

"Yes, Doctor, I will do my best."

"David, I didn't ask you to do your best. I told you that you were going to make me come. Am I clear?"

"Yes, Doctor. You are clear." A faint frisson of fear was mixed with his arousal. He had no idea whether or not he was going to be able to make her come, and he didn't want to fail this test.

He felt her warm cunt on his chin, and he used his tongue to explore her contours. He could taste the salty, musky, tangy taste of her, which he loved from the first lick. He could feel where her folds came together at the top, and he rolled his tongue around the small button of her clit. He experimented, listening to her sounds, feeling her energy, feeling her weight shift and move on top of him. He found that when he moved his tongue up and down one side of her cunt, she moaned more loudly than other movements, so he returned to that spot several times. Each time, she moaned louder.

"Fuck, David, that feels so good."

Her words made him happy. Even though he couldn't see her, he almost felt at this moment that he could feel all of her and feel the movement of her erotic energy upward and outward. That energy crested and she was shuddering, making loud noises, losing control for the first time since they'd first locked eyes on each other.

"That was so good, David. You are a very good boy. You please me. Now it's time for you to come."

It was another command, one he was more than happy to oblige. David felt the pinch of her fingers on his nipples as she twisted both at the same time. That sent a jolt of heat from his chest to his cock. She moved one hand down to his cock, exploring and then giving it small strokes up and down—first slowly, then quickly. He was surprised by the deftness of her hands. His climax was fast and explosive. He grunted loudly in release. He was out of breath.

After a pause, he felt her undo the cuffs.

"Sit up."

He did. He was still a bit disoriented by the experience—he had been craving this kind of submission since his last breakup, and this had been such an amazing surprise.

She took off the blindfold and pointed at his clothes.

"Get dressed."

As he dressed, she watched him with a look he couldn't read.

"You did very well, David. I have only one more night here at the conference—I have to leave early to testify in DC. Come back at eight o'clock tomorrow night."

He nodded.

"Have a good night."

"Thank you, Doctor. You too."

As he closed the door and walked back to the elevator to get back to his room, his mind went back to that moment when

he picked her out of the crowd to answer her question. He had
no way of knowing how his attraction to her then would result
in what happened tonight. His body vibrated thinking about
tomorrow night.

EMBER AND ASH

Oleander Plume

She sings with her eyes closed.

I watch, awestruck. She's lit from within, this woman—no—this creature. Fashioned from myth and bone, wrapped in silk and sprinkled with flame. Her fingers burn the keys. Her voice sears my flesh.

The tone warbling from her throat is smoked caramel. I stare at the skin between her breasts and imagine pearlescent lungs expelling breath past her larynx, mixing with magic on the way out. A siren's song, if you will. Glancing over the scant crowd, it appears I'm the only one paying attention to the seductress behind the piano.

Her last number finished, she looks up. Our eyes meet and my life turns into 1940s celluloid. I'm Bogart and she's a femme fatale, all red lips and shiny tresses. She stands and saunters in my direction. Of all the gin joints, in all the towns . . .

"Buy a lady a drink?" She points her delicate chin at the empty chair across from mine.

"It would be my pleasure," I say, watching the slit of her dress open, allowing a glimpse of smooth thigh as she takes a seat. "What's your poison?"

A pause before a broad smile. "Whiskey. Neat."

"A woman after my own heart."

Next to her, I'm damp matches, all clumsy words and singed fingers, surprised I can string a sentence together. We drink a top-shelf brand and chat about unusual things: the joy of a well-tuned piano, vintage cars, and seashells.

"The beachcombers prize their conch shells, but, to me, they pale in comparison to the sand dollars. Such fragile beauties, you need to treat them with care." She swirls her glass against the tabletop between flat palms. "What's your name, handsome?"

"Ari. And yours?"

"Morgan."

I want to tell her she's beauty personified, but surely she's heard enough booze-soaked platitudes in her lifetime. Instead, I lean in and whisper, "You're the closest thing to a dream I've ever met."

"Smooth talker." Slow motion, she steals a kiss and I taste the ocean. When our tongues collide, the flavor explodes—sea and shore and waving palms—cocoa butter on sunlit skin.

She leans back and tilts her head at me as charming as a coquette. "What brings you to this island, Ari? What made you leave home and settle here?"

"How do you know I'm not a tourist?" I ask, wondering if she's a seer, or just a mind reader.

Her fingers dance over my hand. "I can spot a tourist a mile away. They flitter about, eager to drink in every sight before their time here runs out. You move slowly, with purpose. As if you have all the time in the world."

"If only that were true."

"You have more time than you think, my love."

She signals to the bartender. More whiskey. More kisses, hot and wet. Buzzing hornets fill my head, and my heart is a honeycomb. I feel them moving through arteries until my chest is alive with their motion. Punch drunk, we stumble into the night toward the beach.

"Inhale deeply, Ari. Drink in the sea's perfume. Feel how it intoxicates," Morgan says as she slips off her shoes. I expect her to pick them up, but she tosses them aside.

"I think the booze already did that." I struggle to keep up with her quick pace but then hang back, enchanted by the view of her curvy backside. It's then that I notice her bare feet leave wet footprints behind, a curiosity I decide to blame on the alcohol.

Morgan stops to let me catch up. "Would you like to fuck me, Ari?"

"Oh, I'd like to do much more than that." Hands on her waist, I nip her collarbone and taste salt.

"That was the correct answer." She points north to a tiny island I've never seen before. "Swim home with me."

"Home?"

"A cottage I inherited from my grandmother." She unbuttons my shirt. "Perfect for fucking."

"Any place would be perfect with you, my lovely."

Her lilting laugh echoes across the empty stretch of beach. "You're different, Ari. Innocent, yet worldly, without agenda. You go where the path leads, correct?"

I run a hand over my bald head, grinning despite grim memories of IV bags, months of puking, and endless surgeries. "I do now," I say. "Time is not on my side."

"It is when you're with me." Morgan strips, devoid of

shame, her crimson dress a beached sea urchin amidst the rocks. "Come on, handsome, don't be shy. You can't swim with your clothes on."

How I undress in front of this goddess is a mystery, baring my ravaged frame one article at a time. The old Ari ran marathons, while this shell struggles to walk. I glance at the isle and judge the distance. A mile and a half, at most. I can make it. For Morgan, I will.

I hope.

"You're safe with me, Ari," she says, taking my hand. "I'm a strong swimmer."

Her comforting tone is a balm and my hesitation wanes, but once we're neck deep, it returns. Our destination appears farther away. Arms leaden, legs quivering, I gasp her name.

She turns to face me, as easily as if on land. Her smile beckons. "Accept the sea's embrace, Ari. Her arms welcome you, as a mother welcomes her child. Trust her. Trust me."

The water hugs my body, creating a head rush that steals my breath. Giving in, I find I'm buoyant—a bounced pebble skimming the gentle waves. Calmness dispels fear and I notice the sky as if for the first time. A Van Gogh-like canopy stretches above, swirling purple and indigo dotted with glittering stars. A strange yet familiar sensation fills me.

Peace.

When was the last time I experienced such contentment? I'm still pondering this when my feet touch velvet sand. The island is now in reach, as is my siren. Standing on shore, we kiss and touch. I cup her ass. She grinds her mound against my hardening cock.

"Eat me up, Ari, like a wolf," she says.

First her neck, then each pert nipple. Licking. Sucking. Dead man walking. She's my last meal and I savor every nuance, every hint of spice and nectar. Taut skin over ribs, hip bones, soft thighs. I kneel on the wet sand and flutter kisses over her abdomen before moving lower. Parting her plump lips, I find her clit.

"Yes, Ari."

I suck that pearl while my fingers dive deep, massaging her target until she bucks against my hand. Moaning softly, she floods my palm with fluid sweeter than the brine of a freshly shucked oyster. I lap every drop, wanting more, but so does Morgan. Sand under my back, a pile of sea grass for a pillow, she rides me hard while I sing her praises to the night sky.

Fucking.

Delirious fucking.

Inside her, I'm reborn.

Alive.

"Fill me," she says. "Give me all of you, and then take all of me." Pussy squeezing my cock, she grinds, smiling. "All of me. All of you."

I grip her legs and we climax together. She's ember and I'm ash. One puff of air from her pursed lips and I will surely dissipate, my body nothing but tiny specks that float to the stars. I long to live in this swoon of bliss forever, but my siren has other ideas.

"That was a good start." Morgan rolls off my body and lithely rises to her feet. "Come with me. I have much to show you."

Hands clasped, we head down a sandy path that winds through lush vegetation. She stops to point out an orange blossom as big as a dinner plate. "These only bloom at night. The fragrance is divine."

I beg to differ, as I can still smell her nectar on my lips, but she only giggles a response before leading on. A cabin appears, straight out of a fairy tale. Before we can enter, Morgan insists we bathe under an outdoor shower.

Our hunger barely sated, we still slow our pace. I glide the bar of soap she hands me over her wet skin, taking care to lather every crevice of her exquisite form. My face burns when it's her turn to wash me.

"What are these dots?" she asks as she rubs soap across my sternum.

"Radiation tattoos. They're part of the reason I look like a reanimated corpse."

She clucks her tongue. "All I see is a beautiful man."

"A bald man with a giant scar down his chest isn't beautiful."

Dark eyes flash a warning. Morgan is not a woman to argue with. I kiss her lips and suck her tongue. She pulls away and nips my chin. "Beautiful man. Beautiful cock. Both belong in my mouth."

She leads me through the cabin in the dark. Double bed, white linens, crisp and cool against my fevered skin—skin that grows even hotter under her touch. She kisses and licks a trail from my lips to my nipples, taking soft bites that make me growl in delight. That growl turns to a gasp when she cups my sack.

"Did I hurt you, lover?"

"No, not at all. It's just . . ." I turn shy.

"Oh, you like that." She strokes the skin behind. "How about this?"

Before I can answer, her mouth is everywhere all at once. I'm on my hands and knees, face down in the pillows while her fingers explore and her tongue slithers in places I've only dreamed of. Who is this goddess and why has she chosen me for her supplicant? Now on my back, she takes my full length behind her lips.

"Morgan," I whisper, lifting my head to see her. Those eyes stare up at me while her tongue brushes the crown of my cock.

"Ari," she whispers back.

"Is this a dream?"

"Does it matter?" She mounts me and eases down, taking me back inside her warmth. "All that matters is this moment. All that matters is you and me."

We tongue kiss and fuck, slower this time. With every thrust, every kiss, every breath, I fall deeper and deeper in love. Why now? Why not years earlier, when I had strength and vigor? Yet, here I am, by some miracle, keeping up with this voracious creature.

"All of me. All of you," she says that same phrase, but this time with her lips against mine. Her voice fills my mouth like a prayer—like a chant—and I swallow her words to keep them inside me forever. If only.

If only.

Once again, we soar together, high enough to drink the stars and eat the moon, which I imagine would melt against my tongue like shortbread. When linen brushes against my back again, Morgan is pressed close, singing a lullaby into my ear. Her sweet voice makes fighting sleep impossible, and I succumb.

I wake bathed in sunshine streaming from an open window, alone in the bed, sheets twisted around my legs. At first, I think it was all a dream, until I see Morgan's red dress draped over the back of a chair.

"Morgan?" I say as I rise to a sitting position. "I hope you swam back for my clothes, too."

The cabin is silent, save for the chattering of birds outside. Standing, I'm still a bit drunk and a lot giddy. I call her name as I wander naked through the house, but she's not there. Confused, I rub my hands over my head, stunned to find a full shock of hair. The bathroom mirror shows a man I barely recognize.

It's me, only the way I used to be. Strong and muscular, with a scar-free chest.

"Am I dead, or have I gone back in time?" I ask the man in the mirror.

After searching the house again, I stand on the tiny back porch and stare into the dense jungle beyond. I know I could search the island for hours but not find her, know this with absolute certainty. Perhaps this is heaven, a place where I will live in vibrant health with only the memory of her to keep me company.

Back inside, I sit in a worn rattan chair and gaze out the front window at the endless sea, my head flooded with images of last night. Morgan's haunting eyes. Her luscious lips. The way she tossed her shoes aside without a care and left a trail of footprints in the dry sand.

Wet footprints.

The screen door slams behind me as I exit the cottage and sprint toward the shore on my new, strong legs. The closer I get to the water, the faster my heart beats. A splash first and then a mermaid's tail emerges from the water, glinting crimson in the sun.

I smile. Tonight, when the moon winks back into view, Morgan will return to me.

All of me. All of her.

Forever.

ABOUT THE
AUTHORS

LYNX CANON was founder and host of the Dirty Old Women reading series, and editor of the Dirty Old Women anthology. She writes crime, science fiction, and erotica, mixing genres with abandon. In her alternate universe, she produces content for tech companies from the San Francisco Bay Area.

LIN DEVON is a mixed-race pansexual bibliophilic sci-fi, fantasy, and horror fan more at home in a book sipping hot tea with cats than just about anywhere. Her previous work can be found in *Best Women's Erotica of the Year, Volume 8, The Big Book of Orgasms, Volume 2*, and *Crowded House*.

KIKI DELOVELY is a witchy, kinky, polyamorous, mixed, nonbinary femme who moonlights as an erotica writer when she's not weaving magic through energetic healing and spiritual coaching. Their work has appeared in dozens of publications and they have toured both nationally and internationally, living and traveling all over the world.

ASH DYLAN (ashdylan.com) is a writer based in Texas. When he is not writing romance novels, he is reading them.

EM FARRIS (@EmDashFarris) is a volunteer zine librarian who lives on the east coast of Canada. They are a settler on Mi'kma'ki, the unceded, unsurrendered land of the Mi'kmaq.

D.J. HODGE writes stories that center witty and relatable Black heroines living their sexiest, best lives. Her short story "Wanna Bet?" is out now in *The Big Book of Orgasms, Volume 2*, by Cleis Press. Her short story "The Feeling's Mutual" in *Cunning Linguists* by New Smut Project is also available. In her free time, she enjoys a quality snack and spending time with her cat Lulu.

A.J. HARRIS (biomechanoidblues.wordpress.com/about-a-j-harris/) is a native of the Washington, DC, metropolitan area who indulges in a bit of photography, spends entirely too much on books, and uses Twitter to comment on old movies. A.J.'s spicy romance stories have previously been published in the anthologies *Stranded* and *The Big Book of Orgasms, Volume 2*.

DR. J. (drjauthor.com), a retired sex therapist, writes and edits erotica while enjoying the island life on the Atlantic coast of Florida. When not doing authorly things, you can see her on the pétanque court perfecting her competition moves while sipping something cold.

FRIEDRICH KREUZ was a historian of psychiatry before becoming a pornographer. He writes erotica for the gay BDSM site Recon and writes and performs in adult films for

Erika Lust's XConfessions, Sensate Films, Ivan Sobris Films, Charlie Forde, and Thousand Faces. His movies have been shown at the porn film festivals in Berlin, San Francisco, Vienna, Seattle, Athens, London, etc.

LYDIA LOOMIS writes monster romance. She enjoys looking at the weird, fantastical, and otherworldly, and finding where the beauty and love are. When Lydia is not writing she is most likely indulging in one of her other nerdy hobbies. She lives with her partner and two pugs in Providence, RI.

BARTHOLOMEW MAXWELL is a Black, trans, multigenre writer and lives in Northern California, in unceded Kashia Pomo territory.

SIENNA MERIT is a lifelong writer, devoted to all things romance related. E lives in Pennsylvania with er partner.

JORDAN MONROE (@AuthorJordanMonroe) believes there is no such thing as a guilty pleasure. She enjoys playing her French horn, attempting to bake, and buying too many books to fit on her bookshelves. She lives in Maryland with her husband and spoiled cat. Her debut novel, *Ill-Fated Mate: A Steamy Monster Romance*, is available now.

OLEANDER PLUME (oleanderplume.com) writes erotica while sipping martinis, and yes, they are dirty martinis. When she's not writing, she can be found somewhere near Chicago, creating art and haunting thrift stores.

NIKKI RAE (@NikkiRaeAuthor) is an independent author who lives in New Jersey. She explores human nature through fiction, concentrating on making the imaginary as real as possible. Her genres of choice are mainly dark, scary, romantic tales, but she'll try anything once. When she is not writing, reading, or thinking, you can find her spending time with animals, drawing in a quiet corner, or studying people. Closely.

JESSICA LEIGH ROODE ((https://medium.com/@softapocalypses) is a writer and poet from New York. She uses this pen name specifically to share her erotica and romance fiction works. She is forty-one, has one child, and loves to be silly on Twitter.

SPROCKET J. RYDYR writes from the heart. They have a passion for storytelling in a variety of media and hold an MFA in studio art. When they aren't writing, they're reading, making art, and fussing over their cats. They live with their wonderfully supportive partner and numerous headcanons.

KATE SLOAN (katesloan.com) is a writer specializing in sex and relationships. She is the author of two books, *101 Kinky Things Even You Can Do* and *200 Words to Help You Talk About Sexuality & Gender*. She writes a blog called Girly Juice and cohosts the Dildorks podcast.

SULEIKHA SNYDER is a best-selling and award-winning author of contemporary and erotic romance, whose works have been showcased in *The New York Times, Entertainment Weekly,* BuzzFeed, *The Times of India,* and NPR. An editor, writer, American desi, and lifelong geek, she is a passionate advocate for diversity and inclusivity in media of all kinds.

ANNITA TERCIO teaches writing by day and by night, practices roller-skating moves on light-up wheels in her living room.

To give her legs a rest, she reads romance novels, sews, and quilts. She has an MFA in Creative Writing and lives in Oregon.

ABOUT
THE EDITOR

RACHEL KRAMER BUSSEL (rachelkramerbussel.com) is a New Jersey-based author, editor, blogger, and writing instructor. She has edited over seventy books of erotica, including *Crowded House: Threesome and Group Sex Erotica; It Takes Two; Coming Soon: Women's Orgasm Erotica; Dirty Dates: Erotic Fantasies for Couples; Come Again: Sex Toy Erotica; The Big Book of Orgasms, Volumes 1* and *2; The Big Book of Submission, Volumes 1* and *2; Lust in Latex; Anything for You; Baby Got Back: Anal Erotica; Suite Encounters; Gotta Have It; Women in Lust; Surrender; Orgasmic; Fast Girls; Going Down; Tasting Him; Tasting Her; Crossdressing; Cheeky Spanking Stories; Bottoms Up; Spanked: Red-Cheeked Erotica; Please, Sir; Please, Ma'am; He's on Top; She's on Top; Best Bondage Erotica of the Year, Volumes 1* and *2;* and *Best Women's Erotica of the Year, Volumes 1–7.* Her anthologies have won eight IPPY (Independent Publisher) Awards, and *The Big Book of Submission, Volume 2, Dirty Dates,* and

Surrender won the National Leather Association Samois Anthology Award. She is the recipient of the 2021 National Leather Association John Preston Short Fiction Award.

Rachel has written for *AVN, Bust, Cosmopolitan, Curve,* The Daily Beast, Elle.com, Forbes.com, Fortune.com, *Glamour,* The Goods, Gothamist, *Harper's Bazaar,* Huffington Post, *Inked, InStyle, Marie Claire, MEL, Men's Health, Newsday, New York Post, New York Observer, The New York Times, O: The Oprah Magazine, Penthouse, The Philadelphia Inquirer,* Refinery29, *Rolling Stone,* The Root, Salon, *San Francisco Chronicle, Self,* Slate, Time.com, *Time Out New York,* and *Zink,* among others. She has appeared on "The Gayle King Show," "The Martha Stewart Show," "The Berman and Berman Show," NY1, and Showtime's "Family Business." She hosted the popular In the Flesh Erotic Reading Series, featuring readers from Susie Bright to Zane, speaks at conferences, and does readings and teaches erotic writing workshops around the world and online. She blogs at lustylady.blogspot.com and consults about erotica and sex-related nonfiction at eroticawriting101.com. Follow her @raquelita on Twitter.